A WRONGFUL DEATH

By
SIDNEY ROBIN

ISBN: 13: 9780615809014

ISBN-10: 0615809014

For Sandi: Without her there could be no story, and without a story there would be no book.

Prologue

Phil Levine and I were working at Laurel's Atlantic Resort in North Haven, Michigan when I met and fell in love with Sharon for the first time. It was at a Friday Night dinner at Laurel's. The last pink and orange streaks of a picture perfect sunset were visible through the large cathedral windows of the formal dining room that overlooked Lake Michigan. Two huge crystal chandeliers added a soft glow to the room.

I was a waiter, in my third summer at the Resort, and had carefully set my tables with starched linen tablecloths and matching napkins rolled into the shape of candles, stuffed neatly into the wine glasses. The two ears of each napkin stood stiffly upright as if they had been invigorated with Viagra. There was a glass of ice water at each place setting, menus and wine lists were on each plate, and the centerpieces were in place, along with bountiful baskets of fresh-baked rolls, covered with napkins to keep them warm.

Seated at the head table was Mr. Laurel himself, the guy who created the Resort. He had the guts to buy a large chunk of land on the shore of Lake Michigan, about 120 miles from Chicago, and to borrow the funds to erect a large pink stucco hotel. Folks in the area laughed at first, branding it the "Pink Elephant," but he plowed ahead and over the years built up the resort, adding new and better accommodations, an Olympic sized swimming pool, a marina, and a recreation hall that at night was converted to a nightclub with a live band, and on weekends featured acts who worked the Comedy Club circuit. By the time Phil and I began working there, Laurel's Atlantic Resort was already a long established institution.

Laurel geared his resort to attract folks from nearby Chicago and Detroit, mainly married couples vacationing with their children, upper and upper-middle income couples, they were the ones who could afford his prices, who were looking to spend one or two weeks bonding with their kids, relaxing on the beach or at the pool during the day, or golfing at the nearby links, and dining on three good meals a day. Ever higher airfares and offish airports prompted more and more Midwestern families to opt for the vacation he offered.

Hugh Heffner hired Playboy Bunnies as servers to attract his male patrons. Hooters followed a similar plan. But Laurel knew his clientele. He recruited young men, students, future professionals, to act as waiters, busboys, bellboys and pool attendants. No girls—they were too much trouble. He encouraged his staff to mingle with his patrons, to act as role models for their sons, and to socialize with their daughters. "Just don't get too physical, you know what I mean, be discreet, and don't get anybody in trouble. If things DO go too far, for God sake, make sure you wear protection."

What Bugsy Siegel was to Las Vegas, Mr. Laurel (nobody who worked for him ever addressed him by his first name), was to Southwest Michigan.

As he lorded over his domain that night, Mr. Laurel was clothed in one of his perfectly draped dark blue suits with a crisp white shirt and solid blue tie, not too dark or too light. He sported a deep tan, and held his head erect with dark hair flecked gray at the temples, not a strand out of place, and a part as straight as Cary Grant's. If this were a cruise ship, his table would have been designated the Captain's table, and before the meal began he rose, tapped his glass with a spoon until he had everyone's attention, welcomed all the guests in his deep baritone, and bade them dine.

The job of bussing my tables fell to Ruben Weinstock, a chubby pre-med at Northwestern University who wore thick glasses, and had curly dark hair that was already thinning at the top. He meticulously soaked up the spills with extra linen napkins from Laurel's cupboard, and took care of the crumbs with an antique sterling silver crumb scoop, worth over $1,000.00, that he had swiped from the locked credenza of his parents Glencoe home. He said his folks would never miss it, and that it added a touch of class to his job. Weinstock, like the rest of us, was given free room and board, paid a small salary, and relied mainly on tips. Since he was my busboy, I gave him a portion of my gratuities. If he was obsequious enough, some patrons would also tip him directly.

I was heading toward the table of a patron who complained his soup was too watery. "If the London fog was as thin as this pea soup they wouldn't have any trouble seeing through it." Mr. Split Pea was only there for one week, and as I recalled from prior years, was a chintzy tipper. I just shrugged and ignored his complaint.

I detoured to respond to another summons. "Stan, Stan Seger!" Harold Heller, boomed out to me from his table across the room. His mouth was stuffed with bread, but I was able to make out my name, and hustled to his side.

"When my onion soup comes, make sure the crust is crisp, and that there's plenty of melted cheese. The last time I ordered it, the bread was soggy." I winked at him reassuringly, and rushed toward the kitchen to make sure it got done.

"And Seger," he yelled after me, "when they bring out the roasted chicken, make sure mine has crisp skin. I like it to crackle." I didn't suggest he call Kentucky Colonel and order a bucket of extra-crispy, but I sure wanted to.

Heller was one of the two-week guests. The rates were by-the-week and included the room and three meals a day. I can never remember whether that is called the American plan or the European plan. To this day I think of it as the Laurel plan.

I knew Heller and his wife because this was their third year at Laurel's, and I regularly was assigned their table. They always checked in for two weeks, starting the first Sunday in August. In one of their early stays they mentioned having a daughter, Sharon, who wasn't with them because she spent her summers at a Sports Camp on the Upper Peninsula.

When Heller arrived he would search me out right away, and with a Cuban in his mouth he would slip me an advanced tip of $100.00 and say "treat me like the Maharajah, and make sure the other boys do the same."

It was at the end of the dinner, during that third summer, that Heller approached Phil Levine and me as we were standing out on the front porch, enjoying the night. Phil had the best job at the resort, cabana boy. He worked out a lot more than I did, he was a hell of a lot more muscular than me, and he looked terrific in a bathing suit. The girls crowded around him at the pool, but Phil shied away from involvement with any of them, repeating his mantra that he preferred the town girls to the princesses staying at the Resort.

"Phil--Stan--I've got a little job for you to do--it's very important to me. But keep it strictly between us." Heller was talking softly, very unusual for him. I wanted to lean closer to better hear what he was saying, but he had that damn cigar in his mouth, and even outdoors the smoke was choking me.

"You see that little cutesy standing over by the bushes. That's my little girl, Sharon"

"I don't remember seeing her before," I said. "She really is beautiful." And I meant it. Long blond silky hair that looked natural, and a great figure in cut-offs and a halter top. How did the Hellers produce someone who looked like that? I found out later they adopted her when she was three, after she bounced around between foster homes.

"She got up here an hour ago—she took a cab from the Bangor train station." (Bangor was really the name of the town, not a description of what you wanted to do to the girls that got off there.) "She was away at summer camp the last few years instead of coming with us. Learning to paddle a canoe and shoot bows and arrows and shit like that. And don't get any ideas. Sharon's only 16 years old."

I had her figured for at least 18. I can understand how Roman Polanski got kicked out of the country.

"My daughter has a crush on this guy, his name is Wally Smalley, can you believe. He was a swimming coach at her camp the last two years. We only found out about it recently when my wife happened to see a page of her diary when we were up at the camp for parent's weekend."

Just happened to see it, bullshit. They probably searched through all her belongings until they found it.

"We yanked her right out of camp, and made her join us here. And I thought I was being smart, but it turns out that of all the fuckin luck, that guy Smalley's family lives in this town, and he followed her here. The bastard is 21 years old. I want you guys to break that thing up. Keep her away from him." And he leaned closer and jabbed his cigar at us. "But don't let her know I said anything. She's a very stubborn girl with a temper, I'm ashamed to say, like that that shrew, Katherine."

"I'm impressed. I didn't know you knew Shakespeare."

"What Shakespeare?---the Cole Porter musical---the one with Howard Keel."

"Screw Heller," Phil said. We were relaxing on our bunks in the dorm, having finished serving the evening meal. "I'm not getting involved."

Ruben Weinstock came in while we were talking. He had to clean up the dining room, and always finished later than we did. "What are you guys talking about?" We told him about Heller's problem.

"I could always put the make on her--every girl has the hots for a doctor."

"A third -year pre-med isn't exactly a Board Certified," I shot back. "I've seen Dr. Kildare, and you're no Richard Chamberlain."

I wanted Sharon for myself, even if she was a kid. I know it sounds crazy, but I couldn't help it. Maybe once in your life, if you're really lucky, or maybe really unlucky, you see a girl and magic happens. Call it cupid's arrow, call it moon dust, call it whatever you want, poet's write about it and Sinatra sang about it, and you may call me a hopeless romantic, but I know it's true. In old English novels they would have said I was smitten or besotted. I wasn't living in old England, and I wasn't in the South Pacific either, spotting a stranger across the crowded room, but when I saw Sharon Heller standing by the bushes I knew how Ezio Pinza felt. And it was a feeling that could last a lifetime. As a matter of fact, it did.

"You go for it man," Phil urged. "I'll stick with the townies. Getting tied up with a Princess, I swear, it would kill me."

As it turned out, starting up with Sharon Heller almost killed ME that summer. I take that back. It's probably overstating it. Starting up with Sharon almost got me beaten to an inch of my life by Wally Smalley, her crazy ex-boyfriend.

Sharon and I had clicked immediately, and a week after we met we were sitting on a blanket at the beach, Sharon with her head resting on my shoulder, watching the sunset. Someone came up behind us and kicked me viciously in the back, between the shoulder blades, and I fell forward, my face landing in the sand.

Sharon sprung to her feet, stood arms akimbo, and looked up at the gigantic attacker who loomed over us. I was wiping sand from my eyes as she shrilled, "Wally, are you crazy!" It was like a revival of King Kong and Fay Wray.

Wally was huge and very angry---a dangerous combination. I stretched out my hands in supplication, and long before Rodney King echoed it, implored ---"can't we all be friends?"

He slapped my hands aside and went into a boxing stance, left hand forward and right hand cocked. "Come on and fight," he barked. "Whattsa matter—you a coward?"

The guy was a head taller than me, and outweighed me by at least 40 pounds. He was Goliath and I didn't have a slingshot.

Sharon was watching silently. My head told me I had to stand and fight, but my legs were saying let's get the hell out of here. We stood there for a minute, staring at each other, and I could feel my legs slowly winning that argument. But before I could turn and run, if that is what I was going to do-- to this day I'm not sure-- Phil Levine came out of nowhere and rolled into the back of Goliath's legs, causing his knees to buckle, and sending him to the ground. Phil immediately stomped on his back, and then knocked him senseless with a piece of the driftwood he had been gathering for our bonfire.

If Phil had been a little later coming to my rescue, and if I had chickened out and run, there is a good chance my affair with Sharon would have ended right then. As it was, it lasted for about three years before we broke up. It wasn't that we stopped loving each other, nothing as simple as that. The passion was still there, the love was still there, but the timing was lousy. I was now a lawyer, ready to marry and start a family. Sharon was younger, intent on finishing her education, and not yet prepared to make a lifetime commitment. "I want to taste the world before we settle down," she said. And she had a hearty appetite.

She wanted me to wait while she had more of a chance to experience life. I was impatient. I was headstrong. So was she. And so we parted.

Eventually I married someone else and so did Sharon. I developed my law practice in Chicago. And Phil Levine became my Private Investigator. Sharon moved with her husband to L.A. No chance of us ever seeing each other again. That's what I thought. But I never forgot her.

CHAPTER 1

The Smith Case

The Smith case was a Medical Malpractice suit against the doctors and hospital who were treating Celia Smith at the time of her death. We were seeking damages for her *wrongful death*, a legal term meaning she died because somebody really screwed up. The case was referred to me by my former classmate, Ted Mizell, a fast rising partner in one of the prestigious corporate law firms in the City.

Most of the blue ribbon firms like Ted's wouldn't dream of representing injured persons, no matter the merits of the case. They professed it was an area of the law that was beneath them. But the potential fees were too big for them to ignore. So they would keep their virtuous eyes opened for serious injury cases, and refer them to P.I. specialists like me, and seek a healthy referral fee.

P.I. stands for personal injury, in case you didn't know, and a P.I. lawyer is one who handles personal injury cases, hopefully serious ones. Phyllis, my ex-wife, after one drink too many, once proposed a toast to my clients, saying, "To your clients, who suffer and die so that you may prosper and live well." I hate to admit it, especially since Phyllis said it, but that pretty succinctly sums up my practice. Phyllis shouldn't complain too strenuously. She came out pretty well in the divorce as a result of all that suffering and death.

I met with Ted Mizell in one of the plush conference rooms in the large suite of offices his firm occupied. Dark mahogany paneling on the walls, and a massive stone conference table that weighed multi-thousand pounds. Its legs sunk deep craters into the expensive wool carpeting. Not very good planning there.

We were both seated in rich brown leather swivel chairs with high backs, ornamented with burnished brass buttons that would have dimpled my suit jacket if I leaned back too far. The soft indirect lighting was a little dim for my taste, and when I suggested we might brighten it Ted summoned a lackey to adjust the dimmer switch hidden somewhere in the wall. I declined Ted's offer of a drink from the well-stocked bar at the end of the room. It was still morning, a little early for alcohol, even for me. Ted was really spreading it on thick.

I knew he would like it if I was impressed by the surroundings, so I complimented him on the decor. His smug response: "It doesn't make any sense to practice alone anymore. The economics don't permit it. And you--- you don't even advertise, not even in the yellow pages. The days of the lone ranger are over. You should join a firm---head up a litigation department. You're a fucking dinosaur! Get some support so you don't kill yourself."

To shut him up I told him I'd think about it.

"Do you still have that guy Phil Levine working as your investigator?" Ted was still ticked off at Phil for something that happened when we were at a Blackhawk's game together, me, Phil Levine, and Ted with his date, a redhead he had been bragging about for weeks, and was sneaking around with whenever his wife was out of town. Ted prided himself on always being accompanied around town with stunning "arm candy."

An over-excited fan in the upper balcony spilled some beer over the railing, and it landed all over the redhead's blouse. When she left to clean it up Ted leaned over to Phil, who he considered a connoisseur of women, Phil being the perennial single swinger, and asked, "What do you think of her? Gorgeous, isn't she?"

"Not bad," Phil said, not too enthusiastically.

"'Tell me the truth," Ted said.

"'She's O.K.." The tone wasn't an endorsement.

"I know her face is not exactly a ten."

"No, she's not a ten," Phil agreed.

"You think she's below average?"

"I'm afraid so." Phil admitted."

"But a sensational body, don't you agree?"

Phil didn't say anything.

"You think she's a little chunky?"

Phil just shrugged.

"So you think she is," Ted said, now getting agitated.

"Maybe she is a little chunky," Phil agreed.

"'So that's what you think, huh----- tell me what you really think. Tell me!!"

So Phil told him she was fat and ugly, and he didn't understand why Ted didn't just stick with his wife who was at least as good looking and a hell of a lot smarter. After the game, when I got Phil alone, I told him he should have kept his mouth shut. "The guy is a referring lawyer, an important source. You know how sensitive he is."

"But he was asking for it," Phil insisted."

That happened a couple of months before the *Smith*, meeting, but Ted hadn't forgotten. "You should really think about getting rid of that asshole."

"He's a great investigator. Let's forget about that, and tell me about the case we're here about."

"This fellow Smith who I want you to represent, I don't know his first name, works at one of the factories we represent, and he called his employer right after his wife died on an operating table, and the plant manager called us. I think he might have a good case for her death and my firm wants to refer it to you." And then, almost inaudibly, in case somebody was listening to our conversation, though God only knows who that could be since we were alone in the room, he mumbled, "Of course, we'll expect a referral fee."

"Of course you'll get a fee." I enjoyed watching him squirm un-comfortably as I continued, "You understand that ethics require that the client be advised of any fee-splitting arrangement, and that our referral fee agreement will be included in bold face in the Retainer Agreement the client will sign."

"We wouldn't want that. Our corporate client might be upset if they learned of a referral fee."

"Do you have any other suggestions?" Of course he did. We had been through the dance before.

Ted doodled on the pad in front of him for a few moments, and then looked up. "Forget the referral fee. We can still have you take on the case. But I know you would have trouble handling it alone. We'll let one of our young associates assist you, and you can pay us for the services." To his credit, he kept a straight face while he made the proposal.

I needed an inexperienced associate like I needed a case of lar-yngitis. "And how much would you propose to charge me for those services?"

"Let's make it contingent on the recovery in the case. Of course, the payment you make for those services will come out of your fee, and since it is a fee for services, not a referral fee, the client doesn't have to be told of our agreement."

"That works for me. I suppose I should meet your associate. Is he available?"

"It's a she, not a he, the associate, I mean."

And that's how I got the case without paying any referral fee, but instead contracted for the services of a part-time helper, and that's how I first met Geri Sapperstein.

"This is Geri Sapperstein, a brand new associate with our firm, who just moved here from Los Angeles. She's a recent graduate of Southwest Law School out there." He tried to make that sound impressive. I wasn't impressed. Southwest wasn't exactly a law school with a national reputation. As a matter of fact, I never even heard of it, and I keep up with those things.

Don't get me wrong. Plenty of very good lawyers graduate from local schools, but fancy firms like Ted's almost never hire graduates from schools like Southwest. I figured that she was either in the genius category, or that someone in the firm was planning to bop her. The way that Ted was eyeing the blonde, I guessed it was the latter.

"Geri is familiar with the Celia Smith case," Ted said. "She's already done some of the preliminary work, and is free to work with you on it whenever you need her, as long as it doesn't interfere with her duties here, and her studying for the Illinois Bar. She's already admitted in California. "

Geri was wearing a severely tailored gray suit with a chalk stripe, and one of those skinny ties that lady lawyers like to wear. The skirt hit almost to the knee. She had blonde hair, cut very short, probably so she didn't have to fuss with it as she rushed to work in the morning. She presented herself like so many of the pretty young lawyers. Mannish and very stern, putting a hard edge on her femininity so you'd judge her solely on her ability. It never works.

I'm very partial to blondes. My ex-wife is a blond and so was Sharon, my first true love. So I studied Geri carefully, her looks and her demeanor. Trim body. Pretty features, but thin lips. I don't like thin lips. After careful consideration I sized her up as a lousy fuck.

At Ted's prompting, Geri began telling me what she knew about the case, and I made some notes on one of the yellow legal pads on the conference table. There wasn't much to write because Geri had very sketchy information.

Celia Smith, a 28 year old African-American woman, had given birth to twins at the South Side Community Hospital in Chicago, decided that she didn't want any more children, and 6 weeks later returned to the same hospital for a tubal ligation. During the course of the tubal ligation, while she was still in the operating room, she suffered a cardiac arrest and died.

"The ultimate form of birth control. Kill the prospective mother," I said.

Nobody laughed.

"Who are the survivors?"

Geri read from her notes. "The twins, of course, and a 5 year old son, and her husband, who is a factory worker."

The value of a wrongful death case depends in good part on who survived the victim. This is because the jury would be awarding money to the survivors for their loss. If a woman died leaving a husband and minor children behind, this gave us the potential for a very large verdict, even if she was a wife and mother from hell. If another woman of the same age was single and had no kids, her case was worth much less, even if she was as saintly as Mother Teressa.

"Sounds like a great case, doesn't it?" Ted was fired up.

"Well, it has potential. But it's really too early to say. I'll need to know a lot more. Her medical history. What was the cause of death? What happened in the operating room?"

Ted had no answers.

" Sometimes people die even if the doctor did nothing wrong. It could be an amniotic fluid embolism. Or it could be a high spinal. Was this a spinal or a general anesthesia? What drugs were used? What more information do you have in your file?"

Ted looked to Geri. Neither had much idea of what I was talking about. It was clear that Geri was in way over her head, and that she had been given no guidance.

"Do you have the death certificate and autopsy report?"

She handed over the death certificate, which indicated that Celia Smith had died 6 weeks ago, and listed the cause of death as cardiac arrest. Nothing more specific.

"How about the autopsy report?"

"I didn't order that yet."

"When did your firm first get involved in the case?"

Ted answered that. "We got called the same day she died. As I told you, her husband worked in a client's factory. When Mrs. Smith died the hospital wanted permission to do an autopsy and Mr. Smith didn't know what to do. He called his boss for help, and they referred him to me, their attorney. I was out of town, so Geri took his call."

"He was of course very broken up when I spoke with him that day," Geri continued. "I told him it was all right for him to sign the consent for the hospital to do an autopsy, and I........."

"You let the hospital where she died do the autopsy without someone on our side observing it? Jesus Christ! That's like letting Richard Nixon supervise the investigation in Watergate. "

Geri registered a blank look. She knew who Nixon was, but "Watergate" was too long ago.

"It's like Bush and Cheney investigating the vote fraud charges in Florida." This was more current, and she caught the gist.

"What should I have done?" Geri was somewhat crestfallen.

"You should have hired your own pathologist to do the autopsy, or at least observe it being done. He could have made sure that a thorough examination was performed and recorded accurately."

"Maybe we could exhume the body and have it re-examined," Ted suggested.

"It's probably too late for that. After the autopsy and the embalming, and then 6 weeks of decomposition, any additional examination would probably be worthless. Let's see the hospital record."

"I don't have it yet," Geri said. "I wrote for it but they wouldn't send it to me because I didn't have an authorization."

"Didn't you have the husband sign an authorization for you to get medical records when he signed the retainer?"

"I didn't have him sign a contract, but we do have a verbal agreement to represent him," Geri assured me.

"To paraphrase Samuel Goldwyn, a verbal agreement isn't worth the paper it's written on. All contingent agreements are required by law to be in writing. Some chaser could get hold of Mr. Smith and sign him up, and you would have no standing at all. You better get in touch with Mr. Smith pronto, tell him to talk to no one about the case, and bring him to my office at ten tomorrow morning."

Ted walked me to the elevator and asked "What percentage do you anticipate paying us for Geri's assistance? She's a smart girl, and a quick learner."

"Probably 25%."

Ted shrugged. He didn't look too happy.

I didn't mind that. I wasn't anticipating a lot of help from Ms. Sapperstein.

"O.K.," Ted said. "We'll leave the value of Geri's services open for now, but figure it at a minimum of 25%. And she's really good looking, don't you think?"

I wasn't going to go there again, and stepped into the elevator without responding.

CHAPTER 2

Orwell Washington

I'm pretty much a one man operation, just me, my secretary, a paralegal, and, until he got himself killed, Phil Levine, my investigator. And I relish the autonomy. Ted said that makes me a dinosaur. Maybe so, but if I am, I want to be a Tyrannosaurus Rex, and I'm gonna fight against extinction.

My little enterprise usually has an inventory of forty to sixty cases. I don't see a penny out of any case until it is resolved, and every case requires an investment of time and money, sometimes a lot of time and even more money. When a case is concluded the inventory has to be replenished. I work the practice like a farmer, who each season plants new crops, tills his fields, and brings in the harvest. But unlike many farmers, I get no government subsidies if I let the field lie fallow.

So when I left Ted's office with the skimpy Smith file under my arm I went directly to the Mount Zion Hospital to meet another new client. His name was Orwell Washington and he had been hit by a car and had a fractured femur. A bread and butter kind of case. Not complicated, little investment in time or money, and usually a fairly quick turnover. Orwell had been referred to me by a neighborhood lawyer who sent me cases from time to time.

I phoned my office from the car and told my secretary, Julia, where I was headed and to expect me back in a couple of hours. Julia told me that Geri Sapperstein had already phoned and that she would be at my office at ten the next morning with Tom Smith.

I drove toward Mount Zion, located on the West Side of the city. It was a beautiful clear day, and I had the top down to get some fresh air. I passed Greek Town and the newly yuppified area just west of the loop, and then drove past the sparkling facade of the United Center, home of the Chicago Bulls and Chicago Blackhawks. The same stadium where Phil Levine had critiqued Ted's redhead.

I pulled to the curb to admire the monument to Michael Jordan , and before leaving I raised the top on the convertible and made sure the doors were locked before driving through the blighted area to the west of the arena.

That neighborhood was a long way from being gentrified. Most of the blocks resembled Berlin at the end of WWII. Several of the apartment buildings were now just rubble. The wooden porches at the back of the surviving edifices sagged dangerously, and some had completely collapsed. Many windows were boarded up, and those that had survived were a filthy brown.

Other structures, formerly stately homes, were now divided into overcrowded multi-residences, and the stone facades, once clean and sturdy and imposing, were now grimy, chipped, and pockmarked, some of the chinks probably from stray gunshots. Many were decorated with spray painted gang signs and slogans.

On one building an admirer, I like to think it was an admirer, had printed in large red letters "JUANITA IS A GREAT FUCK!!" Or maybe it was just an ad posted by Juanita's pimp. There was a pretty girl in a white tank top and impossibly tight short skirt standing on the sidewalk in front of the building, and she smiled provocatively as I waited for the light to turn green. Maybe she was Juanita.

The cars parked along the curb looked like they were on their last wheels. Little African-American kids, some as young as three or four, dashed half-dressed out into the street mid-block, and dodged between the approaching cars. My clients of the future.

I stopped for a red light, glanced to my left, and noticed a nasty looking teenager sitting behind the steering wheel of a parked car. He wore a red checkered bandanna around his head and concentrated on cleaning the barrel of a rifle. He noticed me looking his way, pointed his forefinger at me as if it was a pistol, moved down his thumb as if it was the hammer, and mouthed "BANG!" I floored the BMW and got the hell out of there.

Parking at Mount Zion Hospital is a bitch. You don't park on the street unless you have an extra set of hubcaps at home. The hospital parking lot is a few blocks away, and the one-way streets in the area are arranged so that it is almost impossible to reach it. I have a lousy sense of direction, and I wasn't about to get lost in that neighborhood, so I pulled into a No Parking zone directly in front of the hospital entrance and negotiated with the police officer standing nearby. I parked my car right there and sauntered into the hospital twenty dollars poorer.

I spend a good deal of time in hospitals, what with meeting new clients or deposing doctors and nurses. I hate every hospital visit, and can't wait to escape and breathe in fresh air.

I told the volunteer at the desk that I was visiting Orwell Washington. Visiting hours hadn't started yet, but attorneys are given the privilege of visiting clients at any time, and she handed me a pass for Ward 3 East, bed 22 without even asking for identification. My briefcase identified me as a lawyer. That and my go-to-court suit and tie.

Happily, the elevator was working, although it took an interminable amount of time to get to the third floor. When it lurched to a stop I got off and headed to Ward 3 East, bed 22. Lunch was being served. If the food didn't encourage patients to opt for early release, nothing would.

There was a man standing beside bed 22. He was wearing a pearl gray suit, red shirt, and white silk tie. On his head he wore a matching gray fedora with a large red feather. He always wore a feather. The lawyers on the street called him "Cochise." He worked for a group of lawyers who were being investigated by the ARDC for ambulance chasing.

My client to be, Orwell Washington, was trapped in his bed with his leg in the air, fastened to a pulley for traction. Cochise was harassing him, waving a contract in his face and urging him to sign. There were two nurses directly across the aisle serving dinners and totally ignoring what was going on between Cochise and Orwell. It was a common occurrence at Mount Zion. The nurses were probably the ones who called Cochise in the first place.

"Cochise, back off," I shouted.

Cochise turned and glared at me, brazen and angry.

"He's mine," he said. "We already made the deal."

"Are you Mr. Seger?" Orwell hollered from his bed.

I assured him I was as I elbowed Cochise aside and handed him my card.

Cochise refused to give up.

"He ain't no good. Man's a fuckin honky. He'll fuck you over. Sign wiff me, Brother."

"Back off, you motherfucker," I said, language Cochise would understand. "Get the fuck outta here or I'll have your ass locked away."

"Nurse!" I yelled. "Get a security man up here-----RIGHT NOW— or you'll be going there along with him!"

As the nurse scurried from the ward Cochise raised his hands in mock surrender.

"Cool it man. I'm splittin. See ya 'round." He was smiling as he backed off, and a diamond in his front tooth sparkled at me.

I pulled up a chair and spent about a half hour with Orwell getting acquainted and showing an interest in him as a person, making myself as likable as I could and dropping comments that would foster confidence. When he told me he was crazy for the White Sox, I didn't mention I was a lifelong Cub fan, and instead praised Ozzie Guillen, commiserated his leaving, and promised Orwell box seats for a game as soon as he was out of the cast. Then I got down to work taking notes regarding the accident, his injuries, and his medical treatment. When I felt we had established a good rapport I had him sign a Retainer Agreement and a HIPPA Authorization for me to get his medical records, and to consult with his doctors. I cautioned him not to give any statements to anyone and to refer all inquiries to me. We hand bumped, and said goodbye.

As I walked down the corridor I noticed that the nurse I had sent for a guard was in her office taking a coffee break. I walked toward the elevator, stopped, turned, and peeked back around the corner. Cochise was sneaking out of the nurse's office and heading back toward bed 22. Instead of waiting for the elevator, I pounded down three flights of stairs to the lobby, grabbed a security guard who was stationed there, and by employing a combination of threats and promises, persuaded him to hustle up to the third floor.

Cochise was back hovering over Orwell, who looked ready to break out crying.

"Arrest that fucker," I said. "I'll prefer charges against him and the pricks he works for."

I waited around until the paddy wagon arrived.

"You cocksucker," Cochise muttered. "I blow you fuckin head off fo this"

When I finally got back to my car the cop on duty tacked on ten dollars more for overtime.

CHAPTER 3

Meeting Tom Smith

Geri Sapperstein was in my office promptly at ten the next morning. I knew she would be. All lawyers who bill on a time basis have little clocks in their heads. *Tempus fugit, tempus fugit.*

Tom Smith, the client, was another matter. He showed up about 45 minutes late, and mumbled about traffic and parking problems. I couldn't be upset with him. The poor guy was grieving the loss of his wife, and was saddled with caring for their five year old son and two newborn daughters.

Tom and I chatted for about an hour, with Geri taking notes. He and Celia had a warm and loving marriage, and he would be a terrific Plaintiff. A jury would love him.

Without even reading it over, Tom Smith signed the retainer agreement I handed him, and the HIPPA authorization. By federal law, no health care provider could release any medical information or consult with me without the authorization of the patient or, when dead, her survivor.

Phil Levine had joined us for the meeting with Tom. He would play a key role in preparing the case and I wanted him in from the beginning. I wasn't anticipating much of a contribution from Geri, who Phil was appraising like a lamb chop I was serving up for dinner. I ignored it. Geri was a big girl, and would have to take care of herself.

I had already established that Dr. Mijeck, the doctor performing the tubal ligation, was not in private practice, but was in fact an employee of the South Side Community Hospital. This was important because it meant that he would be considered an agent of the hospital. They would be legally responsible for his acts, and he would be covered by their malpractice insurance policy. That policy would be certain to have much higher liability limits than those usually carried by individual doctors. We had a nice deep pocket to go after.

I was anxious to get my hands on the hospital record as soon as possible, so I asked Phil to hustle out to the Hospital immediately with a copy of the HIPPA authorization and get a complete copy of the records.

Phil said that since he would be out South, he would stop for lunch at Elliott's after the hospital, and then we could meet back at my office and review the records. "Do you like pulled pork?" he asked Geri. "Elliott's has the best Barbecue in Chicago." She said she loved pulled pork. Either she found him attractive, or she preferred a ride to the South Side over returning to a desk stacked with paperwork. Or maybe she really liked pulled pork.

As I walked Phil and Geri out to the waiting room, an enraged Cochise came bursting through the door. His gray suit was crumpled and dirty from a night in the County Jail. There was blood in his eye.

"Mother fucker---------I'm gonna get you, you cocksucker!" He had a very limited vocabulary.

He towered over me, and as he leaned closer he reached for something in his inside jacket pocket.

I backed away and stumbled over a magazine rack.

Phil grabbed a lamp and swung it like a baseball bat into the side of his head, sending Cochise's hat and red feather flying.

Cochise staggered to one knee, and Phil finished him off with a kick to the face. Phil searched his pockets and held up a wicked looking knife.

"Thanks pal," I said as I got to my feet and straightened my jacket.

I called the lawyer who employed Cochese, a guy named Morrisey, told him what had happened, and demanded he come over immediately and retrieve his chaser, who was now sleeping comfortably on the floor of my waiting room. Leaving him there would look bad for business. I also told Morrisey that he owed me the price of a table lamp.

A breathless Morrisey arrived at my office within a few minutes, just as Cochise was coming to. He was an overweight balding guy wearing a bold plaid sport jacket challenged to stay buttoned over his expansive belly, a wide gravy stained tie reaching only halfway down his chest, and a frayed white shirt with the buttons struggling not to pop.

Morrisey said that the kid in the hospital, Orwell something, he couldn't recall the last name, was fair game, that they took their shot and I won, so no hard feelings. I should have been satisfied with getting the case, he said. "It's just business." His ethos made it impossible for him to understand why I would turn Cochise over to the police, and I didn't waste my breath lecturing him.

"I bailed him out this morning, but I didn't know he was coming after you. Honest."

If Morrisey ever knew what "honest" meant, he forgot it during his first year of practice, but I believed him because I didn't think he was stupid enough to send a thug to attack a lawyer, at least not in broad daylight in front of witnesses.

"I'll keep him on a tight leash. This won't happen again. You have my word."

But Cochise seemed to have other ideas.

As he struggled to get to his feet, still very wobbly, he turned to Phil, who was testing the mechanism of the knife by repeatedly pushing the button and making the blade flick out.

"Fuck you Hymie, you ass is mine," he hissed.

"This is sure a lot more exciting than corporate law," Geri said, as she and Phil left to get the hospital record.

CHAPTER 4

The Hospital Record

Phil and I didn't have time to give any more thought to Cochise because we were too busy concentrating on *Smith* and playing catch-up. The Risk Management people at the hospital had the jump on us. Geri's letter requesting the medical records was a red flag that triggered the hospital personnel into action. Everyone involved in the case was warned to stonewall us.

I had hoped the hospital record Phil and Geri were bringing back hadn't been "doctored," excuse the pun, and would give us enough information to discover what really happened in the operating room. But the record they brought back contained no smoking gun.

The operative report was more condensed than a Readers Digest synopsis of the Second World War. *Germany and Japan conquered much of Europe and Asia. The U.S., England and Russia beat them.* The hospital record gave about that much detail. *The patient was undergoing a tubal ligation, the procedure had begun, and somewhere along the line, it didn't say when, just at some time before the tubes were tied, the patient stopped breathing, and died.* The nurses notes, what there were of them, gave no more explanation. The anesthesia record seemed to indicate that the patient stopped breathing shortly after the procedure was begun. *But where was D-Day, The Death Camps, Hiroshima?* Nothing in the records gave a clue as to the reason for the death.

The staff pathologist who performed the autopsy obviously wanted to shield the hospital and had made no real effort to explain the underlying cause of Celia's death, or if he did, he didn't record his findings in a way that made any sense to me. His totally unhelpful conclusion was that the cause of death was "cardiac arrest, cause undetermined."

Of course, they couldn't cover up the fact that a healthy twenty-eight year old woman went in for a voluntary simple procedure, the tubal ligation, and that her six week old twins were orphans before her body left the operating room. But if you believed the record, (at least those records that could be deciphered---typically some of the handwritten notes were illegible), all medical personnel performed flawlessly, and God must just have decided that it was time to take Celia away.

It was our job to prove that God had gotten a big assist from somebody in the operating room, the surgeon, an anesthesiologist, or maybe an operating room nurse. I explained for the benefit of Geri Sapperstein, whose knowledge of Medical Malpractice law seemed to be limited to the one week they spent on the subject in her first year course on Torts, that the plaintiff had the burden of proving that one or more persons in the operating room was negligent and caused the death.

"If I had only gotten the hospital record right away there might have been more in there," a crestfallen Geri realized, "and an independent autopsy would have told us more."

There was no sense bemoaning what could have been done. We had to deal with what we had, a minimal record that had been laundered to hide the truth. Our first hurdle was to come up with a plausible theory explaining the cause of death---I needed direction from a pathologist for that, and I needed a good gynecologist who could find flaws in the procedure that was performed. It was also possible that I would need an anesthesiologist, if the case pointed in that direction. But that could wait a little while.

I found the pathologist, Eugene Kramer, who practiced in Los Angeles. Phil came up with the gynecologist, and in the process of doing that, he also found Sharon Heller, my long lost love.

CHAPTER 5

Reconnecting With Sharon

I had attended the first six years of grammar school with Eugene Kramer, and couldn't erase the image of him as the geek who wanted to grow up to be a sportscaster and walked around mumbling to himself, announcing imaginary Blackhawk games. "It's a shot and a goal!" he would shout out excitedly, as he stumbled along on his way to school. In seventh grade Kramer was whisked away to the University of Chicago Lab School, along with a couple of other of our resident geniuses. Now he was a Board Certified Pathologist practicing in Los Angeles. We had to go out of State for almost all of our Malpractice experts, because local guys would almost never testify against each other.

I telephoned Eugene, and after being switched around several times and suffering two disconnects (one caused by his receptionist, one by my inability to master the new complex phone system installed in my office), I finally reached him somewhere in the bowels of Cedars Hospital. We hadn't spoken in some time, and he was surprised to hear from me.

After exchanging pleasantries, I told him about the *Smith* case, and after expressing some reluctance to work on the Plaintiff's side, he called it 'The Dark Side,' he agreed to review the record. "Give me a few days to look over the chart, and then I'll give you my thoughts. But no guaranty I'll come down on your side."

We set a date for the meet at his office in Los Angeles. He suggested that after the conference we could have dinner for old time's sake. He would like me to meet his wife. I said I would look forward to it. We made a firm date.

A week before I was scheduled to leave, Phil and I met to review our progress in the *Smith* case. "As long as you're going out to L.A. for a pathologist," Phil said, " I figured you could kill two birds with one stone and enlist a gynecologist from L.A. as well, so I called Ruben Weinstock."

"Who's Ruben Weinstock?"

"Don't you remember. He was your busboy at Laurel's Resort."

"A name from the past. He made it through medical school? And he's living in L.A.?"

"He is, and he's a gynecologist with outstanding credentials. I talked to him last week. And you know who else is living out there, and who he told me he sees from time to time?---Sharon Heller----remember her?"

It was eons since I had last seen her, but how could I forget Sharon. The love of my youth.

"And Weinstock told me Sharon is divorced, and living in West L.A. I figured that since you and Phyllis are divorced, you might be interested. Why don't you give her a call." Phil handed me Sharon's phone number, which he just happened to have handy.

Here I was, newly divorced, free and over twenty one, actually way over twenty one, and my old flame, the true love of my life, was available. Kismet.

It only took the one phone call. Even after all those years. It was like we had never been apart. She felt it too, I could tell. We talked on for hours, both of us reluctant to hang up the phone.

When I flew out to L.A. the next week, Sharon was there to meet me at the airport. She was even more beautiful than I remembered, and the old feelings surged to the surface. We drove straight to her home, a duplex apartment that she lived in with her fifteen year old son, who, fortuitously, was spending the week-end with his father. Despite the beautiful California weather, we never got outdoors. I called Eugene Kramer Saturday morning, cancelled our meeting and dinner plans for Saturday night, and told him I would be back in L.A. soon. By the time Sunday rolled around I was madly in love with Sharon all over again.

And after that I fell into a routine of flying out to L.A. for a long weekend about twice a month, leaving Chicago on Thursday afternoon after work, and returning Monday morning. The only exception was when Sharon could get away and fly to meet me in Chicago, or wherever I happened to be taking out of town depositions. I did plenty of work on the planes, and I had my laptop, but it still played hell with my law practice.

About a month after we first reunited in L.A., Sharon flew into Chicago, and we took Phil out to dinner at Gene and Georgetti's Steak House, to thank him for getting us back together. We sat at the bar, waiting to be seated, and reminisced about the old days in North Haven. Phil mentioned that he had gotten Sharon's address from Ruben Weinstock.

"So that's how you found me. I wasn't clear on that."

"Phil contacted Weinstock to act as our expert in a malpractice case," I explained, "And while they were schmoozing about old times, Weinstock mentioned you. But how did Weinstock find you in L.A.?"

"He didn't find me--I found him," Sharon said. "My regular gyne had retired and a friend suggested that I try to get in to see Dr. Ruben Weinstock who was a gynecologist with an office in Westwood, not far from me. So I contacted him." She took a sip of wine, and complemented my on the selection. "I didn't even realize I knew him until we met in his office. He told me he was very busy, and ordinarily wasn't taking on new patients, but he had recognized my name and was very nice about taking me on. He's been my regular doctor ever since."

I knew it would be gauche to say that Ruben had always wanted to get in her pants, even when we were kids at the resort, so I just kept my mouth shut.

But Phil of course said "He always wanted to get in your pants."

I explained to Sharon that I hadn't met with Weinstock yet, hadn't seen him since North Haven days, and was having trouble thinking of him as an expert witness because the picture I conjured up was a fumbling busboy at Laurel's.

"He's a very competent doctor, successful and well respected," she assured me. "I think he would make a great witness."

"Let's hope he's willing to testify for a Plaintiff in a malpractice case." More and more of the gynecologists I contacted were reluctant to get involved. Many expressed a growing hostility to plaintiff's malpractice attorneys. They blamed us for their rising malpractice insurance premiums. The animosity was throughout the country. Just a few weeks before, all of the obstetricians in one County in Texas uniformly announced they would refuse to deliver the babies of the wives of malpractice lawyers.

"He has no reluctance to testifying," Phil had assured me, "and his credentials are solid. I checked him out thoroughly. The only thing you want to be careful about," warned Phil, who was always tuned in to the nuances of selecting experts, "is that Weinstock has been head of a team doing sex change operations, and he has published on that subject, and some jurors might be offended by the idea." And turning to Sharon he said, "I assume you didn't get that kind of treatment from him."

"No problem on that score," she said.

I could testify to that.

CHAPTER 6

Another Trip To Los Angeles

Two weeks later, at the end of a work day that had begun in my office at six a.m., I affixed my briefcase atop my rolling overnight case with the compartment for my laptop, double-checked to make sure I had my Droid, bid goodbye to Julia, saying I would be back Monday afternoon, and thus encumbered pulled my portable office to the elevator, rode down to the lobby, walked the short distance to the subway station at Lake and Clark Streets, and boarded the C.T.A. train to O'Hare. I was embarking on my bi-monthly commute to see Sharon in the City of Angels.

The train was not yet crowded with homebound commuters, and I was able to sit comfortably in one seat and park my belongings on the seat beside me. We zoomed along the tracks down the middle of the Kennedy Expressway and passed the barely moving line of cars stymied by the never ending construction work.

When I had been married and living in the far north suburbs I used to drive to the office every day, and I was often stuck in that same kind of traffic going to and from the loop. My daily commute took about an hour each way.

Now I would be commuting to California and back about twice a month. When I tried to convince Sharon to move to Chicago by complaining that the travel time would seriously cut into my law practice, she responded with typical Sharon logic. She calculated that when I lived with my former wife I spent over 40 hours a month commuting in the car. "You'll only spend half that time each month traveling to California. I have my career too, my friends are here, and the weather is great." She gave me a light kiss on the lips. "And, our weekends together are terrific." End of argument.

A fat balding guy, wearing a sweatshirt that advertised he belonged to "The International Skeptics Society," whatever that was, was standing in the aisle alongside me. Despite all the other empty seats, he elected to sit next to me, and to accommodate him I had to transfer my suitcase and briefcase to my lap. *Your appearance could be enhanced if you had your barber trim the hair in your ears, and your doctor burn the black mole off your forehead,* I wanted to say, but I restrained myself. I did tell him that I doubted he was a skeptic. He didn't laugh.

Our train rolled along smoothly and unimpeded, and I tried to concentrate on the Law Bulletin and the Illinois Bar Journal, but he repeatedly distracted me, loudly proclaiming his doubts concerning the Warren Commission findings, Obama's birthplace, Armstrong's moon walk, and whether Romney paid any income tax or even filed returns for those earlier years. A lot to worry about during the 40 minute ride to the airport.

Our plane sat on the ground for 20 minutes behind a long line of other jets before we were cleared to take-off. Then I downed a couple of martinis, did some paper work, and took a short nap. I declined dinner on the plane and telephoned Sharon, using the phone on the seatback in front of me. The call cost me $8.50 and the sound quality was terrible. But I was able to get across that our flight was on time, that she should pick me up at LAX, and that I'd take her to dinner.

I also reminded her that I was meeting with my pathologist, Eugene Kramer, on Saturday, and that we were going to dine with him and his wife in the evening. She either said "love it" or "shove it". Because of the static I wasn't sure which. We signed off just as the plane hit an air pocket over the Rocky Mountains and dropped several hundred feet.

As we touched down I set my watch back two hours to California time, and willed my body systems back to 7 instead of 9 p.m. But my empty stomach was starting to growl.

Sharon was waiting for me, standing on the sidewalk beside her car. She ran forward to meet me. She was blond and beautiful, and when she threw her arms around me and kissed me, pushing her body tight into mine, the weariness disappeared.

"You've had a long trip and you look tired," she said. "Let's have a quick dinner and then get on home."

I suggested we just have a bag of potato chips and a candy bar in the car.

She laughed, and we agreed to skip the restaurant.

Sharon drove straight to her apartment. She did most of the driving when we were in L.A. I always had trouble finding my way around. The angle streets and curving coastline were very confusing to me. I was used to the perfect grid of Chicago, and the water of Lake Michigan always being to the east.

Her bi- level apartment was a yellow stucco two story duplex in West L.A. It was a lived in place with oak wood floors, Indian throw rugs, white stucco walls covered with woven wall hangings, and vaulted ceilings. The living room was furnished with comfortable couches and chairs you could sink into, and there was even a small wood burning fireplace.

The formal dining room had a large dark mahogany table with eight chairs, with a matching credenza, all of which Sharon had assured me were very valuable antiques, originally in the McCormick Mansion, and purchased by her in Chicago before she and her former husband moved to California.

We didn't use the dining room table, but instead sat at the scarred old wooden table in the kitchen, and I watched Sharon expertly scramble eggs, adding green peppers, onions, plenty of salt and pepper, and a touch of garlic. She placed an iron skillet on her gas stove, added some type of butter substitute, and poured in the egg mixture. My contribution was to put a couple of English Muffins in the toaster, and push down the handle.

We washed the meal down with a bottle of chardonnay, I cleaned up the dishes and the skillet, and then we headed for bed to make up for the ten days we had been apart.

After playtime ended, and as we were dropping off to sleep, the phone at the bedside rang. But when Sharon answered the caller hung up. It happened a second time, just a few minutes later. She looked disturbed, maybe a little frightened.

"Do you have any idea who it was?"

"I don't know. The calls are blocked. It happens once in a while. He never says anything... but sometimes I can hear breathing."

"Maybe you should call the police."

"It's probably just some crank. Don't worry. I keep all the doors locked, and we have those gates on the windows. I'm safe."

We turned off the telephone, and drifted off to sleep.

CHAPTER 7

Consulting with Eugene Kramer

The volunteer receptionist at Cedars checked her map three times, and then gave me detailed directions to find Dr. Eugene Kramer's office. The pathology department was housed in the dungeon of the old building. I had no problem finding the elevator she told me to use, but when I got off at the lowest level I began wandering around the maze of dull green hallways with minimal lighting, was forced to reverse course twice at dead ends, and finally stumbled across a sympathetic young lady in a blue surgical gown who took me by the hand, led me along another dim corridor, and pointed to a laboratory at the far end.

I walked past an unattended secretary's alcove, and found Eugene seated at a metal counter, hunched over a microscope and dictating the description of a tissue sample. He didn't look up as I came into the room. The bald dome of his head, glistening under the fluorescent light, was framed by a fringe of gray hair. His pudgy fingers, encased in thin rubber gloves, delicately exchanged one slide for another under the microscope. His gray lab coat was opened, and his belly hung over his belt. But he did have a nice California tan, at least on the top of his head, which was the only skin visible to me.

"You look wonderful Eugene. This California sunshine agrees with you."

"Bullshit. I got old and fat, but you look the same as when you were a kid. How do you do it?" He had looked up at me for a second, and then went back to his slides. I was lucky. I still had all my hair, just a sprinkle of gray had appeared, and I was within five pounds of my weight when graduating law school.

"Genes, abstinence, and a lot of airline meals."

Eugene pivoted around on his stool to face me. "I had a chance to review the Celia Smith file. That was one of the most incomplete autopsies I've ever seen reported. They didn't do half the things they should have done---they didn't even cut open and describe the chambers of the heart. Are you following me?"

I assured him I was.

"They attribute the death to electrical mechanical disassociation. But this is merely a mechanism of cardiac arrest, not the cause. Based on the findings they reported there was absolutely nothing abnormal, and," he chuckled, "if you accepted these findings as true you would conclude that Celia Smith was still alive." Eugene's idea of a joke.

We moved over to his desk, and he thumbed through the hospital record I had sent him. He had dog-eared several pages.

"It doesn't look like a high spinal or other anesthesia problem. If it was, the vital signs during the administration of anesthesia wouldn't look this way. If it was the anesthesia, I would expect to see a precipitous drop in blood pressure. There would have been a tachycardia preceding the bradycardia, and I don't see that here. I'm not an anesthesiologist, but the anesthesia is the type and amount that seems appropriate. So I think it is pretty safe to rule out anesthesia as the cause of death. But without a better autopsy, I really can't say with certainty what happened. And I don't want to just make a guess."

Under the laws of evidence, an expert can't give an opinion that is merely a guess or conjecture. But he can give an opinion, to a reasonable degree of medical certainty, that he believes something is more likely true than not true. Couched in those terms, he is permitted to give an opinion for a jury to consider.

In my experience, doctors, especially those practicing in the more precise disciplines such as pathology, are reluctant to give opinions unless they are certain.

I told Eugene that I could always find a professional witness who would say anything I wanted. But I was looking to discover the truth. Who was culpable? Why did she die?

"I'm not a gynecologist, and I can't give you all the minute details, but I'll give you a general picture. When they do this procedure, the tubal ligation, they want to make it easy to isolate and get to the tubes. In order to do this they blow up the abdomen like a balloon by injecting carbon dioxide. It's like inflating a beach ball with an air pump, only instead of putting in air you put in carbon dioxide. This gives them the room to work."

I nodded to show that I was following him.

"It's possible that somehow the carbon dioxide got into the blood stream by mistake, traveled to the heart, and killed her. As a matter of fact, when they execute a murderer by lethal injection that is exactly what they do....inject carbon dioxide into the blood stream."

"Wouldn't an autopsy show that this is what happened?"

"A careful examination of the right side of the heart would have shown that carbon dioxide caused the cardiac arrest. But the pathologist didn't do that examination. He didn't open the heart chambers. And there was no examination of the blood vessels for evidence of a puncture. He might have suspected what a careful type of examination would reveal, and he didn't want to establish a case against the surgeon or the hospital. After all, he was employed by the hospital. But he didn't do that exam, and that is why I may suspect it, but I can't absolutely prove it…. They might tear me to pieces on cross." He was wavering on whether to commit to testifying. He wanted to take a little time to think it over.

Sharon and I met Eugene and his wife for dinner at an upscale sushi restaurant. The wife had a personality just a shade above that of the cadavers Eugene worked on, and the looks to match. Eugene (no one ever thought to call him Gene, or give him any type of nickname) was as much a geek as ever. Too bad the restaurant didn't allow smoking. I would have lighted a cigar just to mask the scent of formaldehyde that clung to him, and I don't even smoke.

I struggled to find topics for conversation during dinner, and failed miserably. Sharon stepped in and saved the evening. She drew them out and got them talking about their pet poodle, gardening, and cruises they had taken. Then she got Eugene and me to talk about our school days together, and seemed fascinated as Eugene went into a long and boring reminiscence.

By the end of the meal, outsiders would have thought us to be close friends. Sharon leaned over to me and whispered that she could take a pass on any more dinners like this. I nodded.

I grabbed the $500.00 dollar dinner check, which I intended to charge to the file. Eugene didn't fight me for it. More importantly, he leaned back, slapped his hand down on the table, and said he decided he was willing to testify for me in *Smith*. "And it will give us more chances to get together again, the four of us. This has been so great."

Sharon kicked me hard under the table. I smiled at the three of them and sat there, waiting for the pain to subside.

So now we had our pathology expert. I just hoped he wouldn't drop the ball like he used to do when he played right field in the park.

CHAPTER 8

Venice Beach

I spent the next day studying female anatomy at the Venice Beach. After a quick dip in the salt water and an hour of lounging under a beach umbrella, Sharon grew tired of my leering at girls, and suggested that we stroll the Boardwalk to shop for sun glasses and tee shirts.

We stopped at Jodi Maroni's for duck and orange sausage sandwiches, and devoured them at a beachside table while we watched the muscle boys pumping iron. Now it was Sharon's turn to ogle the glistening bodies, and comment on the "nice butts." When we finished eating we resumed walking, stopping to watch the guy juggling chain saws, and a little further on some idiot chewing on ground glass. I almost got run over by a grandmother on a unicycle, and had to dodge out of the way of a Hindu strumming a guitar while gliding along on rollerblades.

Sharon browsed the blocks of stalls, all run by Koreans, each stall exhibiting the same sun glasses, tee shirts, beach towels and other assorted discount merchandise.

We finally headed back to our blanket, following behind a teenage girl wearing a tee shirt that said in large red letters:
"Wanna Get Laid?
Climb up a chicken's ass
And wait a while"

We dropped back so nobody would think we were with her.

CHAPTER 9

Orwell Washington Calls

My brief California sojourn ended Monday morning. Sharon and I overslept and awoke at 6:30a.m. to the sound of birds chirping outside her window. It was always like that in California, where the streets were quiet at night and we could sleep with the cool night air blowing in through an opened window. Back at my apartment in Chicago I had to keep the windows closed at night to shut out the traffic of the city. I even replaced the glass in the windows and sliding door to my balcony with heavy duty triple-panes that the salesman assured me were thick enough to block all sounds, even ambulance sirens. "And not only will they shut out all sound," he added, " they are so thick they are bul-let -proof." I supposed that could come in handy if the terrorists ever attacked.

We didn't even have time for a quickie, so we showered and dressed, and headed for LAX. Sharon dropped me at the United terminal, I kissed her good-bye like a commuter heading for his morning train, and waved as she drove off to work. I was back in my office by mid-afternoon.

I returned a call from Orwell Washington, the boy with the fractured femur, whose case I had signed up at Mount Zion Hospital. He sounded frightened.

"He after me again, lawyer Seger (he pronounced it cigar). Cochise say I should switch over to his man or he gonna break my other leg an both arms too. He's seriously mean."

"He's bluffing. Cops are watching the situation. He wouldn't dare do anything."

"Ain't no pigs where I live. Just assholes like Cochise. Ain't nobody gonna protect me in the hood. Cochise he own the fuckin projects. I gotta fire you Mr. Seger. Besides Cochise is gonna give me bread up front for signing with his man. I know you say you a good lawyer, but you ain't done give me shit."

This wasn't the kind of problem I needed my first day back in town. Sometimes I seemed to spend more time keeping clients happy and in line, than I did working on their cases. It was a necessary part of the practice. I wasn't even sure that Cochise had really threatened Orwell, or if Orwell made up the story to shake an advance out of me. I suspected the latter, and was tempted to tell Orwell to fuck off. But the kid had a good case and someday, probably reasonably soon, it would bring in a nice fee. So I bit my tongue.

"Why don't we sit down and talk about this. How about meeting at Edith's."

He was surprised that I knew about Edith's, a terrific barbecue shack in the heart of the ghetto. Lean spare ribs, St. Louis style, tender but you had to rip the meat off the bone, and a secret sauce with just the right amount of sweetness, and a kick that cleaned out the sinuses. Piled on top of the slab was white bread to mop it all up. One of my great fears was that Chicago Magazine would write Edith's up, and then the yuppies would ruin it.

"I be there in an hour Mr. Seger." He sounded more relaxed already.

CHAPTER 10

Dining at Edith's

You don't go to Edith's in a suit and tie. As a matter of fact, if you're a honky maybe you shouldn't go to Edith's at all. Not that Edith wasn't friendly. She kept up a good natured chatter as she splattered the ribs with sauce, and served up the heaping plates. And although it could get rowdy, her husband, Henry, who did the butchering and cooked the slabs on the smoldering hickory, kept decorum as he periodically patrolled the aisles wearing his chef's hat, his white apron splattered with sauce, and a frown on his mahogany face that glistened with sweat from the heat of the coals. Nobody could miss the sharpened cleaver he held by his side.

When I walked in, the customers shifted their attention to my white face, the only one in the place, and stayed focused on me as I took a table near the window so I could see out onto the street and keep an eye on my hubcaps. I fiddled with my silverware and waited for Orwell to arrive.

He was only a half hour late. Cochise was with him, feather and all. Shit. Orwell hadn't been bluffing.

Orwell sat down, but Cochise remained standing, rested his hands on the table and leaned down over me.

"Man, you are mother fuckin crazy coming in here." He reeked of Jack Daniels, his eyes were bloodshot, and he slurred his words. It didn't take a breathalyzer to make the diagnosis. He had a switchblade knife in his hand, still unopened. He must have bought a new one. Even closed it looked very threatening.

"Now, like Moses said to the Pharaoh---LET MY PEOPLE GO--- you understand that, don't you--Jew lawyer," he hissed. "You don't let him go, the angel of death might visit you."

I didn't bother pointing out to him that it was the Egyptians, not the Jews, who were slain by that particular angel. It didn't seem to be the right time for a bible lesson.

Orwell was taking this all in, and so far I was losing on points.

Cochise's thumb moved toward the button on his new knife, and just in time Henry stepped up behind him and placed his cleaver at Cochise's throat.

"That's enough, Mr. Cochise. Put that piece on the table real slow like, and then step back." A thin red line had already appeared on Cochise's neck, and a trace of blood oozed down onto his silk shirt.

He slowly put his knife on the table, and as he did so Henry's cleaver flashed down and nicked off the very tip of Cochise's little finger. Henry would have made a great moyle.

He handed Cochise a napkin to stem the flowing blood.

"Now I gonna say this just once. You turn around and walk outta here real peaceable like, or I gonna slice you up for barbecue."

Cochise walked quickly to the door holding his bloody finger, and exited without a backward glance. He left his switchblade on the table and Henry dropped it in his pocket. That made two knives Cochise had lost.

Orwell stayed with me. We transferred to a clean table, one without any blood on it, and ordered dinner.

"You plenty lucky that cook was here or you be a dead man," Orwell said.

"Well, sometimes it helps to be lucky."

Henry brought our slabs of ribs to the table and sat down with us.

"How you been Mr. Seger. Long time no see. I was real happy when you called me to say you was coming down. And thanks for the heads up that there could be trouble."

"I've been pretty busy Henry. It looks like you've been busy too."

"Business goin through the roof. But you really saved our ass when you defended us." He turned to Orwell.

"We got sued when some folks came down with salmonella. And the Board of Health climbed all over us, tryin to shut us down. But Mr. Seger here proved they got it from some ice cream at 39 flavors where they went for desert. And he didn't even take a fee. But we gotta feed him whenever he comes in."

"Tonight makes it all even, Henry, but I would like you to do me one more favor. Put Orwell on the cuff whenever he comes in. You feed him real good. Send me the tab."

Whether it was the tip of the finger or the prospect of free food I'm not sure. But Orwell never said anything further about firing me.

When I got home that night I called Phil Levine and told him of my newest run in with Cochise.

"I just wanted to alert you. Henry probably scared him off, but he's pretty crazy and you can't be sure. Just watch your back."

As it turned out later, that was a prophetic warning. The 'watch your back,' I mean.

CHAPTER 11

Dr. Ruben Weinstock

Our case against Dr. Mijeck was shaping up nicely. I arranged to meet Ruben Weinstock during one of my California trips. Another rendezvous with Sharon that I could write off to the *Smith* file.

The *Curriculum Vitae* of Dr. Weinstock was appended to a memo that Phil had prepared. It ran 30 pages and was most impressive. Weinstock had come a long way from the summers he worked as a busboy at Laurel's during his pre-med summers in North Haven.

He had gone on to be educated and trained at the finest Ivy League Schools. Then he did his residency at Cedars in L.A., where he was now on the staff, and was a full professor at U.C.L.A. Medical School. He was in private practice in Westwood. He published numerous papers in Medical Journals, and was the co-author of a medical textbook. The publications would be impressive to a jury

The title of his most recent publication was "Reconstructing the Sexual Organ---Size Does Matter." I winced at what the Defense might do with that on cross-examination, and considered how a jury might be affected by it. The slightest misstep can sometimes shatter the expert's image.

I hadn't seen Weinstock since the Laurel Resort years, and still pictured him as the awkward chubby pre-med. I arrived at his office about 5 minutes early, introduced myself to a stunning red headed receptionist, and had barely settled onto one of the rather stiff leather chairs that were designed to make it easier for his pregnant patients to rise to their feet, when Weinstock himself came out to personally greet me. Weinstock was on time for our appointment, a rarity for doctors.

I was pleased to see he looked like a beardless Santa Claus, and had Santa's twinkling blue eyes. He even had a substantial pouch, the product of good living, that he couldn't quite hide beneath a beautifully tailored Armani suit. Weinstock had developed a charming and courtly manner, and a deep resonant voice, with just a trace of a Boston accent he picked up while at "Hahvahd", and must have worked hard to preserve. I am sure it played well in Westwood, and it would be impressive in a Chicago courtroom too.

He led me back to his private office, and on the way we walked by several austere examining rooms, each with a paper covered examining table with stirrups at the foot. None were presently occupied. By contrast, his plush office was richly paneled, had soft lighting, and a thick carpet. He settled into a huge leather swivel chair behind his beautifully grained desk, and I perched uncomfortably on another of those hard chairs. His chair was raised so that I had to look up to him as we spoke.

We chatted casually, catching up on our lives since North Haven. He told me that he was recently remarried to a "beautiful young thing." He said he was surprised to learn that I was back together with Sharon, we had been apart so long.

"You two must have had a lot of catching up to do, so much happens to people over the years."

"It was a lot of years, but it seems like we were never apart."

"Well, I'm pleased to hear you're together. Really happy for both of you. I usually shy away from testifying in malpractice cases," he said, "whether it is for the plaintiff or defendant. But when Phil contacted me and started schmoozing about old times at Laurel's he softened me up. And then when he mentioned that you were the attorney handling the case I got more interested. The idea of a reunion of sorts kind of sealed the deal, and I agreed to review the case. I'm looking forward to all of us reminiscing about those summers together. It will be almost like old times, you, me and Phil working together again."

"But this time you won't be bussing my tables."

"And I'm going to cost you a hell of a lot more than twenty percent of your tips."

"Sometimes those tips were pretty good."

"I'll review the records and give you an honest opinion. If I see something wrong, I'll say so. And I'm willing to testify. But I'm not going to say things I don't believe or am not comfortable with."

"Of course. I only want your honest opinion." In this case I felt an honest opinion would be sufficient.

I agreed to Weinstock's outrageous fee schedule, and at his request gave him a hefty check up front. So much for his doing this for old time's sake.

Now that the clock was running on the consultation, I wanted to get right to business, and quickly highlighted the important facts of our case. I got up and walked around his desk and leaned over him as he examined the Smith hospital record. The hell with it. Let him look up at me for a while.

While he read the operative report, and the autopsy report, I told him that Dr. Eugene Kramer, the pathologist at Cedars, had consulted with me on the case, and felt it LIKELY, *when I said 'likely' I was fudging more than a little, so far he hadn't committed to more than the possibility,* that carbon dioxide being injected into her abdomen during the insufflation was the likely cause of the death. Ruben, of course, knew Kramer, since they were both on the staff at Cedars.

"Good man, Kramer. If he's right about the cause of death, you might have a case of malpractice against Dr. Mijeck. I'll comb the record carefully and send you a report." He also promised to mail me some medical literature and a videotape of a laparoscopic tubal ligation being performed.

We concluded with a few more pleasantries, and he wished me the best of luck with Sharon. He declined my offer of lunch because he had to deliver a lecture on the construction of a vagina. We shook hands, and he hurried off.

CHAPTER 12

The Video

These days there is a lot of discussion about the police videotaping all arrests and confessions so that there can be no later claim of coercion or undue force. If surgeons agreed to videotape every operation, it could be a powerful weapon in establishing whether or not a malpractice claim was valid. But you can bet any video tape showing a mistake would meet the same fate as those CIA Interrogation tapes Congress was never able to see.

Leading surgeons make videos of procedures, along with a running commentary, that are available to medical students and physicians, for teaching purposes.

It was one of these videos, recording a tubal ligation, covering it step by step, with a running commentary emphasizing the steps to be taken, the safeguards to be followed, and the pitfalls to avoid, that arrived by UPS from Dr. Weinstock a few days later.

"Geri, I just got a new X-Rated video from our O.B. Gyne expert, and if you'd like, we could watch it over a pizza at my place tonight."

She said she'd be over at 8:00.

On the way home I picked up a large frozen half cooked deep dish sausage pizza from Uno's, the world's greatest pizzeria, popped it in the oven, and it was cooked to perfection by the time Geri arrived. I uncorked a bottle of Chianti, and we dined as we watched the video.

It was about as riveting as the training films the army shows recruits during basic training. In a monotone, the lecturing doctor, at each step of the procedure, told us what he was going to teach us, then taught it to us, and then, for the third time, told us what he had just taught us. It's a teaching technique that may be appropriate for army trainees, some of whom never graduated high school, but it seemed an overly simplistic method for individuals who had already reached medical school. On further reflection, thinking about some of the doctors I had encountered, maybe it was the appropriate technique.

As Geri picked a piece of sausage off of the pizza and put it aside on her plate (I made a mental note to order plain cheese if we ever did this again), I re-ran the portion of the video where the doctor demonstrated a test to insure that the hollow needle used to introduce the carbon dioxide into the abdomen was properly placed.

"You have now inserted the hollow needle into what you believe to be the hollow space of the abdomen. As I have stated previously, this is done so that we can attach to the needle a tube leading from the carbon dioxide tank. We have to insert carbon dioxide into the abdomen so that we expand the space and have room to identify the fallopian tubes, examine, and close them off.

But as I said earlier, you want to make sure that the tip of the hollow needle is in the open space of the abdomen. You want to let the gas flow into that space. You must make sure that the tip of the needle has not been inserted into a blood vessel. If that were the case, the gas could pass through the vessels into the chamber of the heart, and result in the death of your patient. Obviously, that is a result best to be avoided (chuckle, chuckle).

One way to determine the location of the tip of the needle is by feel. You can usually tell if it is properly placed because after entering the abdominal space you feel no further resistance. This would indicate that you have not entered any blood vessel. Every experienced surgeon learns to rely on feel.

But in order to insure that the tip of the needle is not in a blood vessel, it is best to perform the following test, which I will now demonstrate.

*Before (**underline before**) attaching the carbon dioxide tube to the verres needle that is inserted into the abdomen, attach an empty syringe to the end of the needle. Make sure that the plunger of the syringe has been fully depressed before you attach it. After the syringe has been attached, and the needle is inserted, slowly pull up on the syringe. If only air is drawn out, you know that the needle is properly placed in the abdominal space. But if you pull up blood into the syringe, then you know you are in a vessel, and you cannot attach the carbon dioxide tube. It* *could have very serious consequences. You must first withdraw and re-insert the hollow needle and do the syringe test again to make sure it is properly placed.*

The placement of the tip of the needle into a blood vessel is a very rare and unusual event, but it can happen, and that is why I mention it.

For the purposes of this demonstration we will assume that no blood has appeared, and that the needle has been properly placed. You then detach the syringe from the end of the needle, attach the carbon dioxide tubing in its place, like this, and begin introducing the carbon dioxide."

I turned off the TV.

"That was very educational," Geri said.

"I'm not ready to perform a tubal ligation, but it gives me a better idea of what to cover with Dr. Mijeck when we depose him." We compared the notes that we had taken during the viewing. I told Geri her handwriting was almost as bad as mine.

"But my notes aren't spotted with pizza stains."

I used a napkin to wipe the spots off my note pad, and Geri helped me clear the dishes.

We went out onto the terrace. I pointed out Phil's apartment, just down the block, across the street. I asked if she wanted to help me finish off the bottle of wine.

"I'd like to, but I really should be going. I have to be up early tomorrow for an office meeting. Thanks for the dinner and the show."

I walked her to the door. We didn't kiss goodnight.

Sharon called about midnight (ten o'clock her time in L.A.). When I'm on trial I turn off the ringer on the phone next to my bed, but otherwise I leave it on so I won't miss her nocturnal calls. She always apologizes for calling so late, I always tell her "no problem--I was up anyway." We make small talk about the events of the day, say we love each other, kiss goodnight, and I struggle to fall back asleep.

To lighten things up I told Sharon I spent the evening at my apartment with Geri Sapperstein, watching a nudie movie that Dr. Weinstock had sent me.

"Did you and Dr. Weinstock ever talk about me?"

"We didn't have much time for socializing. We talked mainly about tubal ligations, and whether he would act as my expert, and agreed to a price for his work. I'll get to spend more time with him when we meet to prepare for his deposition, but that will be further down the road. These goddamn cases take forever to get to trial."

Sharon said that she would be coming to Chicago for a few days the following month, so that would spare me the agony of one of my flights to L.A.. She said she wanted to meet Geri.

"A hint of jealousy?"

"Don't be stupid. I'm just curious."

We said we loved each other, and kissed goodnight.

CHAPTER 13

Phil---I Never Really Knew You

Phil and I had known each other since we were kids. When I became a lawyer, he joined me as my investigator. When we weren't working on cases, we spent many off hours socializing. I didn't think there was anything I didn't know about him. But I was wrong, dead wrong. I found that out one evening when we both already had far too much to drink, and Phil let slip his secret.

The night started out full of good comradeship. A jury came back in our favor earlier in the day and I was buying the drinks. We started discussing what was left to be done in the *Smith* case, and there were plenty of loose ends Phil had yet to take care of, but neither of us was in the mood to talk work, so we switched to lighter subjects.

The outer bar was overflowing with young lawyers on the make, and scores of pretty women, mostly young lawyers and legal secretaries, there for the making. Uniformed Andy Frain ushers controlled the crowd, and people were lined up into the street, waiting for someone to leave so that a few more bodies could be shoehorned inside.

Long time patrons such as Phil and me were seated in a private section on a balcony overlooking the teeming multitude below. You didn't get jostled, the service was good, and it afforded an excellent birds-eye view of the crowd. If you spotted any interesting talent, you could swoop down in a minute and have her accompany you upstairs.

But I wasn't hunting for women that night. Sharon was more than I could handle. I just needed a little breathing space. I wanted to unwind with some heavy drinking and easy conversation.

On Friday during Happy Hours they served two drinks for the price of one. And the drinks were very generous. I was just ordering us our third round of R. J. Hudson martinis (one half Sapphire Blue Gin, one half Absolute Vodka---the vodka mellows the gin, the gin gives the vodka character) when Phil returned from the men's room.

"Ted Mizell is still pissed at you for saying his girlfriend was fat and ugly."

"That was years ago," Phil said. "You mean he's still seeing that pig."

"Yes, and it still eats at him. He brought it up again the other day. We were scheduling a progress meeting on *Smith*, and I said you had been doing a lot of work on it, and suggested you sit in. He didn't want you there---said you had called his girlfriend, the red-headed one, fat and ugly."

"She is fat and ugly. And she isn't even a redhead. Believe me. I checked her out."

Phil and I were half way through our third R. J. Hudsons.

"What do you mean you checked her out? Did you fuck her---Ted's girl. Are you crazy? The guy refers me a ton of business."

"I didn't have to fuck her to check the hair on her pussy," Phil said. He stopped talking, looked down at his drink, swirled the martini around 5 or 6 times, took a sip, and put the glass down. His eyes had morphed into slits, like those of a cat. His eyes always got that way when he drank too much.

I looked at him, waiting for him to continue. The jovial mood of earlier that evening had vanished. We seemed to be surrounded by a wall of silence that blocked out the din from the bar below. Sort of like the security cone that came down in *Get Smart*.

Neither of us said anything for what seemed like several minutes. He finally made up his mind to continue. First he took a large gulp of the martini, tried to carefully replace the glass on the table, but banged it down harder than he intended, and the residue poured onto the table. "Sorry." He wiped the table with a napkin. "Where was I?"

"We were talking about your being at the meeting with Ted, and maybe that's not such a good idea."

"No, that wasn't it. I was trying to tell you something important. It was about the redhead." He looked at me, directly into my eyes. "I didn't have to touch her to see her pussy." His voice was slurred. "All I had to do was get her up to my apartment."

"What are you talking about?"

"Do you remember Big Marlene?" Phil asked. My God. We hadn't talked about her in years, but I immediately remembered her. Who could forget your first childhood sexual experience.

Phil and I were eleven years old. We lived in the same three story multi-unit courtyard apartment building. Phil lived in an apartment with an entrance on Congress Street. My apartment had its entrance around the corner on Central Avenue. Both of our apartments were on the second floor. When we stood on our wooden back porches, we could look across the big concrete yard and waive at each other.

Big Marlene, who was thirteen years old, two years older than Phil and me, lived on the first floor, in an apartment just below mine.

Phil and I liked to play in the concrete back yard. Big Marlene liked to play in the basement, where the washing machines were located. Her favorite pastime was inviting kids like me and Phil to come down to the basement so we could watch her take her clothes off and squat and pee into a can. This was Phil's and my favorite form of entertainment for many months until, to our great distress, Big Marlene's father, a hat manufacturer's representative, got transferred to Cleveland, and she moved away.

"I haven't thought about Big Marlene for a long long time," I said.

"Well, I never forgot Big Marlene. Never. When I was a kid I had a wet dream 'most every night, picturing her in the basement, squatting over the can. And to this day, every time I think of her pissing I get a hard-on."

"Jesus Phil, that's sick." It was a lot more disgusting than that, but we were both plenty drunk and my vocabulary wasn't working so well.

He paused and then mumbled in the slow somber tones of a drunk trying to control his speech. "Better than Viagra."

I wasn't sure where this conversation was leading. But it seemed Phil was at a stage where he needed to unburden himself, and who better than to his oldest friend. I had even shared Big Marlene with him.

Phil ordered us another round, took a large sip from his fresh RJ Hudson and looked to me for a response. First he encouraged me to taste the new drink before me. He waited while I took a deep gulp. I had consumed as much gin and vodka as Phil. I had been matching him drink for drink. I was getting foggy from the alcohol.

Phil looked down and pushed his glass further away from him, but it was too late for abstention. The alcohol had already completely unlocked any control. "I watch women without them knowing it."

"What are you talking about? I don't want to hear any more of this bullshit." My tone was shrill, and for a moment Phil clammed up. But The floodgates were opened. He had waited a long time to share his secret with someone. I remained silent, played with my drink, and after a few moments he continued.

"Ever since high school I had trouble making it. I would get started with a girl, and then I would just shrivel. And I couldn't cure the problem. Remember when we worked at Laurel's. I wouldn't date any of the guests, and not even the maids working there for the summer. I was afraid they would talk. Tell everybody how I couldn't keep it up."

He took another sip.

"I only went out with townies, like Bonnie Rifkin," he chuckled. "You remember Bonnie, the dentist's daughter who was saving her virginity but loved to give blow jobs. And with Bonnie, when I couldn't get it up, I just made the excuse that blow jobs didn't turn me on. And she believed it. Once, she even offered to fuck me, but I persuaded her that she was right to save her virginity for marriage."

"Well, anyway," Phil continued with the slur, "I had a lot of problems earlier." I held my hand up signaling him to stop, but he was on a roll.

"Then one day I started thinking about Big Marlene. And that turned me on. And I realized that if I could watch a girl pissing I would have no problems when I went to fuck her."

He was talking faster now.

"So I found me a setup where I could actually watch them. And things have been fine since."

And then he rhapsodized over his apartment on Elm Street. It was an old apartment where the door to the bathroom was a little too short, where the hinges were set a little low, and where the frame was warped at the top. The result of these flaws was that when the bathroom door was closed there was a gap at the top between the door and the frame. By standing on a stool and peering through the crack Phil was afforded a full view of anyone using the toilet.

Over the years Phil finely honed his technique, he rambled on. He would find a girl, make sure she drank lots of liquids (he found coffee worked the best) and then take her back to his apartment. Eventually she would end up in the can. Slacks were better than skirts because they permitted a less obstructed view.

"And you've never been caught peeping in all these years?"

"Well first, I always pretend I'm on the phone across the room when they head for the John. I have a set-up where I can make the phone ring. There is a stepstool by the door that I can stand on. And you know what I noticed--- they never look up. None of them. When they sit on the pot they either look down or straight ahead."

I tried to keep my face blank, but the distaste I was feeling must have shown because he tried to justify his conduct.

"Look, it's not just so I can watch a broad wipe her pussy. It's so I can get to know them better. Everyone has a facade. Their dress, their grooming, their manner. When they sit on the pot they let their guard down. They pick their noses, they scratch themselves. They're real. That's all I want. To see them as they are. And it helps me get it up when we hop in the sack."

He paused only momentarily when he saw that I had my hands waving, trying to signal him to stop. But he couldn't. He wasn't finished yet.

"Last year I went high tech, and put in a new door with a hidden lens so I get better views, and less chance of ever being caught."

I sat there, not knowing what to say. My lifelong best friend was a pervert. I had always thought of him as this bold tough guy. He had been a good and reliable friend, and a lot of fun to be around too. I owed him for reconnecting me with Sharon. And he was a great investigator. We made a good team. But the guy was clearly a pervert. As he watched me, I sat there weighing all those things.

"Well," Phil finally said, "now you know. What do you want to do?"

I mulled it over, thought about the *Smith* case that was going to be on the trial call soon, and the work I needed Phil to complete. His last progress report indicated he hadn't finished an in-depth background examination of Dr. Mijeck. He was following up on rumors, so far vague and unsubstantiated, that Dr. Mijeck had previously been involved in surgical procedures that resulted in the injury or death of two women, and some hints that at one time his license was temporarily suspended, or he had been kicked off the staff of some hospital. Also Phil said there appeared to be time a gap between the time Mijeck came to this country from Europe, and when he surfaced as a doctor in Wisconsin.

And, maybe most important of all, Phil was still searching for the operating room nurse who had gone missing right after the surgery. Maybe she knew nothing, or maybe she held the key to the whole case.

"What are you thinking?" Phil suddenly sounded more sober.

"Remember the story of the three-legged pig? The visitor was sitting in the farmhouse, looked out the window and saw a three-legged pig hobbling around in the yard. He asked the farmer about it, and the farmer said:

'That pig saved our lives more than once. Last year we had a fire at night, and the pig raced into the house and woke us up and got us out. And a few weeks later my baby son fell into the pond out there, and the pig jumped in, picked him up gently in his snout, and carried him out. Saved him from drowning.'

'But how did the pig lose his leg,' asked the visitor.

'Well,' replied the farmer--- 'a pig like that you don't eat all at one time.'"

"You're sickened by me, aren't you," Phil said.

"We had a lot of good times, Phil, a lot of years. A friendship like ours--- I couldn't kill it all at one time." *I'd wait until Smith was finished.*

"The three-legged pig is going back to work," he said. He staggered down to the bar and started chatting with a girl dressed in slacks, chug-a-lugging a large stein of beer.

CHAPTER 14

The Garage

Phil Levine stepped from the steaming shower, carefully toweled off with a Chocolate Matouk Bath Sheet, Monogrammed *P.A.L,* a gift from a former girlfriend, and then rushed into his bedroom to dress. He was in a hurry to leave, but before stepping into his slacks he stopped to admire himself in the full length mirror. Not bad for a guy in his 40s. Tall, trim, and just a touch of gray at the temples of the $100.00 razor-cut. The tanning parlor color went well with his whitened teeth. *I still look pretty damn good.*

He was to pick up Stan Seger at O'Hare, and according to United's flight arrival information the plane from Texas would be touching down 15 minutes early. *Not that you could believe those fucking airlines.* He was especially eager to talk to Stan tonight --- couldn't wait to see Stan's reaction when he told him what he had discovered.

Phil checked his watch again and hurriedly threw a change of clothes into an overnight bag. Stan was flying into O'Hare from Houston, where he had been taking depositions. He was scheduled to deliver a paper at a conference in Wisconsin the next morning. The plan was that Phil would drive Stan's car to the airport, pick him up, and he and Stan would head directly to the Abbey Hotel in Lake Geneva, the site of the seminar. Stan would be able to get a good night's rest before his speech the next morning, and Phil would be free to troll the halls and maybe pick up a young female barrister hanging out at the bar. There was always an abundance of young associates at those Bar Association meetings.

Phil went to his battered desk and shut down his computer, grabbed a light coat from the closet----it was chilly in Chicago and would be even colder in Lake Geneva, turned out all the lights, and made sure the front door of his third floor condo was double locked. Phil lived in what real estate agents termed a vintage building, which meant that it was very old, and if the warped oak door wasn't pulled shut hard before double locking, it was likely to pop open.

Phil bounded down the three steep flights of stairs and walked out into the October night. He pulled his hat down low on his head, and raised his collar against the howling wind. He moved quickly to the dark alley where Stan's car was garaged. Stan lived in one of the older elevator buildings on the lakefront, about a block from Phil's apartment, one of those expensive 1920's vintage co-ops that had beautiful apartments with high ceilings, but wholly inadequate parking facilities.

Stan was forced to pay an exorbitant amount to rent a parking space a short walk away in a free standing garage behind an old mansion. The garage was a solidly constructed brick structure with a green overhead door that opened onto the alley behind Elm Street. In its glory days it had sheltered horse-drawn carriages.

Phil ducked his head and bent into the wind that skimmed over chilly Lake Michigan about a block to the east, and gusted to 30 miles an hour as it was channeled through the alley. Dry leaves swirled around and made a crunching sound beneath his feet. The temperature near the Lake had dropped to the mid-40s, and the wind chill factor made it feel much colder than that. Phil pulled his hat down further.

When Phil reached the garage he fumbled in the dark to find the garage door opener and Stan's car keys. He didn't notice the broken pane of glass in the window at the side of the garage, or that the window sash had been lifted high enough to admit an intruder.

As Phil clicked the opener, the door slowly rumbled up. It was noisy, but not loud enough to disturb the people in their home across the alley, not the parents on the first floor who were absorbed in watching yet another rerun of *Law and Order*, nor their teenage son upstairs in his room, who challenged himself by blasting *Arcade Fire* on his I-Pod while puzzling over a geometry problem.

Curiously, the garage light did not go on when the door went up. Phil figured the bulb must have burned out and silently cursed whoever was responsible for maintenance. In the gloom he was barely able to make out Stan's BMW convertible, the only car in the garage. At least it had been backed in and was facing out toward the alley, so that it would be easy to exit. He cautiously felt his way along the driver's side of the convertible until he reached the door handle. It was unlocked.

When he opened the car door no interior light went on. *Shit*! He slid behind the wheel and fumbled for a light switch but was unable to find it. He felt along the dashboard, searching for the ignition switch. He wasn't sure where it was. He had never driven Stan's car before. *A lousy night for all the lights to be out.*

He finally located the ignition and got the car started. Phil then adjusted his seat, almost crushing the person behind him who had been crouched in wait in the cramped space between the front and back seats.

As Phil fumbled to fasten his seat belt, a figure silently rose behind him, raised a small caliber pistol to a place a few inches behind Phil's head, and squeezed the trigger twice. There were two popping sounds, very muffled. Phil's hat blew forward. His hair, which had been carefully sprayed, did not move out of place.

Phil's body slumped across the front seats, a dead weight which prevented his murderer from pushing the back of either seat forward to exit the vehicle. In a panic, the killer reached over the seat, and wrestled the body around, frantically trying to move the obstruction. Phil's body moved only slightly. The killer sat back—defeated. The headlines would be terrific: "KILLER TRAPPED IN MURDER VEHICLE."

Think…Think you idiot. Don't blow your cool. Finally the killer realized the problem, and reached around and released Phil's seat belt. Phil's body rolled to the floor. Sweating profusely, the killer folded a seat forward, managed to open the passenger door, and finally escaped the vehicle with gloves and one sleeve smeared with blood.

CHAPTER 15

The Funeral

Parlor C of the Weissman Brothers Funeral Home was one of their smaller chapels. It provided seating for about 300 mourners. On this day it was less than half full. The mahogany casket holding the remains of Phil Levine rested on a pedestal at the front of the room. The casket was closed.

Phil's mother was in the front row, sobbing hysterically. She was being comforted by her husband who was very pale and appeared to be in shock. Phil was their only child, a 42-year-old bachelor, and the family line ended in that casket.

The mourners consisted mainly of lawyers Phil had worked for, a sprinkling of distant relatives, and a group of social friends, the few males greatly outnumbered by several casual girlfriends, none looking terribly distressed. I can't remember Phil ever dating anyone more than a handful of times.

Oh yeah, and my ex-wife, Phyllis was there, looking trim and sexy in a black Anne Klein suit that she probably purchased new for the funeral with money from one of my monthly alimony checks. She had come to know Phil pretty well during our years of marriage, but I doubt that she had any contact with him in the two years since our divorce. I myself only saw Phyllis on those rare occasions when she would be downstairs at the house *we* formerly owned, but now was solely hers, when I picked up my daughter, Danielle, for our twice a month week-ends.

I was surprised to see Phyllis at the chapel. She never liked Phil. She said there was something weird about him, but couldn't put her finger on it. And during our marriage she resented me spending any evenings with him. I think it was because she feared that his confirmed bachelorhood would rub off on me.

I suspect she came to the funeral because she knew I would be there, and she wanted me to see how good she looked. And she did look good. Blond and tanned and trim, her hair cut a little shorter than it used to be. Her legs, always very shapely, looked particularly fine in the sheer black hose. As she walked to the front of the chapel to offer condolences to the family, I could tell that she was watching me out of the corner of her eye, so I gave her the old up-and-down once-over, and nodded approvingly. She pretended not to notice, but her slight smile told me that she did.

After chatting briefly with Phil's parents, Phyllis took a seat as far away from me as she could get, and we had no further eye contact. Other than for brief discussions about Danielle, I don't think Phyllis and I had spoken more than ten words in the last year, and that wasn't about to change today.

Phil's folks had asked me to deliver a eulogy. "You were his oldest friend, actually his only close friend," his mother had said. "You even roomed together at Illinois. And he loved working as your investigator."

I declined to speak at the funeral. She couldn't understand it.

"You two were almost like brothers." She said. "Why won't you speak?"

I said I just couldn't. I told her I was just too broken up by the loss. I lied. I couldn't bring myself to deliver a speech honoring Phil. I would have felt like a hypocrite. It was true that he still worked as my investigator, that was business, but our friendship ended on that night Phil and I got drunk and I learned of his perversion.

The family had to settle for having the rabbi deliver the eulogy. It was obvious that he didn't know Phil, never even met him. He had to rely on notes of information furnished by the family, embellished by the usual platitudes. But that didn't mean it was going to be brief. *Au contraire.* He droned on and on. He was going to give the Levines their money's worth. At the rate he was going, the eulogy was going to last longer than *Gone With The Wind*.

Every time he paused briefly, took a deep breath, and launched into a new segment, he evoked a fresh flow of tears from Phil's mom and dad, and muffled groans from the lawyers in the audience, who grew ever more fidgety as the billable minutes ticked off, never to be recaptured. You could tell how important each lawyer was by how frequently he glanced at his Rolex.

I searched the room for Sharon, who had insisted on flying in from L.A. for the funeral. I told her she didn't have to attend, it was a long flight to Chicago, but she said she felt obligated because Phil was there all those years ago when Sharon and I had first met at Laurel's Atlantic Resort, and it was Phil who was instrumental in bringing us together again after our long separation. But so far Sharon was a no show, and by the time the rabbi finally ran out of gas she still hadn't appeared. Probably her flight had been delayed, a common enough occurrence with United Airlines.

As I checked one last time for Sharon, I noticed a police detective standing at the back of the room, scanning the crowd for suspects. He tried to remain innocuous, but he was easy to spot. He was a big guy with a full head of white hair, and the yarmulke he wore as a disguise was too small, and slipped off whenever he turned his head.

CHAPTER 16

To the Cemetery

I moved up to join the other pallbearers in the second row, directly behind the immediate family. Ted Mizell was sitting alongside me, nervously rubbing together the gray pallbearers' gloves we had been given, as if he was trying to smooth the felt. Ted was certainly no fan of Phil's, but when they were short of pallbearers, he agreed to serve.

Ted turned back toward the other members of his firm, who were seated a few rows behind us, and signaled that when the service concluded they could return to the office. I nodded toward Geri Sapperstein, who was dabbing a tear from the corner of her eye with a white silk handkerchief.

After directions were given for assembly of the funeral parade to the cemetery, and information about the *Shiva* at the parent's home, the pallbearers were summoned forward to transport the casket to the hearse.

Phil's mother asked us to wait a few moments while she viewed her son one last time and kissed him goodbye. A curtain was drawn around her and the casket so she could have that one final agonizing moment with her only child.

From the other side of the curtain we could hear her sobbing, and her husband pleading with her that it was time to leave.

The detective from the back of the chapel came up to me and introduced himself as Inspector Hollman. He looked more comfortable now that he had replaced the yarmulke with a soft brown fedora like they used to wear in '40s movies.

My father wore a hat like that. We used to call them men's hats. Whenever I try one on I always feel ridiculous, like a little kid impersonating Humphrey Bogart. I still feel that way, even now when I'm past my fortieth birthday. But I had to admit that the soft brown fedora with the slouch brim looked perfect on the head of Inspector Hollman. I didn't ask to see his identification.

"I'd like to ask you a few questions," he said, impervious to the wailing of Phil's mother in the background.

"It doesn't seem like a very propitious time," I replied, all the while keeping my eyes on the curtain.

I agreed we could talk at the cemetery, after the burial was concluded.

There were only ten cars in the procession following the hearse. The rest of the mourners had gone from the chapel to their offices, or out for a two-martini lunch.

Geri Sapperstein got Ted's permission to go to the cemetery, and asked if she could ride with me. I was glad of the diversion. Too many things I didn't want to think about yet.

It was a clear and unseasonably warm autumn day, and although I wasn't sure it was appropriate to do so in a funeral procession, I had lowered the top on the convertible I rented. The police had finished examining my BMW for evidence, and I had it towed to a detailer to have it thoroughly scoured and cleaned. Then I would sell it. No matter how good a job they did I never wanted to drive it again.

The breeze softened Geri's severe hairdo, grief had softened her face, and she looked more feminine and less lawyerlike than usual. She was saying what a nice guy Phil was. She couldn't get over the tragedy.

"Were you and Phil very close?"

"We spent a lot of time working together on *Smith*. It was strictly business. He was a nice guy, easy to be with."

"Did you ever do any work up at his apartment?" I couldn't stop thinking about *that* bathroom.

"What a strange question. Why would you ask that?"

"Just making conversation. Just wondering, that's all. It was an unusual place."

"Our work was in the field, or in the office. I don't make it a habit to visit men's apartments. Watching the video at your place was an exception. Did Phil tell you anything different?"

"Of course not. I didn't mean to offend you. I apologize if I did."

She changed the subject. "Did Phil keep you up to date on what we were working on---the progress we were making?"

"I've was really busy lately, out of town for depositions on other matters, so I didn't have a chance to talk to him since I left Chicago last week."

"Didn't you call him while you were out of town---like to tell him when your flight was arriving?"

"I just texted him my flight number. We hadn't spoken since I left town Thursday."

"Do you need me to bring you up to date on *Smith*?"

"Probably not. Phil routinely sends memos to the office on the progress. I'll check them over, and let you know if I need more information. I probably will need your help in the future on the case though. 'Specially since he's gone."

She was quiet after that, and I didn't feel much like talking either.

When we arrived at the cemetery I joined the other pallbearers and carried the casket from the hearse to the grave. Ted Mizell was gripping the casket handle opposite me, and we spoke in a low tone across Phil's body.

"I see that Geri rode out to the cemetery with you."

"Yeah, she asked to come along."

"I was hoping she'd ask *me* for the ride. She's a good looking piece. I hit on her, but she turned me down cold. And I could have done her some good with the firm."

"Maybe she doesn't like dating married men."

"Everybody knows I'm not that seriously married."

We placed the casket on the rollers that would lower Phil into the ground.

Phil's mother was still crying------she had a bottomless reservoir of tears. She was being supported by her husband and another relative as they shuffled along the strip of green indoor-outdoor carpeting that led to the gravesite.

I once had a case against a cemetery where the widow tripped on the loose carpet and fell into the grave on top of her husband's casket, breaking her arm. I noted that today the carpet was secure.

CHAPTER 17

Talking to Inspector Hollman

After the graveside service Inspector Hollman approached me. "You have time to talk now?"

Geri excused herself and said she would get a ride back to the office with Ted Mizell.

Hollman and I walked over to a wooden bench in a carefully manicured memorial area and sat down. The sun was still shining brightly. As Phil's mother had said earlier, it was a beautiful ugly day.

He wanted to know how Phil had been behind the wheel of my car when he was shot. I explained that I had spent the weekend in L.A. with Sharon, then flew to Houston on Monday for a deposition, and was flying back to Chicago on Monday evening.

"Phil was going to pick me up at the airport in my car. I was going to drive directly to Lake Geneva where I was scheduled to give a talk the next morning and then chair a program on "Sudden Acceleration of Jeeps". Phil was going to accompany me to Lake Geneva and just hang out---maybe make some contacts for future business."

"When did you find out he was dead?"

"I was supposed to call Phil on his cell phone when I got off the plane. Since 9/11 they don't allow cars to park by the curb, waiting to pick up passengers. So he was supposed to be at a McDonalds near the Airport, waiting for my call, and by the time he got to my portal I would be outside, on the curb, waiting for him."

"So you called his cell when you got off the plane?"

"And no one answered. I called him two or three times. I couldn't understand what happened, I thought maybe he got into an accident or something, and I really didn't know what I should do. I called his home too, but no one answered there either. I called my secretary, Julia, but she didn't know what happened either."

"What time did your plane land?"

"At about nine o'clock, right on time, surprisingly enough. I figured maybe Phil got tied up in traffic, so I waited around for another half hour, but no Phil."

"So did you go home?"

"I couldn't. This was a big conference in Lake Geneva in the morning. I had spent a lot of time preparing. The meeting had been publicized for months, and lawyers with sudden acceleration cases were coming in from all over the country, along with a very expensive automotive engineer we had hired to consult with all of us. So I rented a car at the airport and drove to the Abbey."

"So you didn't go home first?"

"No, I got on the toll road and drove straight to the Abbey. That's the resort where the meeting was being held. Actually, I stopped off at the Brat Stop on Route 60 for a sandwich and a beer on the way. I hadn't eaten on the plane and was starving. And then I stopped at a tavern in town for an Akvavit Martini to unwind, and cool off before checking in. They do a dynamite Akvavit Martini. I was really pissed at Phil for not picking me up. I figured maybe he got the date mixed up, and thought I wasn't coming in until the next night. I tried calling him again. But no answer. I left him another very nasty message. I probably didn't get to the Abbey until close to midnight."

"Can anyone verify the times you were at the Brat Stop and that tavern in town?"

"I doubt it. Both places were pretty busy, and I didn't really talk to anyone, except to order food and drink. The desk clerk at the Abbey should be able to confirm when I checked in, because he was dozing at the desk and I had to wake him up. Also, I had him cancel Phil's reservation, but I had to pay for that room anyway because of their cancellation policy. I was going to make Phil pay me back for that one."

"So when you went to bed that night, you didn't know Phil was dead?"

"I didn't hear about it until the next day. We broke for lunch and I called the office for messages, and Julia told me she had just heard that Phil was dead. That he had been shot. She heard it on the radio. She wasn't supposed to listen to a radio in the office, but when I'm away she doesn't pay much attention to my rules. She doesn't much listen to me even when I'm in the office, as a matter of fact."

"So you spent the weekend in Los Angeles?" Hollman had taken out a small spiral pad and was making notes as we spoke. He squinted as the smoke from the cigarette dangling from his mouth drifted into his eye.

"I spend every other weekend with Sharon, usually in Los Angeles, occasionally in Chicago."

"Being separated like that must make it tough on a relationship"

"Well she's stuck there right now because of her kid and her job. She's a teacher. And my law practice is keeping me here. We're making the best of it, and hopefully it will work out where we can live together someday. But what does this have to do with Phil?"

"Probably nothing, just curious." But he wrote it down.

"Is Sharon's last name Heller?" he asked.

"Why do you ask that?"

"When we went through Levine's papers we found a note that said 'Sharon Heller >>>>>W. S.' Do you know what W.S. means?"

"I don't have any idea." And I couldn't figure out why he would have a note with Sharon's name.

When did you say you left L.A.?"

"I flew out of LAX Sunday night. Sharon drove me to the airport. I flew into Houston, and checked into a Radisson right by the airport. I took the depositions at a conference room at the hotel Monday, and then caught a plane back to Chicago, just like I told you."

"And nobody can really verify your whereabouts from the time your plane landed in Chicago until you checked into the Abbey."

"There would be a record of when I rented the car. I told you where I stopped. I don't think I talked to anybody, and I can't give you the names of any bartenders or waitresses or patrons."

"Any phone calls that night, other than to Phil Levine and your secretary?"

"The only other call was to Sharon. I called her on her cell several times while I was at the airport waiting for Phil, but I couldn't reach her. Finally I got her on the home phone, and we just talked a few minutes, and then I went to rent the car."

"And your cell phone carrier will have a record of all your calls—you don't mind giving me access to those records, do you?"

"Be my guest."

"When you stopped at the Brat Stop and that tavern in town, how did you pay for those drinks, cash or credit card?"

"Cash. What am I, a suspect or something?"

"Just covering all the bases. It only takes about ninety minutes to get to Lake Geneva, faster if you rush. So if you really hurried, you could have had time to get to the garage, kill Phil Levine, and then drive to the Abbey."

"And why would I kill him,--- because he didn't pick me up at the airport?"

"And if the desk clerk was as sleepy as you said, he probably couldn't be sure if it was midnight or even one o'clock when you checked in," he said, ignoring my comment.

"This is such bullshit. I would never kill anybody, especially Phil. The guy was my lifelong friend. He was still working on a big case that's going to be called for trial soon. I needed him."

"Did anyone know that you were leaving town that weekend, and that Phil was going to use your car?"

"I normally don't make announcements that I'm leaving town. I like clients and attorneys to think that I'm available at all times, and when I am away I keep in touch with the office on a very regular basis, and return calls promptly as if I were there. When you run a one man show you want to give the appearance of always being available. Otherwise people get skittish. But there was publicity in legal publications about my speaking in Lake Geneva that Tuesday. And I send out a monthly newsletter to all of my clients, new and old, as a sort of Public Relations tool. Telling about recent verdicts and settlements, and mentioning speaking engagements. I'm sure there would have been an item about my speaking at the upcoming Lake Geneva conference."

"So plenty of people knew you would be going to Lake Geneva."

"I guess so."

"And if you were speaking Tuesday morning, they could figure you would be driving up there on Monday." He was making more notes.

"What about Phil using your car. Anybody know about that?"

"Not unless he told somebody. He wanted to go with me to the conference and I said O.K. We agreed he would pick me up at O'Hare in my car when I arrived from Houston, and we would drive there together."

"But why drive in your car instead of his?"

"No particular reason. I kept my car in the garage very close to his place. We only live--lived---a half block from each other. It was no problem for him to get my car. My building, it's an old one--- doesn't have parking in the building itself. That's why I rent space it in that garage."

Hollman was intently scribbling in his pad. As he wrote, a fresh cigarette drooping from his lip, he squinted one eye to block out the irritating smoke, and I watched without comment as the ash at the end of his cigarette grew dangerously longer, until it finally fell onto his jacket. Unperturbed, he brushed it off, and it wasn't until the ember of the glowing tip almost reached his lip that he gingerly removed the last remnant of the cigarette with two fingers, and flicked it to the ground.

He irreverently ground the butt with the heel of his shoe into the well-tended turf at the base of the headstone of Hyman Solomon, who, according to the inscription, lived to ninety years, and was a beloved husband and father.

I reprimanded Hollman for littering, and suggested that he at least field strip the cigarette. I learned to field strip a cigarette years ago, during my smoking days, while I was on active duty with the Army Reserves. You remove the tobacco from the cigarette and scatter it on the ground, and roll the paper into a ball, and put the ball of paper, and the filter, if there is one, in your pocket. "If you field strip your cigarette the enemy won't find any evidence that you were there," I said.

He looked around at the graves, and told me that there was no enemy in the area.

"Were you and Phil lifelong friends?"

"We knew each other since we were kids. We went through school together. He was my investigator, and we worked together on cases. Socially, we kind of drifted apart."

"Mrs. Levine told me you refused to deliver a eulogy for your 'lifelong friend.' She was quite upset by that---couldn't understand it. What caused you to drift apart? Sounds like it must have been some serious differences to cause that big a split."

I didn't want to destroy Phil's reputation. "Nothing that serious. We just kind of migrated to different groups. Different interests, I guess. But we still worked together."

Another entry went into his notebook.

"Who were his closest friends?"

"He was kind of a loaner. I suppose I was as close as any."

"Was he going with anyone----dating anyone special?"

"I don't think so. He dated, but nobody special."

"Was he a queer?"

"Maybe a little odd, but not queer."

"What do you mean by that?"

"Nothing. I didn't mean anything. I can only tell you that he liked girls, and he certainly never made a pass at me."

The interview went along that vein. Holman's questions were getting annoying, but he was persistent, so I answered as fully as I could.

Finally he asked if Phil had any enemies.

I mentioned our run-in with Cochise, but added that it was almost three years ago. I could pinpoint the date because it was the same day we started working on *Smith*. "That was a long time ago, and I don't think he and Cochese had any further contact, but Cochese did make the threat, and it sounded very serious at the time."

Hollman said he would look into it.

The interview had lasted about forty five minutes, and during that time Hollman had lighted, smoked, and mashed out three cigarettes under heel.

As we rose to leave I glanced at the butts on the ground, and then at Hollman. He sheepishly picked up the butts and put them in his pocket. "That's showing proper respect for the dead," I said.

"Speaking of the dead, did it occur to you that maybe someone wanted *you* dead, not Phil? Maybe they thought it was you behind the wheel of that car."

"Phil didn't look much like me."

"But it was dark, and he was sitting behind the wheel of your car, and we think the killer was crouched and hiding in the back seat. Phil could have been mistaken for you."

It was something to think about. Seriously think about. I could conjure up a pretty long list of people who at one time or another were very unhappy with me.

CHAPTER 18

Back to my Apartment

I left the cemetery and drove to Phil's parents' house to sit Shiva. Shiva is the Jewish version of an Irish wake. There's an old joke that goes:

Question: What is the difference between an Irish Wedding and an Irish Wake?"

Answer: One less drunk.

Well the difference between an Irish Wake and a Shiva is that a Shiva has no drunks. Usually there is one bottle of liquor and everybody takes the compulsory shot "neat" and grimaces as it goes down. Not a pleasure, but a tradition. The typical guest gets his pleasure from gorging himself on the huge platters of food that are provided.

When I arrived at the Levine house there was the ritual bucket of water at the front door, provided to rinse your hands after coming from the cemetery. As was customary, there were plain wooden crates scattered around the home for everyone to sit on, and all the mirrors were covered with sheets.

A table was stacked with cold cuts and other delicatessen items, and friends and relatives were eating off of paper plates perched precariously on their knees. Between plastic forkfuls of potato salad they were all lamenting the tragedy of Phil's death.

Mrs. Levine, now a little more composed, approached me and sat down on the crate next to mine. After I again expressed my sympathy she asked if I would please retrieve Phil's personal effects from the police, and if I would go through Phil's apartment to gather any personal papers, records of savings and checking accounts, wills, insurance papers, etc.

She offered to pay me for my services, but of course I told her not to worry about that.

When I left the Levine's I drove straight home. I parked the rental car in my garage, the garage where Phil had been killed. The yellow crime scene tape had been removed. Then I walked quickly down the block to my building, checking out each passerby, ready to break and run if I spotted anything in the least suspicious. I willed myself to calm down.

My building, a magnificent old edifice protected from demolition as an architectural treasure, is called "The George House," named after the guy who constructed the building as a monument to himself in the early 1920's. He went bust later that decade. Our principal doorman is coincidentally also named George. We call him "George of the George House." George, the doorman, not the builder, greeted me warmly.

George had worked there forever, and had a pipeline into the private lives of every tenant. As he opened the door for me he said:

"How's California? How's the lady?"

"Great as always," I replied.

He winked.

After checking my mail, all junk and bills, nobody writes letters anymore, I took the elevator to the twentieth floor, and walked down the thickly carpeted corridor to my apartment. I paused before putting my key in the front door. I was remembering Inspector Hollman saying that maybe someone had tried to kill me.

I carefully examined the front door and saw no sign of forced entry. But the door was not double locked. I could have sworn that I bolted it that morning.

I opened the door a crack, making plenty of noise to let anyone know I was home. I was ready to slam the door and race back down the hallway if anyone jumped out at me, but nothing happened. I stood at the doorway for a few moments, listening for any sounds. Heard nothing. Now I entered the apartment, and went from room to room, peering in closets and even looked under the bed. Nothing.

The door to the terrace wasn't locked. I always locked that door. But I saw no one on the terrace. Just to make sure, I slid open the heavy door, always a struggle, and stuck my head out. Nobody there.

The phone rang and I almost jumped out of my skin. It was only Julia, calling from the office to remind me that an Appellate Brief was due the next week, and I better get moving on it. It had slipped my mind completely.

I told myself to calm down and not be so stupid. I tried to stop my imagination from running away with me, but I kept envisioning a bullet crashing into the back of my skull.

I poured some Scotch over ice and downed it in a single gulp. It didn't do much to calm me.

I had a strong urge to take a piss. My hand was shaking as I stood over the toilet and tried to unzip my pants. A hand shot out from behind the shower curtain and clamped onto my arm, sending my stream onto the wall. I screamed.

It was Sharon. She had been taking a shower, heard me at the front door, turned off the water, and waited in the tub until I entered the bathroom. She stepped out from behind the shower curtain, laughing. She was nude.

"What are you doing here? You were going to meet me at the funeral."

"My flight was delayed, and when we landed at O'Hare we sat on the tarmac for an hour waiting for a gate, so I missed the funeral and the Shiva. I figured I'd come right to the apartment, clean up, and wait for you."

"George didn't tell me you were here."

"I asked him not to. Said I wanted to surprise you."

"You surprised me alright." My heart was just starting to slow down. "Now do you mind letting go of me so I can finish my business."

"I'll just help you aim." And she did.

"Why don't we go in the bedroom and continue this," she suggested

"I doubt I could get it up. I just left a Shiva for a dead friend."

But the friend she was holding in her hand wasn't dead. She was getting my full attention.

" Maybe we'd better finish this in the bedroom."

And we did.

"You ready to do it again?" she asked. I was already dozing.

But I kept waking, and was plagued with thoughts of Phil lying under the ground. A very strong wind kicked up off of Lake Michigan, and set off the ghostly whistling sound through my apartment that always occurred when the wind hit my patio door from the east, even with the fancy new glass panels.

Sharon was deep asleep. I quietly got out of bed, being careful not to displace the cover, put on a robe, poured a generous Remy Martin VSOP into a snifter, and stepped out onto the terrace. It was about 50 degrees and there was a fine drizzle. The cool moisture felt good on my face.

Only a few cars, widely spaced, were moving silently along Lake Shore Drive at this hour, their headlights reflecting off the wet pavement. Occasionally there was a flash of lightening over the lake, but no thunder. The wind died to a light breeze, the water was still, and the whistling sound in my apartment stopped.

By leaning over the railing I could see Phil's old brownstone apartment. It was a block down and across the street from my place. And I could just see the tip of the roof of the garage, the place where he had been murdered. The Victorian style street lights, perched atop ornate iron poles, designed to resemble gas lights of old, cast a warm yellow glow onto the streets. Charming, but not much illumination. I slowly sipped my cognac, raised my glass to the insomniac staring out the window of his living room in the high-rise across the street, and went back inside. I crawled back into bed as quietly as I could. Sharon was still dead to the world, and she didn't move even when I kissed her on the neck. I turned over and finally fell into a deep sleep.

CHAPTER 19

A Morning Run

I woke up at 5:30 the next morning. I always wake up at 5:30, no matter what time I go to sleep. This is true whether I'm weekending in California or working in Chicago. My mental alarm clock seems to automatically adjust to the time zone. I snuggled up to Sharon, plugged in an earphone, and listened to Public Radio in one ear, and the sounds of Sharon's soft breathing in the other.

I tried to focus on the world news, but my thoughts kept shifting back to Phil. At about 6:30 a.m. I again slipped out from under the covers, took a pair of shorts and a shirt from the dresser, retrieved my running shoes from under the bed, and tiptoed out of the bedroom. Sharon didn't stir.

I ground some coffee beans in the kitchen (a dark roasted Sumatra priced at about $16.00 for two and a half pounds at COSTCO--screw you Starbucks), started the coffee going, and dressed in the living room. Then I headed for the lakefront jogging path, which is only a few blocks from my apartment.

The sky had cleared and the sun was just rising over Lake Michigan. I've told Sharon that this morning view is as beautiful as a California sunset over the Pacific, but she said it didn't matter because she'd never be up to see it.

There are plenty of people who do get up early, and the joggers like me had to keep to the right to avoid being run over by the in-line roller skaters and cyclists. I settled in behind a bobbing blonde ponytail with a bouncing derriere (wouldn't that make a great song title) and let her set the pace. I felt like a greyhound at the dog track. I would never catch her, but I really didn't want to. The view was too good. But not distracting enough. I kept mulling over the question of whether the killer was after Phil, or me, and who the killer might be. And if I was the target, would they try again.

I ran my usual slow six miles, and got back to the apartment a little after 7:00, after buying a Tribune from the news lady who stands alongside the running path. Her home is on a park bench, where she sleeps alongside all her worldly possessions. But she's more than a bag lady. She's an entrepreneur. Early every morning she walks to the corner newspaper box, invests one dollar, and instead of taking out one Tribune, she removes as many as she can carry, never less than ten. Then she camps out on the running path and hawks them to the runners and cyclists for two bucks apiece, plus whatever tip she can wrangle.

When I near the finish of my run every day, rain or shine, she's standing there ready to hand me my paper and take my three dollars, two for the paper and one for the tip. She always gives me a toothless grin. That's a lot more than you get from a machine. It would be easier to use home delivery, but I like to patronize the small neighborhood businesses.

When I got back to my apartment I peeked into the bedroom and found that Sharon was still sound asleep, dead to the world. She hadn't even moved.

I rewarded myself with a cup of the freshly brewed coffee, and sat out on the balcony with my paper. It was a great way to start the day.

As I was finishing the Sports Section, the lead story was about the Cubs planning to retool (for the umpteenth time), Sharon sashayed out of the bedroom and poured a cup of coffee. I signaled her to come out and join me.

She had to put her cup on a table and struggled with both hands to slide back the door to the balcony. "This damn door weighs a ton," she complained.

"The trick is to lift up slightly before you start trying to slide it. Then it glides real easy." I showed her how it was done.

"Aren't you a little chilly in just my shirt?" It was all she was wearing.

"I like the breeze. It cools me."

She sat down across from me and slowly crossed her legs. I tried to concentrate on the Editorial Page.

"By the way, do the letters W.S. mean anything to you? Capital W---Capital S."

She was lifting her coffee cup to her lips, and paused for a moment, breathed in the aroma, and took a sip. "Delicious, but still a little too hot." She set the cup down.

"Why do you ask?"

"The police found a note in Phil's desk with your name on it, and the letters W. S. It was written by him. I didn't know what it meant, so I thought I'd ask you."

She played with the handle of her cup for a minute, and then lifted the cup, cradled it in both hands, held it steady, and stared into the black coffee like a gypsy fortune teller trying to conjure up an image. Then looked up at me. "It's about Wally Smalley. You met him once, a long time ago, but you probably don't remember. It was really a long time ago, back when we first met in North Haven. During the summer. You and Phil had a run in with him then. We were just kids."

I knew the name. North Haven, Michigan. Sharon was dating Wally Smalley, a guy from town, and Sharon's dad had asked Phil Levine and me to break it up.

Of course I remembered. Sharon broke up with Wally Smalley, and Sharon and I fell in love. Wally, a really big and beefy guy, went bonkers about losing Sharon to me, and Phil had rescued me when Wally tried to take a punch at me. And a good thing too, because Wally probably would have beaten the shit out of me. But that was so far in the past.

CHAPTER 20

Wally Came Back

"There's something I think I guess I'd better tell you. It didn't seem important before......it still isn't, really.....but just maybe.......because of what happened......maybe it is."

"You sound very serious."

"I am. It's about something that started a very long time ago and it should have ended a long time ago, but it didn't."

I held up my hand to stop her. "I told you that anything that happened before we got back together didn't matter. It was history. I don't care and I don't want to hear about it. You don't have to tell me."

"But I think Wally is crazy and he might want to kill you."

"Wally Smalley? The guy from North Haven? That was finished a hundred years ago. Wasn't it?"

'Not exactly."

"Maybe you better tell me."

And she did. She told me that when her marriage broke up in California, and she started dating again, she bumped into Smalley at the Crab Shell, a waterfront bar on Venice Beach. He was a bartender.

"He told me that since we last saw each other he had been a professional football player, never made the NFL but played some Arena Football, and somewhere in there he had served a tour of duty in the Marines. He also claimed he did some kind of mysterious work for Blackwater, and still got occasional security assignments from them."

"And he was working as a bartender?"

"He said bartending was what he did between assignments. It allowed him to move around, and to stay flexible so he could be available if a security job came up. I know he was probably feeding me a lot of

B.S., but my marriage had broken up, I was lonesome, and seeing him was easier than starting up with new people."

"You don't have to tell me all this….."

"I want to. I really think I have to. After we were together a while, actually it was almost a year, I found out he was also booking bets, and maybe dealing a little drugs---I'm really not sure about that last part."

She sipped the coffee. "Ugh—it's cold. It was shortly after my divorce, I was lonesome, and he was fun. And he cared about me. I needed someone who cared about me. I know it's not a good explanation, but it happened. He lived in a houseboat in the Marina. "

"Sounds idyllic."

"It wasn't idyllic, and after I came to my senses it stopped being fun---as a matter it became terrible."

Finally, she told me, when her head cleared, she decided that Wally and his lifestyle were not at all what she wanted. What she wanted was OUT.

"Wally had been evicted from the Houseboat, and he had nowhere to live, so I let him move into my home. We lived together for a short time. But it wasn't working. Wally would get very jealous and suspicious for no reason. He became horribly possessive and sometimes he got violent. I told him to leave. He refused. So one day I put all of his things on the lawn when he was at work, and I had the locks changed. When he got home I wouldn't let him in. He broke down the door and I had to call the police. Later I had to go to court and get a restraining order. But he kept calling and writing. I refused to respond."

Shortly after she broke with Wally, I phoned her from Chicago and came bounding back into her life. She said I was her knight in shining armor who rescued her from Wally, just like I had done all those years ago in North Haven.

"When we started seeing each other again I didn't tell you about Wally because you kept saying you weren't interested in what happened in our lives before we got back together. And I was relieved to not have to tell you about him."

She leaned over and kissed me on the cheek, and poured each of us some hot coffee. She waited for my reaction.

"We've been seeing each other for almost three years," I said. "You tell me that Wally is in the past. Why should it have anything to do with us now, and why would there be a note in Phil's apartment with your name linked with Wally's initials?"

"Because even after I broke it off, Wally wouldn't stop bothering me. He kept calling. I hung up. I wouldn't talk to him. He sent me letters. I sent back the letters."

"I remember. Those phone calls at night when you said there was just breathing."

"He began following me, and sometimes when you were in Chicago and I was in L.A. he would try to come over. I never let him in or even talked to him through the door. He acted crazy."

"My *femme fatale*."

She ignored my comment. "Finally I told him that I love you, I always did love you, that I'll always love you, and that someday we were going to be married. He said he'd kill you first."

"Why didn't you tell me this was happening?"

"I was afraid it would upset you. I wasn't very proud of it. I got myself into it, and I wanted to get out by myself. I knew Phil was an investigator, so I called him and told him what was happening and asked his help to get Wally to stop. I made him promise to never tell you about it. I was afraid I'd lose you. That must be when Phil wrote that note… when I called him. Phil didn't say anything to you about Wally, did he?"

"No. He never mentioned it. And you almost married that asshole! You've got lousy taste in men."

"Except you."

"Flattery will get you nowhere. Where is this guy now?"

"He moved back here to the Midwest about a month ago. I heard that he had gotten into some kind of trouble in Venice Beach. Something about some money he owes for a drug deal or a gambling debt or something. His family is from North Haven, and I'm pretty sure he's moved back there. At least that was the postmark on the last letter he sent me."

"Do you still have that letter?"

"No. I returned it unopened like all of the others. But I noticed that Postmark."

"Do you have a picture of him? I'd like to see what he looks like so I can spot him if he tries to sneak up behind me."

"Just pictures with the two of us together."

"With your clothes on, I hope."

"I knew it wasn't a good idea to tell you about this. I'll send you the picture as soon as I get back to California. And I'll put fig leaves in the appropriate spots."

"What was his last name again?"

"Wally Smalley..........I usually just called him Smalley."

"Cute.........But I'm glad you thought of him as a smally rather than a biggy."

She groaned.

CHAPTER 21

Phil's Apartment

I grabbed a few sips of coffee, left the rest for Sharon, and headed down the block to gather the material Phil's mother had requested from his apartment.

Phil lives, oops, had lived, on a high third ---one apartment to each floor in his building. There was no elevator. The stairs were steep and narrow, constructed of well-worn oak. Each flight was guarded on the open side by a matching solid oak banister. The walls along the stairwell were covered with flocked wallpaper panels dating to an earlier century.

Phil always said his stairway was steeper than Kilimanjaro, and claimed he didn't need a health club because the climb kept him in shape. Even with all my jogging, I was winded by the time I reached the third floor landing.

The key his mom gave me slipped easily into the tarnished brass lock, and the same key fit the deadbolt above it. The heavy wooden door creaked loudly as it swung open.

All the windows in the apartment were shut tight and the air was heavy and stale. The blinds were down, blocking all light, and as I entered the apartment it was so dark that I banged my shin on a low wooden cocktail table. I swore as I fumbled for a light switch. I raised the blinds, opened the windows, and fresh air and light filled the room.

It seemed like a hundred years ago that I helped Phil lug furnishings up here when he first moved in. I was just finishing law school at the time. I had changed a lot since then. But the apartment hadn't changed much at all. The same carpeting, now a little more worn and slightly stained near the couch. Probably that's where he took most of his meals. The same wallpaper, now more faded. Phil had re-furnished the place periodically with junk, or antiques, depending on your point of view. To me it looked more like junk.

The best feature of the apartment was the living room fireplace that was inlaid with blue mosaic tiles. It was enough to convert the place from crummy to arguably charming. But then, I've always had a thing for fireplaces.

Next I moved to the bedroom.

There was a king sized bed with a canopy. The bed was neatly made, hospital corners and all, and covered with a white chenille bedspread.

The bedroom closet had mirrored sliding doors, and was overstuffed with clothes. Shirts, pants, suits and jackets hung at random with no sense of order, and several pairs of shoes were scattered along the floor.

The wooden bed stand held a reading lamp and an alarm clock with a beam that projected the digital time onto the ceiling. There was an unopened package of Ramseys in the drawer.

A pile of wrinkled clothes was on the wooden dresser. The dresser drawers held nothing of interest.

I moved on to the bathroom. If you didn't know what to look for, there was nothing to alarm anyone using it. A rose colored chenille bath mat covered the tile floor in front of the tub/shower and it clashed with the orange and blue plastic shower curtain. "Go Illini!" There was a small sink, with a ledge barely big enough for his electric toothbrush, and a mug from our fraternity days at Illinois used as a holder for Phil's toothpaste, razor, and comb.

Above the sink was a mirrored medicine cabinet, with shelves inside holding shaving equipment, assorted aftershave lotions and colognes, aspirin, prescription medications for high blood pressure and choles-terol, and a bottle of 100 mg Viagra. The label said 24 tablets but only nine remained.

The one big change was the door to the bathroom. The old warped door was gone. It was replaced by a new extra-thick wooden door that fully filled the frame. No crack for peeping, either at the top or bottom.

The unusual thing about the door was that both the front and back were elaborately decorated with carvings and encrusted with several *faux* jewels of different colors. I got down on my knees, and took a closer look at a clear gem in the door. There was some kind of lens hidden in there. Phil had gone high-tech.

When the door was closed that gem pointed directly at the porcelain throne of a toilet, which sat up on a little pedestal. Very elaborate, quite inviting actually, and certainly looking innocent enough.

I switched off the bathroom light, and headed for the roll top desk in the living room. If Phil had kept any personal papers, this is where they would be. Phil's insurance policy was in the top drawer, along with some bank statements indicating a modest balance in the checking account, and a Morgan-Stanley monthly statement showing holdings of slightly less than $200,000.00. He had named his parents as sole beneficiaries on his $10,000.00 insurance policy. It would almost be enough to cover the funeral and casket.

I scooped up the financial papers and all the bills I could find, and put them in my briefcase. I would give The financial papers to the Levines, and would pay Phil's small bills for gas, electric, and telephone. No sense bothering his folks with those.

Phil's appointment book was on the desk. I didn't find any appointments of interest, except that I saw that I was scheduled to meet Phil and Geri Sapperstein at my office in 15 minutes. We had made the appointment the week before Phil was killed. I had completely forgotten about it. I reached Geri just as she was leaving her office, and told her I was calling from Phil's apartment and we would have to reschedule.

"You must be in pretty good shape. You don't even sound winded from the climb."

"That's only because I've been here long enough to catch my breath."

On my way out I stopped in the lobby and retrieved a few current bills from Phil's mailbox. His mom had given me the key. I added them to the bills I would take care of.

CHAPTER 22

Dorothy Parelli

Because of Phil's death, I was out of the office for a couple of days, and the stacks on my desk were even higher than usual. Julia brought in a fresh brewed cup of coffee, and handed me a letter. It was from a client, Dorothy Parelli. It said she was firing me, I was to do no further work on her case, and she wanted me to return her file. She gave no reason other than she didn't want me to be her lawyer anymore.

"I thought I'd start off your week on high note," Julia said. "First Orwell Washington, now Dorothy. It's getting to be an epidemic."

"Thanks. Did you add a little arsenic to the coffee too?"

The letter came as a complete surprise. Dorothy's case was less than a year old, so it was too soon for her to be unhappy with the progress. I thought our relationship was solid. The case was going to be a huge one--- her husband had been killed when a faulty scaffold he was working on collapsed. It was a clear case of liability.

Many times a face to face can smooth over differences, and I was going to do everything I could to keep this client. Julia handed me the phone.

"Hi Dorothy, this is Stan Seger calling." I forced my voice to sound calm and friendly.

"I just got back in town from a deposition and I was very surprised to get your letter." I noted that it had been mailed the week before, on the day I left for L.A. to be with Sharon. Hopefully she hadn't already signed with another lawyer.

"I think we should talk about it, and I'd like to meet you as soon as possible."

"There really isn't anything to discuss Mr. Seger, I've really made up..."

"Look Dorothy," I interrupted, a little firmer, but still trying to sound pleasant, "there are a lot of things to consider and discuss before you make this decision. I've done a lot of work developing this case, spent a lot of money, and it's coming along beautifully. At least let me show you what we've done, and let's talk."

After much cajoling, she agreed to meet in my office. "But I don't see how I can change my mind. Please have the file ready to hand over to me."

"She's coming in at 3:00. Bring me the file."

Dorothy Parelli was a 21 year old widow. She had met Sal Parelli at a bar, it was love at first sight, and two months later they got married. Just three months after that Sal, a construction foreman, had a scaffold collapse under him and he fell eighteen stories to his death. When the suit was resolved Dorothy was going to become a very wealthy young widow. And if I was still her lawyer at that time I could deposit a nice chunk in my retirement account, and have enough left to put my daughter through a couple of years of college.

The first time we had met, Dorothy was accompanied to my office by her parents. Her father, a bookkeeper, questioned me carefully about Dorothy's rights. I explained that under Illinois law Dorothy would be entitled to all the money we recovered for Sal's death because she was Sal's widow.

"What about Sal's parents, and his brothers and sisters?"

"Once Sal and Dorothy were married, she is entitled to all the money we recover. Sal's parents and siblings get no share."

"Even though they were married such a short time?"

"That's the law."

The next week Dorothy was back in my office, this time with her very agitated in-laws. Her mother-in-law was incensed.

"My boy is dead. My bambino. My youngest son. And you say I won't even be paid for my loss!" The elder Mrs. Parelli was shouting, and rose from the edge of her chair, leaning forward and pounding her small pudgy hand on my desk.

"I'm sorry Mrs. Parelli, but under Illinois law when a married man is killed, his wife, and children, if any, get everything. His parents and brothers and sisters have no right to anything .No matter how close they were or how much they grieve. I'm sorry. I don't make the laws. But I must follow them."

"My husband and I had Sal for 23 years. We'll mourn him the rest of our lives." Then, looking directly at Dorothy and spitting out the words, "this *puttana* had him for only three months, and she'll be in another man's bed before the year is up. And you tell me she gets everything and we get nothing!"

It didn't sound very fair to me either. But sometimes the law isn't fair. Dorothy was looking uncomfortable and I gave her a reassuring smile.

"Look Mrs. Parelli, I know you're upset. But I've told you what the law is. Dorothy is my client, and I have to represent her interests. You're free to consult another lawyer, but I'm sure he'll tell you the same thing."

"Fuck all you lawyers and fuck your law, the old lady shouted as she and her husband stormed out of my office

That meeting was almost a year ago, I hadn't heard from the in-laws again, but it must have been simmering.

"I want to fire you because I am going to get killed!" It was 3:00 P.M. Dorothy was in my office, trembling, and there were tears in her eyes.

"Two weeks ago I got a call. I know it was from one of Sal's brothers, but I'm not sure which one. He said he was going to kill me and no Jew lawyer could stop his mom and dad from getting a fair share of the settlement. He said he was making sure of it. He said I had to hire their lawyers."

"He was bluffing Dorothy. They are an excitable Italian family. It's an emotional time. It's all talk. They'll calm down."

"Calm down, you say. Last week a brick came through my window and shattered a lamp in my living room!"

"Did you call the police?"

"I was too frightened. I didn't tell anyone until now. But you better be careful too."

"I don't know how real the threat is Dorothy. The brick was intended to scare you off, but I don't think they intended to hit you with it. And they wouldn't want to kill you. They need you, the widow, to be alive when the case is tried. In order to recover the full value of the case, they will need a surviving living and breathing widow."

As I was speaking I realized that while they may have needed Dorothy alive, they had no reason to keep me alive, the Jew lawyer they hated, the one who said that if he handled the case they would get nothing. Maybe one of the brothers came after me, and he got Phil by mistake.

I could picture the scene in the garage. Someone waiting in back of my car, sticks a gun in Phil's ear, believing it's me. He orders Phil to drop the Parelli case or he is dead meat. Phil doesn't even know what he's talking about.

I thought of the old Jack Benny routine: Benny was a notorious miser. A thief with a gun threatens him: "Your money or your life," the thief says, and when there is no answer repeats the threat. "I said your money or your life!"

.....Long Pause.......Longer pause.........Still longer pause

"I'm thinking....I'm thinking," Benny said. The audience laughed hysterically.

Phil would have been thinking, trying to figure out what the guy was talking about. But there would have been no laugh.

Instead, just a loud **BANG!**

Dorothy was looking at the two thick files on my desk, her files, containing all the information I had assembled: investigative reports, photographs, expert reports, transcripts of depositions, pleadings, interrogatories, motions, briefs. It was an impressive display of work.

"I like you, Mr. Seger, really I do, and I know you are working hard for me."

"Do you trust me?"

"Yes, but I'm afraid."

"They're angry because they feel they are being cheated. I can calm them down."

"How can you do that?"

"Simple. I'll lie."

With Dorothy's consent I picked up the phone and called the mother-in law. I spent a long time talking with her. I assured the old lady that when the case was settled I would see that she and her family would be fully compensated for their loss. Dorothy would agree to share the recovery on an equitable basis. And I made sure she would tell her sons about my call. By the time we finished talking she seemed to have calmed down.

"Your promise to that bitch isn't legally binding, is it." Dorothy asked. "When the case is over you can renig, can't you?"

I nodded.

"But what happens when the case is over. What is gonna happen then?"

"We'll deal with that when the case is over. The brothers may be in jail by then."

As soon as Dorothy left I called Inspector Hollman and told him about the Parelli threat. He said he would be at my office in half an hour.

"Meanwhile," he warned, "stay away from the windows."

CHAPTER 23

Hollman at my Office

We were both seated on the couch in my office, Hollman and me. Normally I would have been sitting behind my desk with my back to the window, but I had visions of the Magruder film, President Kennedy shot from behind, his head bursting open and his brain splattering Jackie's pink suit.

"I realize you're a busy man, Inspector, and I apologize for having you come over here, but I've got some thoughts I wanted to share."

"No problem. Actually, this is the only case I'm working on, and as a matter of fact it's gonna be my last case. I'm scheduled for retirement, and as a favor to the Commissioner, we're pretty close, I agreed to take on this one last case and clear it before turning in my papers. The Mayor himself is following this one---he doesn't like murders on the Gold Coast." He took out that spiral pad. "So let's hear your thoughts. I'm more eager than you to finish this one up."

"I think you may be onto something when you said Phil could have been killed by accident and they were really trying to kill me." I added timber to my voice to mask my agitation.

"Just calm down Stan." The timber didn't fool him. "We're not all that sure Phil was mistaken for you. I just threw that out as a possibility......as something to consider. I didn't mean to alarm you."

"Of course I'm alarmed. I've been thinking about who might want to kill me, Inspector. It's kind of thin, but I thought I might kick it around with you. Now I'm not accusing anybody, and there's nothing formal about this but..."

"Why don't you just tell me. I'll keep it off the record, unless something is substantiated." His pen was poised over the paper.

I shrugged, and began. I reminded him about Cochise, the ambulance chaser, and his threat to Phil and me. I told him about Wally Smalley, Sharon's old boyfriend, and how Smalley told Sharon he would kill me, and how Phil was trying to get Smalley off Sharon's back. And I told him about Dorothy Parelli, the threat made by her brother-in-law, and the brick through the window.

"You sure seem to have made some nasty enemies for a guy who minds his own business except when he's protecting cemeteries from cigarette butts," he smirked.

"I can give you a much longer list of folks who like me, but I don't want to keep you here all day."

"I'll see if I can get a line on this guy Smalley, at least find out exactly where he is, and where he was when Levine was killed. And I'll talk to Dorothy Parelli, but from what you say, we'll never be able to prove who threw the brick. But I'll see what we can come up with on those Parelli brothers. This gives us some leads to follow up on."

"What about Cochese?"

"Oh, he's got a record. But it doesn't sound like the way he would kill someone. We can roust him and try to shake him up a little but he's pretty tough and odds are we won't get anything. We'll give it a look."

"Is there anything else?" he asked, as he rose to leave. He deliberately left his cigarette burning in the ashtray on my desk

"When you talk to Dorothy Parelli tell her what a good lawyer I am, and that she should stick with me."

CHAPTER 24

Hollman Reports

Inspector Hollman called a few days later. It turned out the Parelli brothers were mob connected, small time enforcers, but not made men. They both had juvenile records that were sealed, and as adults had been convicted of assault, and were currently on probation. He was checking up on their alibis for the night Phil was murdered.

Cochese might or might not be in the clear, he said. Of course he denied any involvement, but said he was glad the motherfucker was dead. His alibi for the night Phil was killed was weak. He claimed to have been in a crap game at the back of a pool hall on Roosevelt Road. A couple of the other players vouched for him, for whatever that was worth.

Wally Smalley was back in North Haven, Michigan, living in the home he inherited when his mother died. He was employed as a bartender. No word yet on whether he was working the night Phil was killed, but Holman had asked the local police to look into it.

"Do you know what Levine had been working on at the time of his death? Any special assignment that might have caused trouble?"

"He was working on the Smith case, a malpractice case. It was set for trial in about eight weeks, and there were still a lot of loose ends. I'm sure he didn't have time to be working on anything else. We were pulling out all the stops."

"Anything about the case that could have put Phil at risk?

"I can't imagine what."

When we hung up I opened my mail, and found a letter from Sharon and the picture she enclosed of Wally with Sharon. "Sorry, it's the only picture of him I could find," she said. The two of them, Sharon and Wally, were standing on a beach in very skimpy bathing suits with their arms around each other, smiling at the camera. Waves were crashing against a pier in the background.

Wally looked to be about 6' 3", and very muscular, with broad shoulders and rippling abs. Pretty much the way I vaguely remembered him from when we were kids. I estimated him to be about 4 inches taller than me, and he outweighed me by at least 30 pounds.

He was well tanned and had close cropped black hair. I examined his face with a magnifying glass and thought I detected meanness around the mouth and eyes, but it could have been my imagination. His hand resting possessively on Sharon's hip was real enough. At least she could have had the decency to crop the picture.

I scanned the picture and E-mailed a copy to Inspector Hollman, for his records.

CHAPTER 25

Pressured To Take a Deposition

Phil was murdered before he could complete his background check on Dr. Mijeck, and he had not yet found Ann Swanson, the operating room nurse who had quit the hospital right after Celia Smith's death. I had deposed all of the other nurses in the operating room during the surgery, and none of them admitted seeing anything unusual. It was a good bet that they had been warned to keep their mouths shut, and if they had noticed anything out of sorts, they weren't about to reveal it. The missing nurse could prove critical.

So there were still dangling ends I needed to tie up. A very snippy Judge had his own agenda, and wasn't sympathetic.

"I don't care about the death of your investigator. That's your problem," he snapped. "I've got a docket to clear. What discovery has to be completed?"

There was a time, long ago, when you would go to trial without knowing what evidence the other side was going to present. There were plenty of surprises, and you dealt with them as best you could. You tried the case pretty much by the seat of your pants.

But all that has changed. Under present rules of discovery, long before the trial begins the parties are required to name all of their witnesses, and the opponents can question them in discovery depositions and find out just what their testimony will be. And you can require your opponent to produce the documents they plan to present at trial.

"We need the deposition of the Defendant, Dr. Mijeck, your honor, and then we have to take the depositions of the expert witnesses for the Plaintiff and Defendant. All the other deps have been taken."

The Judge ordered me to return in four weeks and report that I had taken the deposition of Dr. Mijeck, "or else." He didn't spell out the "or else," but the threat was clear. Comply with his Order, or I was in deep trouble.

"And when you return in four weeks we will set a schedule for the experts to be deposed. It will be a very tight schedule. I warn you, gentlemen, I am losing patience." He said 'gentlemen,' plural, but he glared only at me as he banged his gavel extra hard, for emphasis.

"Everything else goes on the back burner. We have to focus on *Smith.*" We were back at the office, Geri, Julia and me, and moving into crisis mode. "Julia, clear my schedule. Check with our California experts, Kramer and Weinstock, and find out when they will be available for deposition---but first call Bill Masterson and set the Mijeck deposition. It has to be in the next two or three weeks."

Julia headed for her phone.

And then to Geri: "We have to get the file organized. It's a mess. There's shit all over the place."

"I can organize it for you---organization is my specialty."

" It'll take a lot of time. I need every sheet of paper read, tabbed, indexed and put together so that when I need something I can lay my hands on it immediately without having to fumble around for it".

"I have the weekend free. If you'll give me a key to your office, and tell me where the files are, I can come in, spend as much time as I need, and have it all together for you Monday morning."

I gave her the key, and told her the *Smith* files would be on my couch.

"Will it be O.K. if I sit in on the depositions? It would be a great learning experience for me."

"I'd be delighted to have you join us."

CHAPTER 26

The Mijeck Deposition

We were starting the Mijeck deposition, given the Judge's order I had no choice, but we still hadn't found the missing nurse, and I needed to complete the background check on Mijeck. Phil's last memo hinted at something suspicious in his background, but he hadn't yet flushed it out. We desperately needed more time.

The Court Reporter was a sexy looking Asian girl with an English accent. And she was wearing a very short skirt. She had set up a recording device on the table in front of the witness as a backup device. The main record would be made on her stenotype machine that she secured to a tri-pod stand. She was seated on a secretarial type chair, and smiled at me as she moved the stand into position between her legs, causing her skirt to rise a little higher. I momentarily lost my concentration.

"Do you swear to tell the truth, the whole truth, and nothing but the truth, so help you God?"

She ran her fingers over the keys of her shorthand machine. I refocused.

"I do" Dr. Mijeck lied, with his hand raised. He spoke with an Eastern European accent, and I whispered to Geri, "he sounds like Paul Lucas." She had no idea what I was talking about. "Think Bella Lugosi as Dracula," I murmured, and she nodded. Accent aside, he appeared confident as he spoke in a firm and steady voice, and looked me right in the eye, just the way his lawyer had coached him.

I was seated at one end of the long shiny conference table, with Geri to the left of me. She was wearing a blue serge suit that looked much like mine, but with a skirt. She filled out the jacket in a more interesting way than I did, but I had the prettier tie.

Dr. Mijeck was seated at the far end of the table. He was also wearing a blue suit, with a conservative tie. His two attorneys were seated in the chairs to his left, both also wearing blue suits. The five of us looked like either the Blue Man Group, or a class reunion at the Naval Academy.

The court reporter was seated half way down between me and Mijeck, so that she could easily hear the questions and the answers. The recessed lighting was set at a comfortable level.

The lead lawyer for Dr. Mijeck was William Masterson, hired and paid for by Doctors Liability Insurance Company. He was very tall, about 55 years old, with a receding hairline and graying sideburns. He enunciated carefully, had a deep and mellow voice, and spoke with authority. If you didn't listen carefully to the substance, he sounded smart, more intelligent than he really was. But the overall package, with the look and voice, was good enough to attract a lot of insurance company business. And his win record was good because he palmed off most of the losers to his associates, and kept the easy wins for himself.

Seated to the left of Masterson was Terry Frazer, his young associate. He was a U. of Chicago graduate, and joined Masterson's firm 3 years ago to get some trial experience. Chances are that with a few more years under his belt he would strike out on his own and either steal away some of Masterson's insurance clients, or come over to the Plaintiff's side.

Frazer's job was limited to taking notes and feeding documents to Masterson when requested. If there were any objections to be made, they would come from William Masterson.

Geri Sapperstein was Frazer's counterpart. She had before her a neatly indexed file, containing all the documents that I might need during the deposition. She had no litigation experience whatsoever, and had never before attended a deposition, so I had carefully explained the procedure.

"This is a discovery deposition, which means that it's my chance to ask questions of Dr. Mijeck, feel him out, see what kind of witness he will make, and probe for sensitive areas that could throw him off stride. This isn't like being at trial where they teach you not ask a question when you don't know what the answer will be."

"You mean like ..If the glove don't fit, you must acquit?"

"That's the general idea, but that rule doesn't apply when you are taking a discovery deposition. As a general rule the discovery deposition can't be read to the jury, so I can be a lot more freewheeling in my questioning, and fish around for information we can use later. And I can use the deposition to pin Dr. Mijeck to a version of what he claims the facts are. If he tries to change his story at trial, then I can use the deposition when I cross examine him to show that he tried to change what he earlier said under oath."

The doctor had been sworn to tell the truth, and I was ready to begin my questioning. But first I dropped my pen, bent down to pick it up, and snuck another look at the Court Reporter's long legs. She tugged her skirt down. When I straightened up she gave me a little smile, and then we settled down to business.

Geri Sapperstein handed me a copy of the hospital chart. It was carefully tabbed and cross-indexed. She had done a good job with the record.

THE MORNING SESSION

I started by carefully questioning Mijeck about his schooling and experience. Juries normally respect doctors. The Defendant doctor starts off with that edge, but you can knock him off his pedestal if you raise questions about his training, or come up with some evidence that he had screwed up or been disciplined in the past.

"In 1987 I graduated from Julius-Maximilians-Universitaet Medical School in Wurzburg. I then traveled to Argentina and had an internship and general residency in the State Hospital in Buenos Aires. I was licensed to practice medicine there. In 1992 I immigrated to the United States and settled in Wisconsin. I took the examination for foreign medical graduates in 1993, passed it, and had an obstetrical-gynecological residency at the University Hospital in Madison Wisconsin. After completion of that residency I set up practice in Hayward, Wisconsin, and remained there until 2002. I then moved to Michigan City, Indiana and practiced both there and in the South Side Community Hospital in Chicago."

"Give me the name of your Dean of the Medical School in Wurzburg"

"I don't recall."

"Well name at least one of your professors there"

"I don't recall"

"You can't name one of them? Isn't that odd?--- Are you sure you graduated in 1987?"

"Of Course!" He was getting agitated, and raised his voice.

Masterson interrupted the questioning to give his client a chance to settle down. "The question has been asked and answered more than one time. Move on to something else."

I ignored Masterson's instruction as if it hadn't been made. He was a smug son of a bitch, and there was no way I was going to let him tell me how to conduct my questioning. I was entitled to go into great detail, and if it would take several hours to get the information I needed, I was willing to take the time.

We spent the balance of the morning learning where Mijeck's German and Argentinean School diplomas were located (he lost them in a flood in Hayward), why he moved from Madison to Hayward (an opportunity to take over a private practice), why he moved from Hayward (he just got tired of living there and wanted to be closer to a big city), why he moved to Merrillville (there was an opening for an obstetrician at a hospital there), and how he ended up at South Side Community Hospital in Chicago (a chance to make some extra money). He denied ever having practiced in any other States than Wisconsin, Indiana and Illinois, denied that his license had ever been revoked or suspended, and denied that his privileges at any hospital were ever revoked or suspended.

He had never received Board Certification as an expert in Obstetrics and Gynecology, or in any other specialty area, he never held a teaching position, and had never published any papers. A very undistinguished career.

He was getting annoyed with me as I pretty much diddled through the morning, and really, I could hardly blame him. I repeated the same questions again and again, with only the slightest of variations, to a point where even I was getting bored. Geri looked at me puzzled, trying to understand what I was doing.

I was just toying around to see if I could rile Mijeck up, and I always enjoyed getting Masterson agitated.

At noon we adjourned for lunch, and agreed to reconvene at 1:30.

CHAPTER 27

Lunch at the Bismarck

I took Geri to the Walnut Room in the Bismarck Hotel for lunch.

The restaurant was richly paneled in walnut, and was elegantly set out with crisp white tablecloths, sparkling glassware, and polished silver. It was a favorite lunch spot for judges, politicians, and lawyers.

There was a lot of nodding and waving between tables, and somebody was always getting up and walking over and shaking hands with someone else. With all the circulating and kibitzing and handshaking, it was a wonder that any eating ever got done. But everyone looked overstuffed, so somehow they were finding time to clean their plates.

The two specialties of the house were fried breaded fillet of sole and a thin German pancake rolled around lingonberries and sprinkled with powdered sugar. The pancake was probably 3000 calories.

Geri ordered the fish. I had the pancake.

While we were eating, former Judge Irwin Natansky made a triumphant entrance to the dining room after having been absent for a year. He had just completed a federal jail term for bribery. He looked tan and healthy after his stay at one of the country club style minimum security prisons. His colleagues rushed over to greet him warmly. He was a hero. He had refused to wear a wire, and hadn't squealed on anybody.

Geri and I spent a few minutes bemoaning the morality of our society, and then we resumed our discussion of the Smith case and the deposition of Dr. Mijeck.

"I know the bastard is lying about his background."

"But how are you going to prove it?"

"If we make him give enough details, somewhere he'll make a mistake. I wish Phil had finished the background check. Did he tell you anything that wasn't in that last memo?"

"I think he was locating some other doctors who had worked with Mijeck. He was waiting to hear back from them. That's all I know. Sorry."

"Well, I'll fish around with Mijeck a little more this afternoon and see if we come up with something. Then I'm gonna have to move on to his treatment of Mrs. Smith. We have to wrap up this dep today"

On the way out of the restaurant I stopped at former judge Natansky's table to welcome him back and tell him how good he looked. I figured it couldn't hurt. The way Chicago politics works, he could end up being re-elected to the bench.

CHAPTER 28

Mijeck—The Afternoon Session

"Who was the valedictorian of your medical school class?"

"What was the name of the dormitory you lived in?"

"Name your roommates"

I went on like that in a calm manner, ignoring the angry objections to relevance. I was harassing and insulting the witness, Masterson claimed. Of course I was, and I was enjoying it. And through the whole thing, Mijeck kept his cool. If I was ever going to score points on anything in his past, I wasn't going to learn of it in the deposition. I would have to follow up on whatever Phil was working on.

So I moved on and had Mijeck describe in detail each step he took during the tubal ligation. I was meticulous in pinning him down to the exact procedure he followed.

As expected, he claimed that he adhered strictly to required protocol, and was convinced that the death was unavoidable, one of those tragedies that sometimes occurs no matter how careful the surgeon. He admitted that he did not use the syringe test, but argued that with someone of his great experience it was not necessary. He insisted he could tell by feel alone that the needle was properly placed. He had performed numerous tubal ligations over the years, never used the syringe test, and never had a problem. When pressed, he surmised that the death was due to a congenital aneurism that could not have been discovered prior to Celia Smith's death. He expressed sympathy for the family.

We had completed the deposition of Mijeck without doing much to advance our case. If we were going to win, I had to come up with more ammunition.

CHAPTER 29

Smith—The Stretch Run

There had been no progress in finding Phil's killer. Under one theory, the murderer made a mistake and shot the wrong man, and if that turned out to be true I could still be a target. I had to put that out of my mind, and focus on *Smith*.

The case was going to trial in eight weeks, and the Judge made clear that there would be no further extensions.

We still hadn't located Ann Swanson, the missing nurse. The hospital claimed to have no forwarding address for Ann, and as best we could tell, she had simply disappeared. Phil's last memo, dated a few days before he was shot, mentioned no solid leads.

All of the Discovery in the case had been completed, except for the deposition of my OB-Gyne expert, Ruben Weinstock, my former busboy in North Haven. The case was a tough one, and I needed a strong deposition from Ruben. But even if he came through, the case was 50-50.

In every case there were last minute details to take care of, and with Phil dead I would have to deal with most of them myself. My only assistant was Geri Sapperstein, but Geri wasn't always available because her own firm had assigned her to prepare merger documents for some big deal they were working on. She promised to lend whatever help she could.

I was in the process of reviewing the Smith file for the umpteenth time, to make sure I hadn't overlooked anything. I did that with every case. Sometimes you overlook something because you don't realize its relevance until other pieces are in place.

As I thumbed through the voluminous folders, I came to one marked "Miscellaneous Duplicates." I almost passed it by, but then decided to look through it. A good thing I did. It contained a memo Phil had prepared on the day he died. He must have either faxed or e-mailed it to the office, and with all the bedlam after his death, it somehow had landed in that folder without reaching me first.

In the old days, the days we referred to as B.S. (before Sharon), Phil and I would meet at the end of almost every day to review things face to face, but because of all my West Coast travel there was much less opportunity to meet, and most of our communication was by written memo. While I was roaming the shores of Southern California with Sharon, instead of staying home and paying full attention to the practice, details were slipping by me. The old maxim was true. *The law is a jealous mistress.*

In that last memo, Phil said he had contacted some doctors about problems that had arisen at Mijeck's former hospitals, and was awaiting information from them. Phil also said he had learned that Ann Swanson, our missing nurse, had a sister living in Northern Wisconsin. He was going to give top priority to reaching the sister and locating the nurse. How could an important memo like that get buried in the Miscellaneous portion of the file without me seeing it? A stupid mistake on someone's part.

"Don't look at me," Julia said. "I didn't do it."

Geri also denied having filed the memo when she was organizing the file for me. She had come into the office a few minutes earlier, out of breath, saying she was able to get away from the merger papers for a few hours.

"Must have been the office gremlins," I said.

Geri asked if there was anything I wanted her to do. She must have been working out of her house, because she was wearing jeans and a halter top, an outfit that wouldn't pass muster in the corporate world.

I told Geri it was imperative that someone find and interview Ann Swanson, the missing operating room nurse. "We have to locate her and get her statement. Phil thought her sister, he gives us her name, lives somewhere in Wisconsin. But maybe I better track her down myself," I said. "It's crucial that it be done."

"You have enough to do. I'll follow through on it," Geri said.

"You sure you can do it?"

"I'll find her. Just leave it to me."

"O.K., find her. If she won't cooperate we'll have to serve her with a subpoena for her deposition. And make it quick!"

I was a little sharper than I meant to be. We were in the stretch drive. And I was angry with myself for missing Phil's last memo. It was all that flying up and back to California.

And, by the way, I don't believe in gremlins.

CHAPTER 30

Back to Phil's Apartment

The memo I found confirmed Phil was giving *Smith* absolute priority, and he must have been working on the case right up until the moment he headed down to my car and got himself killed. Knowing Phil, he would have been relentless in tracking down Ann Swanson, and he would have gone after rumors of dirty linen in Mijeck's medical history like a pit bull after chunks of raw meat.

"I'm going over to Phil's apartment to see if he had a private file on the Smith case, or a note, or some information that he hadn't reported to me yet. You want to come along?"

"I'd like to join you," Geri said "but I have merger papers to review. It's for one of Ted's--I mean Mr. Mizell's--- biggest clients, and he expects me to finish it this afternoon and bring it over to his apartment tonight so that we can check it over and make any necessary revisions."

Now I understood why Ted phoned me just thirty minutes ago and cancelled our dinner date that night because of a "pressing business engagement."

"And I suppose he said he'll order up a working dinner at his place."

"I think he said his wife would fix us something."

I knew his wife was out of town. "Sounds cozy," I said.

So I went to Phil's alone to search for his raw file, or any notes of work he had done since that last memo.

I found the Smith folder in his file cabinet. The only things I hadn't seen before were a list of names and telephone numbers of doctors who had been in Mijeck' graduating class from Medical School in Germany, and a note printed in Phil's hand, written the day he was killed. "CALL WEINSTOCK ASAP!!!" There was nothing indicating what Phil wanted to talk to Dr. Weinstock about.

I booted up Phil's computer, which the police had returned after searching it and copying the hard drive. The most recent document regarding the Smith case was a letter under Phil's letterhead, dated a few weeks before he was killed.

"Dr. Peter Brunner
241 Sunrise Dr.
Key West, Fl. 33041
Dear Dr. Brunner

Thank you for taking my call the other day regarding your former classmate, Walter Mijeck. This is just a reminder that you were going to check some stories told to you by some of his former classmates, and then get back to me.
I look forward to hearing from you.

Very Truly Yours,

A similar letter had been sent to a Dr. Schwartz in Houston, Texas.

There was no further information regarding Phil's search for the nurse, Ann Swanson.

I tried using my cell phone to call Dr. Brunner, but couldn't get service in Phil's apartment. *Goddamn Verizon!* So I put Phil's file in my briefcase, along with printouts of the letters to the doctors, and left his apartment, being careful to double lock the door. I headed home, rather than fight the traffic back to my loop office.

CHAPTER 31

My Home Office

I had converted one of the bedrooms to a home office (my very cautious accountant still wouldn't let me write it off as a business expense—said home offices always raised a red flag). It was equipped with a copier/fax machine/printer and a state of the art Gateway Computer that worked fine and hardly ever crashed.

The computer was networked to my office so that I could pull up any of my files, and the fax machine allowed Julia and me to send each other letters and documents, and innumerable drafts that were edited and re-edited before they were in final form. Julia came to hate the whole setup.

I shed my work attire and slipped into comfortable pajamas. Now I could work like Hugh Hefner, except my pajamas weren't silk, and there were no Bunnies hopping around.

I tried reaching Dr. Brunner in Key West and Dr. Schwartz in Houston. After long delays wading through menus saturated with Muzak, I finally reached human voices that in each instance advised me that the doctors were with patients, and asked if I would like to leave a message in their mailbox. Since the only alternative was to call back later and repeat the same tedious procedure, I reluctantly opted to leave messages.

Dr. Schwartz never returned my call but Dr. Brunner got back to me at about 10:00 P.M., and apologized, explaining that he had just completed an emergency C-Section.

"After I heard from Phil Levine I began thinking about Walter Mijeck. I never really knew him well myself. We were classmates in Europe, and both ended up emigrating to this country. I promised Levine I would get back to him, but I got really busy and didn't have a chance to call back yet."

"Well you won't be able to reach Phil now," I said. "Phil is dead, died unexpectedly. I'm following up for him. Is there anything you can tell me about Dr. Mijeck?"

"Sorry to hear about Mr. Levine's death. I hope my delay in getting back to him doesn't cause any inconvenience. There were some unsettling rumors about Dr. Mijeck's practice while he was in Louisville, Kentucky, something I had picked up at one of our class reunions. But it was vague, just a comment that he had run into some type of problems in his practice. I mentioned it to Mr. Levine when he called, and at his request I had checked with a couple of our classmates who are still practicing down there to see if they could give me any more specific information."

"Funny," he ruminated, "how Mijeck and two others in our class in Wurzburg had ended up in the same hospital in Kentucky. I think some Lutheran Church Group helped them relocate there."

I cut him short. "But what did you find out about those problems he had?"

He wasn't going to be rushed. "I told them that I was contacted by an investigator, Mr. Levine, who was looking into Dr. Mijeck's background."

"And what did they tell you?" I asked, as I began taking notes.

"The first one I called became very upset with me. He wouldn't say anything, except that he had remained in touch with Dr. Mijeck, that Mijeck was his friend, and he was going to alert Mijeck that a private investigator was looking into his affairs."

"And the other doctor you spoke to...was he more forthcoming?"

"That's why I'm calling you back. Ordinarily you wouldn't find me cooperating with a plaintiff's malpractice attorney"

We both chuckled at that--my chuckle considerably more forced than his.

"But I do have a responsibility to the profession---and to the public."

"So what did this second doctor tell you?"

"He insists on remaining anonymous. I promised I wouldn't reveal his name."

"That's O.K. But what did he say?"

"It was eating away him at for many years. He couldn't keep quiet any longer. He and Mijeck were on the staff together at a small community hospital in Louisville. Mijeck lost his operating privileges--actually he didn't lose them, he was allowed to resign from the staff---because of three deaths that occurred in one year during his surgeries. They may not have been surgical errors. Sometimes bad results occur even if you are being very careful," he added weakly.

"Why don't you just give me the facts." I was sounding like Sgt. Friday from *Dragnet*.

He hesitated before answering. "Two of them were due to sepsis after bowels were punctured during hysterectomies. One happened after he didn't close off a bleeder, and it wasn't found until too late.

"Were suits filed? Weren't there records made?"

"According to my classmate the hospital covered things up. The records of the mortality committee of course, were sealed, and it never went any further. By agreement, Mijeck resigned from the staff and left the State."

"So, I said, "Mijeck began his practice in this country in Kentucky." He never mentioned that on his C.V. or at his deposition. And I doubt he mentioned it when he got his licenses in Wisconsin, Indiana or Illinois."

Then I thought of something else. "When you spoke to that first doctor, the one who was a friend of Dr. Mijeck, the one who was going to tell Mijeck about the investigation, did you give that doctor Phil Levine's name, address and phone number?"

"Sure I did. He asked me for it. He wanted to warn Dr. Mijeck he was being investigated, so I gave him all that information."

"Is there anything else you can tell me about Dr. Mijeck?"

"Isn't that enough," he said. "You damn lawyers are never satisfied. I've done my duty. Don't call me again." He hung up.

CHAPTER 32

Hollman Visits Again

Inspector Hollman popped into my waiting room the next day, just as I was getting ready to leave for lunch. No appointment. No phone call warning that he was coming over. If I hadn't been in he would have been wasting his time and a lot of taxpayer's money. But I didn't mention that to him.

Instead of inviting him to lunch, I took him back to my office.

"Well Sherlock, have you solved the case yet?"

He just shrugged. "Right now I just want to rehash things."

"We're still not even sure whether the killer intended to kill you or Phil Levine. The only person we are aware of who threatened Levine is Cochese, and he threatened you too. But he's a violent man, and hiding in the back of a car and shooting someone in the back of the head doesn't seem to be his style."

"Besides," I said, "the back seat of my car is pretty small, Cochise is a big guy, and he would have trouble fitting back there. It's not impossible, but pretty unlikely. It would be a real tight squeeze."

"We've interviewed several people who knew Levine, and found nobody who disliked him. As a matter of fact, he came across as a very popular guy. Do you have any further thoughts on who might want him dead?"

I thought of Dr. Mijeck. He knew that Phil was investigating him, and he could have lost his license if it was revealed that he hid the Kentucky incidents. But should I sic the police on him on the oft chance that he murdered Phil to keep his secret? Probably not. He might kill someone by his incompetence, but I doubted he was guilty of intentional murder with a gun. It was farfetched to accuse him of murder. But then again, it might help my lawsuit if Hollman were to start investigating him for murder. It might even drive the defendants to settle the Smith case without a trial. So what the hell.

"You might look into Dr. Walter Mijeck," I said. "Phil was digging into his background to see if he could come up with some dirt to help a lawsuit I have against him. Mijeck learned Phil was digging into some old scandal, and he could have lost his license if the scab came off. Maybe he killed Phil to stop him before he got the full story and went public."

I gave Inspector Hollman the home address for Mijeck and the details of his Kentucky misadventures. I gave him the names of the doctors Phil had contacted, the Kentucky hospital involved, and the licensing requirements in Illinois that would have required Mijeck to list all hospitals where he had been denied privileges and the reasons for the denial. He wrote it all down in that little spiral notebook he carried. I knew that he would retrace Phil's work, contact the same witnesses, and dig much deeper than Phil had been able to do before he was killed. And he would check to see if Mijeck had an alibi for time of Phil's murder.

"You met this doctor. Do you really think he's capable of murder?" Hollman asked.

"Yeah, I think he could kill someone." I kept any uncertainty out of my voice.

"Let's look at the other possibility," Hollman said. "It could well be that you were the target. You seem to be a much more annoying personality than Levine."

"Don't let my mother here you say that--she thinks I'm perfect. And my girlfriend loves me."

Hollman thumbed through is notes. "Yeah, but what about the others. Cochese threatened to kill you as well as Levine. And you had that run-in with him at the Barbecue joint. The guy lost part of his finger. Dr. Mijeck may have been pissed with Levine, but he probably had no love for you either. He knows Levine was working for you. And you were as big a risk as Phil was to expose his past, maybe a bigger risk. And then there is that old boyfriend of Sharon's. ....What is his name again, Wally Smalley?"

"I'm impressed. You *have* been busy working on the case."

"I want to close out this case, turn in my papers, and retire."

"You're too young to retire."

"It can't come soon enough for my wife," he said. "But let's get back to business. After you mentioned Smalley's name to me, I thought I better check up on him. He has a history of violent behavior, a few misdemeanors, but no felonies."

"And then there are the Parelli brothers," he continued. "They think you're planning to cheat their family, and give the widow all the money in that case where their brother was killed. They have criminal records, are known to be violent, and were angry enough to hurl the brick through their sister-in law's window. So I think there are a lot of people with a motive to ice you, a lot more than had a grudge against Levine."

"What about alibis. Don't any of them have alibis that would clear them?"

"It's hard to pinpoint the exact time of death. Within the possible time period, any of them could have done it. Cochise says he was in that crap game---but that could be just a bunch of crap."

"What about the Parelli brothers?"

"The Parelli brothers alibi each other. They say they were playing gin rummy together. And according to local police, that guy Smalley seems to have an alibi, but it may not be airtight."

"If the person in the back of my car was intending to kill Phil, it would have to be someone who knew he was going to be getting into the car that night," I said. "Someone who knew Phil's plan to pick me up at the airport."

"And we don't know who that might be, because we don't know who Phil might have told he was using your car. Did you mention it to anyone?"

"Nobody who might have wanted to kill him."

"But what about if they were trying to kill you. Why would they be waiting for you in the back of your car?" Hollman mused.

"Put together this scenario. No one knows Phil is using my car. They expect it will only be used by me. My schedule, going to the Bar Association Conference in Lake Geneva, is well known. The fact that I will be speaking has been widely publicized. It was published in the Law Bulletin. Anybody can buy that paper. I also included it in my News Letter that I distribute to all my clients and referring attorneys every month. Publicizing what a great lawyer I am, you know. The meeting is in Lake Geneva, so the only way I can get there is by using my car. Anyone could have called the hotel and found out I was registered to check in Monday night. My car is parked, as usual, in my garage in the alley, and they assume I will be getting into it to get to the conference. A perfect setup for an ambush."

"It could have gone down that way," Hollman said. "We certainly won't rule it out. But this thing you're telling me about this Dr. Mijeck might be promising. It gives us someone else to look at. I'll follow up. We'll keep in touch."

CHAPTER 33

Moving Closer to a Settlement

And apparently Hollman was true to his word. A few days later I got a call from Dr. Mijeck's attorney, William Masterson. He started with small talk, asking about how things were going, chatting about the Cub's chances for a pennant, all the usual bullshit.

He sounded so friendly that I suspected he wanted to explore possible settlement. It wasn't that my case had gotten stronger. It had to be something else.

"Look, I've been chatting with Dr. Mijeck about this case, and he really wants to see if we can resolve it without going much further. He has a very busy practice, and this pending suit is too distracting."

I assumed that Inspector Hollman had been poking around Dr. Mijeck's business, Mijeck found out about it and told his lawyer, and the two of them decided it might be better to nip any investigation into Mijeck's past by trying to settle the case. If it ever came out that Mijeck had falsified his application to practice medicine in Illinois, if he failed to reveal the episodes in Louisville, he could not only lose the case, he could lose his license.

Masterson continued. "I haven't talked to the carrier yet, but with a little help from you, I think we may be able to persuade our adjuster to consider a reasonable settlement."

When you sense weakness, you push. "Look Bill, this guy is a butcher and shouldn't be practicing. You know it, I know it, and he probably knows it too. We have a powerful case, and your Companies are going to have to come up with their policy limits, both the underlying policy and the excess carrier, and Dr. Mijeck will have to kick in some of his own funds to get the case settled."

"Don't talk foolish. We have a base policy with a five million dollar limit, and I don't even know that they will pay all of that. Anything above that would have to be approved by the excess carrier, and they are murder to deal with. You'll be lucky to get all of the base policy. And it's outrageous that you want Dr. Mijeck to contribute any of his own money."

Mijeck will ante up just to keep his license, because if we go to trial, a lot of dirty stuff is going to come out, even if some of it may be inadmissible before a jury."

"Stan, this is all premature. I don't have any authority yet from my company, and while they usually follow my recommendations, I won't be able to get authority until they hear from your expert. Let's make a deal. You present your expert, Dr. Weinstock, for a Discovery Deposition. Bring him into town, I'll have my insurance adjustors at the deposition, and if Weinstock comes in real strong on the liability question, I'll go to bat with the company to get their full five mil, and explore the possibility of more from the excess carrier. Is that a deal?

I said I would think about it. The trial date was getting close, and I would have to present Ruben Weinstock for a discovery deposition soon anyway, so I really wouldn't be agreeing to anything that I didn't already have to do.

I called Ruben the following day to see when he would be available, and if he was willing to travel to Chicago for the Deposition.

"I reviewed the records, and depositions, and the pathology work-up of our friend, Gene Kramer. He's a good man and he did a good job. We can nail this guy Mijeck pretty good."

When my expert starts saying "we," I know I've got him strong on my side.

"Any chance of me persuading you to come to Chicago to give your deposition, instead of all of us dragging out to L.A.? We can set it on a Monday, and have the weekend before to kick back and prepare."

"I've got a better idea," said Weinstock. "How about I fly into Chicago with my wife on a Thursday, you pick us up at the airport, and we drive straight up to North Haven and have a nostalgic weekend. I always wanted to show my wife where I misspent my youthful summers. We'll have Friday, Saturday and Sunday to prepare for the deposition, and get drunk on the beach at night. Let's make the long weekend in honor of Phil."

"And then we drive back to Chicago for the Deposition on Monday?" I asked. "Sounds like a lot of driving."

"Not if you're used to L.A.," Weinstock said. "We'll have a full weekend in North Haven. I really want to get back there. It's probably the last opportunity I'll ever have. We can get up early Monday, drive right to Chicago for the Deposition, it's less than a three hour drive, and I'll fly back home late Monday night. The deposition won't take more than three or four hours, will it?"

"When are you available to come in?"

"Send me first class tickets for my wife and me for a week from Thursday, with a return Monday night so that I can make my Tuesday poker game. Oh, and Stan, mail me an advance of $7,500.00 to be applied to my deposition fee."

"Will do, but you're gonna have to pick up the tab for Friday night dinner."

I called Masterson and set up the deposition at my office on the Monday Weinstock had suggested. Masterson tried to jockey to take the deposition at his office, looking for whatever little advantage home court would give him, but I refused, pointing out that I was bringing the expert all the way from California, and that was enough. After brief hesitation, he acquiesced. I agreed that he could have his adjustors present at the deposition, figuring it could only help to have the insurance representatives learn first-hand how strong our case was.

I told Julia to make sure that the conference room would be set up for the deposition.

"Have plenty of coffee available, and soft drinks. You better notify Geri Sapperstein that the deposition is going ahead. She wanted to sit in on all the deps. If she wants, she can join us for the preparation in North Haven. She could come in handy."

"How many will there be at the deposition?" She was taking notes.

"Me, Geri, Masterson and his associate. Masterson will be bringing along two adjustors, the one from the underlying carrier, and one for the excess carrier. And there will be Dr. Weinstock, of course, and the Court reporter. And the Defense will probably bring Dr. Mijeck in too." They always like to have the Defendant there, looking our expert in the eye. They hope that waters down the sharpness of the criticism.

Julia was adding up the number of attendees and figuring how many donuts to order.

I phoned Sharon that night and told her I would not be coming out to California the following week because we were bringing Dr. Weinstock in for his deposition.

"But we haven't seen each other in three weeks and I was really looking forward to it. It's been too long."

"I miss you too, but I've really been busy, and this deposition has to go ahead."

"How about this," she said. "I already planned to take the long weekend off. How about if I fly to Chicago. I could come out on Thursday, and we could all go to North Haven together. I'd like a little nostalgia too. As I remember, it's a cute little town, and their beach is beautiful."

"I'll be busy prepping Weinstock most of the weekend, so you may get stuck with Weinstock's wife a good part of the time."

"You sound like you don't want me to come."

"Of course I do. It's just you might be bored."

"You've warned me. I'm coming anyway."

I cleared it with Ted Mizell for Geri Sapperstein to accompany us to North Haven for the weekend, after assuring him it wasn't a ploy to get in her pants. That didn't take much convincing, because he assured me that nobody in his firm had been able to get close to her. They had taken to calling her the ice maiden.

Julia made reservations for all of us at a very pricey bed and breakfast in North Haven. The best suite for Weinstock and his wife---- the only accommodation that included a Jacuzzi, a nice king size bed for Sharon and me, and a single room for Geri. It was off-season so we had no difficulty booking the rooms. I told Julia to make reservations for Friday night dinner at Hawks Head, the one very expensive restaurant in town. I figured that with the fee I was paying him, it was only fair to stick Weinstock with a healthy meal tab.

Julia got tickets for Sharon and Dr. and Mrs. Weinstock on the same flight out of L.A., and I made arrangements to pick up the three of them at the airport and drive directly to North Haven. Geri would drive up in her own car, and meet us at the B and B.

CHAPTER 34

At the Airport

I had timed it well, and the three of them were waiting curbside when I pulled up in the Lincoln Town car I rented for the weekend. We would need the roomy interior for the four of us, and the cavernous trunk for the luggage.

It was the first time I had seen Mrs. Weinstock. She was an attractive woman, if you like hair dyed to a platinum blond, nose sculpted by an expert, and a face immobilized by Botox. Platform shoes with high heels added about 4 inches to her height, and as she stood at the curb she arched her back to show off a very trim figure and perky breasts. She had to be at least 25 years younger than her husband.

Weinstock still looked like Santa Clause, but a slightly worn Santa. One who was coming off a very tough sleigh ride. He had a few more wrinkles in his face than I remembered from our last visit, and his designer suit needed a pressing.

He gave me a big bear hug. I'm not physically demonstrative with men, and would have preferred a handshake, but when someone grabs you with affection you can't just shove them away. So I briefly hugged back, then grasped his shoulders and held him at arm's length, looked him in the eye, and with a sincere smile lied and said he looked great.

Weinstock proudly introduced me to Ros, his trophy wife. She threw her arms around me, ground her body into me a little harder than the occasion called for, and kissed me on the lips before I could turn my head. She had tucked the gum she was chewing into her cheek before the kiss. "Ruben told me all about you," she said. "I know we'll be great friends." Weinstock beamed.

Sharon greeted me with a peck on the lips, and whispered "Stop ogling her."

It's a good thing I had the big car. As a matter of fact, a large SUV might have been even better. Sharon had her usual giant bag for her outfits, and a matching one for cosmetics. Mrs. Weinstock ("call me Ros") was rolling two large trunks, one, I later learned, filled with shoes.

"I didn't want to get caught short, without the right outfits," she explained.

Travelers packed much more sensibly in the good old days before wheels were added to luggage, when they had to carry their suitcases, not roll them.

The others climbed into the car, while I labored to get all the luggage into the trunk. Despite rearranging the cases several times, I couldn't figure out how to get them all to fit. Spatial perception has always been my weakness. I scored miserably on that segment of every I.Q. test I ever took, and have never completed, or even gotten halfway through a jigsaw puzzle.

I stood frustrated, with the trunk lid opened, the trunk full, and one case still on the sidewalk. A lady traffic cop was rapidly approaching and tooting her whistle menacingly, shouting at me to get moving. Sharon hopped out of the car, took one look, and showed me how to re-arrange things so that all the cases fit with room to spare. She was smart enough to not gloat.

We settled into the Lincoln, Weinstock up front with me, and Sharon and Ros in the back, just like old married couples. Ros mainly talked fashion and dieting and makeup, while Sharon mainly listened. Weinstock and I briefly discussed his deposition, and during the rest of the trip we reminisced.

CHAPTER 35

North Haven Revisited

I turned off the Blue Arrow Highway onto the two lane blacktop road leading into North Haven. At that junction there was the remnant of a badly weathered wooden sign. The paint was cracked and peeling, and many of the letters were faded and barely legible, but I was able to make out "Laurel's Atlantic Resort". Ros asked me why a Resort on the shore of Lake Michigan was given that name. "Mr. Laurel told me he chose the name because it sounded classy."

The houses we passed were all neat and well maintained, set back from the streets and resting on large lots with well-tended lawns and carefully sculpted bushes.

The downtown area consisted of one street about two blocks long, intersected by another street of about the same length. The buildings were all of brick, vintage 1930s, none more than three stories high. Short square structures, strong enough to stand forever. There was a bank, two barber shops with those old peppermint barber poles out front, two hardware stores, several restaurants, a drug store that had been there since I was a kid, a sprinkling of offices, a few clothing stores, all but one for women, a shoe store, two groceries, and even a movie theatre. There were no vacant buildings. All in all, it looked like North Haven not only survived, but that it was comfortably prospering.

There is a river that divides the north and south sides of the town, and a single bridge that spans the river.

As we approached the bridge I found that a whole new development had been built along the banks of the river at a place where there had formerly been nothing but an old dock and warehouse. Back in the really old days, long before the Mr. Laurel had built his "Atlantic Resort," the town had been a port for the cutting and processing of lumber. Logs were shipped to North Haven from Sweden, across the ocean and down the Great Lakes in huge ocean going vessels. Once unloaded at the dock, a sawmill converted the logs to usable timber, and the timber was stored in a giant warehouse until it was moved on.

The dock had been replaced by a new marina with moorings for scores of luxury yachts and sailboats, and in place of the warehouse there was now a row of buildings built on two levels, designed to look like a New England Fishing Village. The buildings housed bars, restaurants, and several attractive shops selling everything from souvenir T-shirts to resort fashions. Since this was beyond the end of the summer season, most of the businesses were closed, or in the process of being shut down until the spring. The summer weather seemed to be lingering, and it was unseasonably warm. More evidence that Al Gore is right.

We arrived at the B&B around 4:00 P.M., about two hours before sunset. The owner of the bed and breakfast, a rather prissy looking gentleman named Sheldon Babich, greeted us on the large veranda at the front of his old clapboard mansion. He introduced himself as "the innkeeper." We followed him to the front desk where he had us sign the register. He explained the Rules of the establishment. "No smoking, no loud radio playing in the lobby (there was no T.V.), and no rowdiness."

There was no bellman on duty, and Babich didn't look capable of lifting more than my briefcase, so we had to manage our own luggage.

I struggled up the narrow staircase to our second floor room, lugging Sharon's suitcases, and she floated along behind, carrying my lightweight overnight bag. Meanwhile Weinstock labored up the stairs to his third floor penthouse, bouncing Ros' suitcase up each step, with Ros yelling at him to be careful, "it's a Ralph Lauren." She carried nothing but her purse. Weinstock rested at the top to catch his breath, then repeated the struggle a second time. He declined my offer of assistance, and then lumbered back down for a third tortuous climb with his own suitcase. After settling in our rooms, we all assembled in the parlor, where the innkeeper served us a welcoming round of wine and cheese. Nice touch.

"Let's go down to the beach for the sunset," I suggested. "We can take along a bottle of wine and a blanket."

I always loved to watch the sun setting over Lake Michigan. Sharon and I had spent many romantic hours on the beach when we were kids, watching the sun sink into the Lake. It used to get even more romantic after the sun disappeared.

Sharon surprised me when she turned me down. "I want to take the car and run downtown to pick up a few things at the drugstore. And then I want to rest a little and freshen up before dinner. It was a long flight, and then the three hour drive. I'll wait until tomorrow for the sunset."

Weinstock also declined. I think it was the stairs that got him, but he didn't want to admit that, and instead said, "I'm really beat from the trip. I think I'll take a soak in the Jacuzzi, and have a little nap before dinner. Want to join me, hon?"

"I'd rather see the sunset," Ros said, and then turning to me, "I'd love for you to show me the sunset. My husband was talking about North Beach all the way on the plane, he told me about your beach parties, not everything, I'm sure," she giggled, "and he says that the sunset here is prettier than over the Pacific, and that the sand on the beach is better than the Cayman Islands."

"That's the way I always think of it too," I said.

Weinstock trudged up to his room.

I grabbed a beach blanket and a portable radio from the trunk of the car, and tossed the car keys to Sharon, so she could drive into town.

The Innkeeper sold me two chilled bottles of pinot gris---- at his cost, he assured me--- and threw in the plastic cups for free. In Chicago they would have doubled the price of the bottles, and tacked on another five for the cups.

Ros and I headed for the beach. It was only a short block away. I told Babich to keep an eye out for Geri, who was scheduled to arrive soon, and to direct her to the beach if she wanted to join us.

Sharon stuck her head out the window of the car and hollered "No hanky panky now."

"Hanky panky" wouldn't have been a bad idea, I thought, as Ros sashayed along ahead of me, her ass bouncing seductively in skintight flowered pedal pushers. At least that was what they were called when I was young.

I took my gym shoes off, and Ros kept her Crocs on as we walked through the sand to within a few feet of the water. I spread the blanket, unscrewed the wine cap, and poured us each a glass. The wine was nicely chilled, and to me tasted crisp and dry. Sharon probably would have said it was too fruity.

The sand was clean, and almost white. Not as powdery white as Six Mile Beach in the Caymans, but to me it was a lot prettier. And certainly a hell of a lot better than the stones and pebbles in Cannes. The beach was almost deserted, just a couple of kids at the far end, near the pier, flying a yellow kite. There was just enough wind to keep it up. Out on the pier, less than a block to the south, a lone fisherman sat on one of those little folding canvas stools, with his pole dangling over the edge, not getting much action.

To the west the orange sun was about an inch above the water, sinking slowly. There were a few fluffy clouds on the horizon that should light up beautifully as the sunset spread. A fishing boat and a small sailboat made their way toward the shoreline.

Ros and I touched glasses and toasted the sun. "It's even prettier here than Ruben said."

"Ruben sounds so formal, do you always call your husband that?"

"Why, what do you call him," she asked.

"Come to think of it, I guess that when we were kids working out here in the summers we called him 'Weinstock', or 'tubby'. But 'Ruben' just struck me as kind of formal for a wife."

"I first met him when he was my doctor, my gynecologist. I guess he liked what he saw," she giggled, "so he asked me out. But only after he had me switch to another gyne. It wouldn't have been ethical otherwise."

"We dated on and off for about a year before it got serious. When we started dating I called him 'doc', but he didn't like that, and asked me to call him 'Ruben'. I did, and it kind of stuck. Don't worry, I call him plenty of other things when I'm pissed at him. Maybe I'll start calling him 'tubby'."

I winced. "I shouldn't have mentioned that. Please forget I said it."

"But he is kind of tubby. Now you, on the other hand look plenty tight." She rubbed her hand along my stomach.

I sat up and poured us each a little more wine. I looked back toward the land to see if there was any sign of Sharon, or maybe Geri, but no one was coming. We had already been at the beach for a half hour, and I expected that someone from our party would show up soon.

I switched on a portable radio and fiddled with it until I found a station playing Rod Stewart doing the good old standards, the songs I liked to sing along with at piano bars.

I sipped the wine while Stewart rasped out a love song.

"So, how long have you and Sharon been going together?"

"We have known each other a very long time. As a matter of fact, we met right here in North Haven when we were just kids. At a resort just up the road there, at the edge of the beach. The resort was torn down a long time ago. It stood right where those new condominiums are."

"Sharon is a very beautiful woman," Ros said. "And she has really kept her good looks. I first saw her when we were both patients of Ruben. I only saw her a couple of times in his waiting room, but I remember her because she was so striking. I never saw her again until we were at the airport in L.A."

"Ruben introduced her to me as your girlfriend," she continued. "I mentioned that I recalled seeing her in Ruben's waiting room, but she didn't remember me. Of course Ruben quickly changed the subject because he never wants to discuss his patients. He says because of the intimate nature of some of his work it might embarrass them. And maybe he was right, because Sharon did seem a little flustered when I said I had seen her before."

"Sharon's a pretty tough cookie, and I doubt that your mention of seeing her would bother her. She was probably just a little surprised at what a lovely wife Ruben has landed."

"You really think I'm that lovely?"

"You ain't chopped liver---kid." In my best Groucho imitation I leered at her and pantomimed flicking the ash off of a cigar.

She laughed. "You want to take a dip?"

"We don't have swimsuits."

"I don't mind if you don't," she said

"But I think those boys down the beach would lose their kite, and that fisherman down there would probably fall into the lake. Besides, it's getting a little chilly with the sun going down."

"Spoilsport"

"Try me some other time. Then say that."

Rod Stewart had moved on to describe a lovely face but "the wrong lips," and we emptied one of the bottles of wine.

The sun had settled into the lake, and the sunset was pretty, but not as spectacular as I remembered it to be. We had been at the beach for more than an hour, it was starting to get dark, and nobody else had shown up.

"Let's pack up and head back to the Inn. We have about two hours before dinner. It'll give us time to relax and clean up before we go eat. Geri should be here by now, Sharon is probably back, and Ruben will have gotten some rest."

I shook the sand out of the blanket, Ros helped me fold it, and we trudged up the path to the Inn. Her ass still looked plenty cute, and at her request I helped her brush some sand off the back of her pants. But to paraphrase Stewart, it was the wrong ass.

Our Town Car was back in the lot, and parked next to it was a Lexis with Illinois plates that I assumed was Geri's. The Innkeeper confirmed that it was. "As soon as you left I went into town for some supplies, and when I got back Miss Sapperstein was waiting in the parlor to check in. She wasn't interested in going to the beach, but instead went to her room to unpack and do some work."

Ros headed up to the third floor, and I peeled off at the second landing. Sharon was in our room and opened the door while I was fumbling with the lock.

Just then we heard Ros' hysterical screams from the floor above.

CHAPTER 36

Weinstock Took a Soak

I raced up the flight of stairs two at a time, Sharon close behind. The door to Weinstock's room was opened and a screeching Ros, her face red and tears streaming from her eyes, stood just inside the threshold, gripping the door-knob for support. I pushed past her and saw Weinstock lying on his back, naked, in the Jacuzzi. His pale flabby body and all but the top of his head were completely submerged. The bubbling swirling water was tinted a pale red from the blood that had oozed from a wound to his skull.

I ran to the side of the Jacuzzi to see if there was any sign of life. His arms were moving lazily, but the movement was caused by the pulsating jet streams. His eyes were opened, but they were lifeless. I could feel no pulse in his neck. Through his thinning hair I could see two bullet holes in the back of his head. He was obviously dead.

Sharon had entered the room behind me. I tried to shield her from a view of the body, but was unable to do so. She joined Ros in a cacophony of screams. If there would have been any life left in Weinstock's body those screams surely would have roused him.

Sharon recovered her composure quickly, but Ros only cried harder.

"Cover him up, for Christ's sake" Ros pleaded. "His prick is waving around for everyone to see."

And indeed the water had buoyed his penis, and the current of the Jacuzzi was causing it to sway from side to side. Weinstock would have been pleased by the way the water magnified its size.

We tried to comfort Ros. There was nothing we could do to cover Weinstock because we didn't want to contaminate the murder scene.

Ros broke away from us and threw herself onto the floor next to the body, sobbing "Ruben, Ruben, Ruben." She attempted to cradle his head, and slipped to the floor, landing alongside the Jacuzzi in a sitting position.

I stood behind Ros, placed my arms under her armpits and wrapped my hands around her chest to pull her upright. I couldn't help noticing how nice and firm her breasts were, and Sharon glared at me, somehow picking up on what I was thinking. I just shrugged, and handed Ros my handkerchief to dry her eyes.

Attracted by all the tumult, Geri came up to the room, and she and Sharon each took one of Ros' arms, and supporting her in that manner, they awkwardly walked Ros down the narrow staircase to the parlor on the main floor.

Babich called the police, and a squad car, its siren screaming and its blue lights flashing, screeched to a stop at the front of the Inn, just as we were seating a now exhausted Ros into a rocker in the parlor.

CHAPTER 37

The North Haven Police

The first police to respond were two rookies who looked young enough to still be wearing Boy Scout knickers. They hurried up to Weinstock's room.

The Chief of Police for North Haven arrived a few minutes later. He could have been their grandfather. "I'm Chief Sampson," he boomed out in a strong baritone, obviously proud of his commanding voice. Thinning gray hair, a full shaggy gray mustache, maybe to make up for the loss of hair on top, and obviously painful arthritic joints that caused him to grimace as he moved. But he carried himself ramrod straight. To his credit, Chief Sampson tackled the steep stairway, and by grasping the side railing for support he managed to struggle up to the top. He spent about ten minutes in Weinstock's room, and then walked stiffly back downstairs, wincing as he planted each foot. It was painful to watch.

He shook his head sadly. "We haven't had a murder in this town since I've been with the Department---almost thirty years." And a good thing too, I thought. The Chief looked to me like a guy who couldn't handle anything more complicated than a parking ticket.

"You folks aren't from around here, are ya? It's always the out-of-towners that cause our problems. Where exactly are you from?" Spoken in an unfriendly tone.

"We were up for a vacation weekend, sort of a working, vacationing reunion thing," I said, realizing as I said it that the syntax was off. But the Chief was only half-listening. He was busy trying to figure out what to do next.

"I'm from Chicago. My girlfriend Sharon--that's the one in the white windbreaker, sitting next to the lady with the red eyes--Sharon is from Los Angeles. That's in California," I added.

"The lady doing all the crying--Ros Weinstock, is from Los Angeles---"

"I am not---I'm from Beverly Hills" Ros interrupted.

"The lady doing the crying is from Beverly Hills," I corrected, with a shrug toward Sharon. "That's also in California, adjacent to Los Angeles. Her husband, Dr. Ruben Weinstock, the body in the Jacuzzi, is also from Beverly Hills."

"Also in California," Sharon added.

And the other lady sitting on the couch, the one in the Blue Brooks Brothers Blazer, is from Chicago, like me, but if I recall correctly she also originally came from California."

"I was born in the Valley," Geri said.

"That also is adjacent to Los Angeles," I added.

"A real wise guy group, aren't ya," Sampson said. The geography lesson didn't endear us to the Chief. I didn't really care.

The two uniformed cops came thundering down the stairs.

"What were you doing up there so long," the Chief demanded.

"It took us a while to figure out how to turn off the Jacuzzi. The guy's arms were floating around and his dick was flopping up and back."

The description started Ros wailing again.

The Chief decided to call the county sheriff, who contacted the county medical examiner, and the local boys contented themselves with securing the scene and awaiting competent help.

It took about an hour for the plainclothes detective from the sheriff's department to arrive. He had been umpiring a Little League Baseball game, and it was only the fourth inning when he got the call, and there was no one to take his place so they had to finish the seven innings before he could leave, with the final score being 17-14. His son's team won, he bragged.

The detective's name was Charles Archer, "Call me Charlie." He was a lot more hospitable than the Police Chief, and seemed a lot brighter too. He was all of six feet two, obviously a former athlete, probably football and wrestling at the local high school, and maybe second string varsity at some small college, and now with an expanding waistline. He had muddy brown hair--if he was a girl I'd call it mousy-- and an oval face, browned from the sun, probably from fishing or golf, with wrinkles around the eyes and the beginning of jowls.

He brought the County medical examiner and a crime scene technician with him.

The technician took out his camera as he climbed the stairs. It was one of those old- fashioned Nikon 35 jobs that used film, rather than a digital.

"Are they going to take pictures of Ruben in the nude? I won't allow it!" Ros said.

"I'm sorry mam," Charlie said. He too had a deep voice, but spoke gently to Ros.

"It's part of the procedure. We'll be as quick as we can, and then have the body removed by the medical examiner." He didn't mention that they would take Ruben down to the morgue where they would split him open like a chicken, and scoop out all his organs.

"Can someone take this lady to a room where she can relax while we get this work done?"

Sharon and Geri accompanied Ros to an empty bedroom on the first floor. I wished that the innkeeper had told me before we checked in that a bedroom was available on the first floor. I could have avoided lugging Sharon's luggage up the stairs.

"Why don't you stay here with me," Charlie said to me. "You can fill me in on some of the preliminary matters."

He told the North Haven local police, the uniforms and the Chief, that they could leave, and said he would contact them further if needed.

The uniforms looked disappointed. The Chief seemed relieved.

"In thirty years on the force I never had a murder," he muttered, as he walked out the door.

CHAPTER 38

Detective Archer Interview

"I'm a lawyer from Chicago. Dr. Weinstock is---was--- a gynecologist from California, and he was working with me on a medical malpractice case. His deposition was set for next week, and we are up here on a sort of work-vacation weekend to prep him for the deposition."

"And who are the ladies?"

I explained that Ruben had brought along his wife, I brought along my girlfriend, and Geri Sapperstein was a lawyer working with me on the case.

"And how is North Haven lucky enough to have you gather here?" Charlie asked, somewhat sarcastically. "It isn't even our regular tourist season."

I told him that Ruben and I had worked in North Haven at a Resort for several summers, and that we got the idea to return as a trip down nostalgia lane.

"It turned out to be a pretty lousy idea," he said, in what was a monumental understatement.

"Do you know anyone in this town? Or did Weinstock?"

"I haven't been here in many years. And I'm sure Ruben, that's Dr. Weinstock, hasn't been here either. He was living on the West Coast. And none of the old Resorts are even here anymore. Most have been torn down and replaced by condominiums, and a few like this one where we are staying, are now bed and breakfasts. But none of them are managed by the old resort owners. Those old timers must be dead, or maybe a few have retired to Florida."

"Well somebody knew Dr. Weinstock well enough to want to kill him. And if nobody from town knew him, it seems to me it must have been someone in your party."

"Maybe someone followed us up here," I said. "Plenty of people knew we were coming up for the weekend."

"It doesn't make sense that someone would follow him from the West Coast, just so they could kill him in North Haven." Charlie said.

"No, but they could have come up from Chicago. My secretary made the arrangements, and she had to contact several people. She could have mentioned it. As a matter of fact, come to think of it, the attorney on the other side in our malpractice case knew I was coming up here. I told him so when we made arrangements for the deposition to take place. I didn't tell him where we were staying, but I did mention that we were going to North Haven for the week-end with my expert, to prepare for the deposition. This isn't a very big town, and it would be easy to find out where we had a reservation."

"You think your opposing counsel would kill your expert witness?" he scoffed. "Maybe all those lawyer jokes are true after all."

"No, I don't think he would kill my expert. He's an asshole, but not that big an asshole. But maybe he told his client, the Defendant in our lawsuit. That guy could have been angry enough with Weinstock to kill him. Weinstock was testifying against him, and was gonna come out real strong. Practically call him a quack. That guy, Dr. Mijeck, could possibly lose his license"

"It sounds very farfetched to me," Charlie said, losing interest in my theory as he started to get up from his chair.

"There's something you should know before you disregard it, Charlie. My investigator who was working on this same malpractice case was murdered just a few months ago, shot in the back of the head with a small caliber gun. And they never found his killer. Maybe the killings are related in some way." That got Charlie's attention, and he sat back down.

"How could they be related?"

"I don't know---they both worked on the same malpractice claim--- they know a lot of the same people---it just seemed possible." I said.

"It does sound possible," Charlie said, "but on the other hand, maybe it's just that you hire people who are easy to dislike." And then, shifting gears, and taking out a spiral note pad, the kind with the spiral rings on the top, "What time did you arrive in town?"

"Ruben and Ros and Sharon and I got here in the same car at about four this afternoon. We checked into our rooms by about four thirty."

"So we know that Ruben was still alive at that time."

"Definitely--he looked a little pooped, but definitely alive. I asked him to go down to the beach with us, but he said he was too tired. He was going to relax in the room, maybe take a short nap. Ros and I left for the beach. We were going to check out the sunset."

"What happened to Sharon? Did she go down to the beach with you?"

"Sharon had to pick up something in town, at the drug store, I think. She took the car, and said she would either join us at the beach later, or meet us back at the room."

"Did she meet you at the beach?"

"No, I didn't see her again until we got back here, after the sunset."

"And you and Ros were together at the beach until you came back together. You were together at all times?" Charlie was carefully writing down everything I was telling him.

"I notice you use a ballpoint pen, and not a pencil," I said. "What happens if you make a mistake? You can't erase it."

"I don't make mistakes."

"What about this lady lawyer, Geri Sapperstein," he continued. "Where was she when all this was going on?"

"I don't know. She must have arrived while we were at the beach."

"So when you got back Mrs. Weinstock went right up to her room?"

"That's right."

"And she screamed immediately?"

"As soon as she walked in."

"So unless his wife shot Dr. Weinstock before she left with you for the beach, he must have been killed in the interval between when the two of you left for the beach, and the time you came back and she walked into the room."

"If she shot him before we left, somebody would have heard it."

"Not necessarily. It was a small caliber, and the shot could have been muffled. But I agree with you, it is highly unlikely that she shot him."

"Very unlikely," I agreed.

"That means you and Mrs. Weinstock give each other an alibi. Unless the two of you were in it together."

I couldn't argue with his logic.

"Can anyone vouch for you and Mrs. Weinstock even being at the beach?"

"The beach was pretty empty. There were a couple of kids down there, but they were far away and probably too busy flying kites to notice us. And a fisherman out at the end of the pier, but he wouldn't of seen us."

"Mrs. Weinstock is a nice looking lady."

"Nice ass," I agreed.

"Were you two close?"

"Cool it, Charlie. I never even met the lady before today."

The medical examiner came down the stairs. He confirmed, as if there was any doubt, that Ruben was dead, probable cause being two bullet wounds to the back of the head. He talked in clipped phrases, just spit them out. "Small entrance wounds—no exit wounds—the bullets probably still in the skull—maybe a 22." *The same caliber that killed Phil Levine.*

Two paramedics struggled down the stairs with the gurney bearing Ruben's' body. He was covered by a white sheet. Because of his pot belly the gurney looked like it was carrying a mound of snow that sloped gently from the peak, kind of like a bunny hill. As they negotiated down the steep stairway Ruben's body tilted forward and his pale bare feet, still wet from the Jacuzzi, slid out from under the sheet. Ros Weinstock screamed. It's a good thing he wasn't being carried head first. If his bloody head would have popped out, she would have had a heart attack.

CHAPTER 39

Babich Has His Say

Detective "just call me Charlie" Archer had us assembled in the parlor, just like in a Hercule Poirot novel. He even started to light up a pipe, but the innkeeper, Sheldon Babich, sternly told him the Rules prohibited smoking.

"Too bad you had no rule against murder—then we wouldn't have to be here in the first place," Archer grumbled, putting the pipe back in his pocket.

Ros was sitting next to me on a white wicker love seat, still sniffling into the handkerchief I had loaned her and would probably never get back. She had managed to commandeer the place next to me, forcing Sharon to take the matching wicker chair on the other side of the wicker cocktail table. Innkeeper Babich either loved wicker, or got a terrific buy at a close-out sale.

"I know that you and Ros were at the beach in the hour or so before the body was discovered," Charlie said to me, and then turning to Sharon, "but where were you while your boyfriend was watching the sunset and sipping wine with Mrs. Weinstock?"

"I had taken the car to McConnell's Drug Store in town to pick up a few personal items," Sharon said.

"Wait a minute," Babich interrupted. "I went to town just a few minutes after you left. I went into McConnell's and didn't see you there, and I didn't see your fancy town car on the street. And believe me, I would have noticed. Not many cars like that in this town." He sounded like the kid across the aisle who liked to snitch to the teacher that Johnny was cheating.

"I must have left before you got there," Sharon said. Her glare at Sheldon Babich was enough to wilt him down two sizes and wrinkle his seersucker suit.

"Just for the record," Charlie said, "can you show us what you purchased?" Sharon opened her oversized Donald J Pliner purse and produced a pack of sanitary napkins, and a small bottle of Midol. If Weinstock's death didn't put a kibosh on my hopes for a sexy weekend, that put on the finishing touches.

Charlie was blushing slightly. "You have a receipt for these items?" he asked.

"I threw it away."

"Of course" Charlie said. "But you claim to have been gone for over an hour. It didn't take that long to buy those things. Did you get lost?"

"No. I remember this town very well. It hasn't changed much from the time I was a kid. I just drove around, listening to an oldies radio station, reminiscing. I guess I just lost track of the time. Then I came back here and went to my room."

"Did you see anyone who could verify that?"

Sharon hesitated, and looked at me. She shook her head. "No," she said. "Nobody."

Charlie filled pages of his spiral notebook, nodding to himself every now and then, summarizing what he had been told, and making notes on follow-ups under a page he had headed "To Do". I noticed him crossing out a mistake, but I didn't say anything.

"Do you have the name of the Detective in charge of the investigation of that murder of your friend in Chicago--- oh yeah, and you better give me the name of the friend who was killed." He recorded Phil Levine's name, and the name and phone for Inspector Hollman of Chicago Homicide.

Then he turned to Geri Sapperstein. "I haven't forgotten you, little lady." Geri cringed at "little lady."

Geri explained that she had driven up alone from Chicago, left there about 2:00, and had arrived in North Haven about 5:00. She had parked her car, and gone in to register, but there was nobody at the front desk. There was a sign saying that the Innkeeper would return shortly, so she took a short walk to stretch her legs. She got back to the Inn shortly before Babich returned. Then she registered, went to her room and did a little work, and was unpacking when she heard the screams.

"What time did you get back?" Charlie barked at the innkeeper.

"I was out shopping for some furniture ---actually, cushions for the seats of Wicker furniture," Sheldon Babich explained.

"I can confirm that he needs cushions," I said, shifting uncomfortably. There were probably hatch marks on my ass.

"I hope you picked out cushions with some soothing colors----maybe pinks and blues and yellows," Sharon said, squinting. "All this white is boring, and it gives off a very harsh glare." She slipped the sun glasses that had been perched on the top of her head down over her eyes.

Babich was offended. "Suitable cushions are coming," he said, "and I assure you they will be color coordinated and very comfortable."

"You still didn't answer my question," Detective Archer said. "What time did you get back?"

"I got here about 5:30," and with a sneer directed at Sharon, "and I noticed, by the way, that the town car was back." Turning to Detective Archer, he continued, "I checked in Miss Sapperstein who was in the parlor waiting for me, and then began straightening up. Mr. Seger and Mrs. Weinstock came back from the beach and went upstairs. And then I heard the screams. Someone hollered for me to summon the police and I did. I can't believe that this occurred in my establishment. I have to clean the place up. I can't leave it in this state. There is so much to do. This is going to ruin the reputation of my Inn."

"Well at least you'll have lodgers for the next several days," Charlie Archer said. Stealing the dialogue from an old movie, he looked at us, and somberly instructed "No one is leaving town until we get this sorted out. Make your phone calls, rearrange your schedules, and settle in. And give me your cell phone numbers."

Looking at Ros, he said "I'm very sorry for your loss mam. We'll have to rope off your old room until the crime scene people finish their work. Then I'll have your things moved to another room in the Inn. Your husband has been transferred to the morgue, and we have to keep the body until the medical examiner is finished. That could take a few days. Then we can release the body for burial."

Ros was deep in thought, seemed stunned, but no longer appeared very bereaved. Then she looked at him and demanded "At least let me go in there to get my things, my clothes and make-up. I can't walk around looking like this." Archer gave the O.K., and Sharon accompanied Ros and helped her retrieve the things she wanted.

Charlie Archer got up to leave. He walked out the door with a parting shot. "I have your cell numbers. Stay available."

CHAPTER 40

The Merry Widow

Sharon and I were on the front veranda, rocking gently on a creaky old glider. It was almost 9:00 p.m. A naked yellow light bulb in the ceiling, designed to keep away mosquitoes, was our only illumination, and gave us both a sallow complexion. We were sharing the contents of my sterling silver flask, a present from my former wife, alternating sips of single malt scotch. Actually I was sipping. Sharon was doing more of a chug-a-lug.

"We should never have come back to North Beach. We should have stayed farrrrr away from here," Sharon lamented. "Then this never would have happened. It didn't have to happen like this." She took another swig.

"I don't see how coming here could have gotten Rueben killed. North Beach doesn't kill people. People kill people."

"Not funny." Sharon cried ---real tears. I never saw her cry before, and I didn't know what to do. I put my arm around her and she buried her face in my shoulder. I couldn't even give her my handkerchief. Ros never returned it. Fortunately my windbreaker was waterproof. The sobbing finally subsided, and we sat quietly, slowly gliding back and forth.

"I'll be alright now. Sorry I got your jacket wet. I don't want to talk about this anymore now. Maybe later."

It was well past my usual dinner time. And as inappropriate as it seemed, what with Rueben's death and all, I was getting very hungry.

"Do you remember that old roadside Café on the Blue Arrow Highway, the road we used to take out here before they built the expressway. They had the best spareribs I ever tasted. I wonder if it's still out there."

"Typical. Your friend gets killed because of you, and all you can think of is your stomach? Ugh."

"What do you mean because of me---how am I to blame?"

"If you and Phil hadn't brought him into this case as an expert, and if you hadn't flown him to Chicago and then driven him out here to North Haven, he wouldn't have been killed. It's pretty obvious, isn't it? And the ribs at that Café weren't that terrific---it was the sauce she concocted that made them taste that good. That sauce could make kale taste great."

"But how are they related. Phil's death--- Ruben's death. I just can't figure it out, and I've been racking my brain. It's hard to believe Dr. Mijeck would want to kill people over a malpractice case---it seems too fantastic---but I don't see any other connection. It just doesn't make any sense. But to call the two murders a coincidence --- I just don't know."

"Maybe there is another explanation," Sharon said. "We have to think on it. But let's go eat first. You never could think on an empty stomach. And if you don't eat you'll just get grouchy, like you always do."

"O.K. We'll hit the Blue Arrow Café if it's still there. You can skip the ribs if you want, and just put that terrific sauce over your usual salad."

"We should ask Geri if she wants to join us," I said. "She's all alone in her room. And what about Ros. Can we ask a grieving widow to go out for barbecue?"

"By the time I got Ros packed up and moved into her new room she was over the shock. She seemed more concerned about her makeup than she was about Ruben. She wasn't acting like a grieving widow, more like a Merry Widow. I think it's safe for you to ask her if she wants to go out to eat. You go talk to the widow. I'll ask Geri if she wants to join us."

Ros was settled in her new room, seated at a small desk by the window, writing a letter on the Inn's Stationary, headed "North Beach Inn—Blueberry Capital of the World." In response to my gentle knock she had invited me to come in. Her eyes were dry, and she was wearing her fresh widowhood well.

"We were married less than two years. I was his trophy wife," she said. "He was a lot older than me, but we got along fine. I could go my own way when I wanted. I could keep my old friends. When he wanted me I was there for him—in all ways, if you know what I mean."

I nodded. "It sounds like a nice arrangement."

"He was good to me. And I was good to him, if you know what I mean. We had a pre-nup, but I'll come out O.K., even if it can't be broken. I took out a policy on his life. You know any good divorce and probate lawyers in L.A.?"

I ignored the question. "We're going out for barbecue. I realize you may feel like being alone, but if you care to you can join us." Her short grieving period, might have set a new Guinness record.

"Give me five minutes to change. I'll meet you downstairs."

A little later we all piled into the rented Town Car and headed to the Blue Arrow Highway Café. That was the correct name, and I verified it in the yellow pages. A phone call revealed they were still in operation, and although it was nearing closing time, they agreed to stay open to serve our party. That meant the owner was still there running the place. Employees would never stay beyond scheduled closing.

The café was as I remembered it. In Chicago, they opened a lot of "Diners" to recapture the era, and the layouts were similar, but they could never quite capture the smells and the feel of an original.

"Is Catherine still here?" I even remembered the name of the owner, a chunky grey haired lady who looked like Aunt Jemima, but had the swagger of Muhammad Ali.

"Momma has passed," the waitress said. "Died of cancer two years ago."

I realized I was speaking to the daughter, the one who Catherine used to boast about—the valedictorian of her grammar school class, who someday was going to be a lawyer or doctor, or some other big money professional.

"I'm sorry. Your momma was a terrific lady. I forget your name, but I remember her talking about you a lot. She was determined that you get a good education. Were you able to finish school?"

"I had to take a break after undergrad because we ran out of money--- I'm getting the Diner running good and when I sell it I'll go back. For a Masters in International Finance."

"You still have that same barbecue sauce? The recipe your mom concocted?"

"The best in these parts. By the way, my name is Ellen." She shook my hand and smiled.

"We'll take four slabs."

"Make it 3 slabs and one chopped salad," Sharon said. "And a side of your sauce."

Sharon was delicately nibbling on pieces of lettuce dipped in barbeque sauce, and Geri, Ros and I were absorbed in ripping the meat off of the bones with our teeth, each of us with greasy fingers and smears of sauce on our faces, when Chief Sampson entered the Café.

"I was driving by, and noticed your sign was still on, past closing. Just wanted to make sure everything was O.K.," he said to Ellen. Then he noticed us. "Having a wake, are you? You big city folks are really a piece of cake." He walked out shaking his head.

CHAPTER 41

On The Pier

I called Julia at her home early the next morning.

"You sound kind of sleepy."

"Of course I'm sleepy—what time is it."

"Look grumps—it's almost eight o'clock."

"Jesus, don't you know this is Saturday morning--my hours don't start until Monday. What's wrong?"

"Something has come up. I need you to do a few things for me."

"Can I fix some coffee first and call you back in say two hours?"

"Make it an instant coffee, and get back to me in fifteen minutes."

I was alone, walking barefoot along the beach, with my gym shoes tied together and slung over my shoulder. Just like I used to do when I was a kid. The cool powdery sand felt wonderful between my toes.

When I walked closer to the waterline I left a full footprint in the damp sand. And I mean a full footprint. No arch. I have totally flat feet.

My mother loved to say that the feet were the only thing that kept me from being perfect. Phyllis, my ex, the former Mrs. Seger, would shake her head in disgust every time mom said it. When mom said it to Sharon, she replied that my feet were probably one of my better features.

When I reached the pier I leaned against a piling and put my shoes back on. The concrete surface was rough, and if that wasn't enough to cut or bruise your soles, the discarded bent fish hooks and lures presented an additional hazard.

My harem, as I began to think of them, Sharon, Geri and Ros, were still asleep at the Inn. I needed some air, some time to think. What the hell was happening? Why were my investigator, and now my expert

157

murdered? I checked my cell phone to make sure I was getting a signal, and then cautiously sat down about half-way down the pier with my feet dangling over the water.

There are two piers that jut out into the water, parallel to each other and about sixty yards apart. I was on the north pier. The channel between the piers provides boats access from the Marina out into Lake Michigan. At one time there was a lighthouse at the end of each pier, but sometime in the last several years the one on the North Pier was destroyed, leaving just a stump of rocks as a memorial. The lighthouse on the South Pier was still sending out its beacon.

I looked across the channel, remembering back to when we were kids, me, Phil Levine, and Weinstock, and the races we had, swimming across the channel from one pier to the other, and then back again. Weinstock always lagged far behind, and come to think of it, I didn't have many first place finishes.

The air was clear, with a slight chill, but there was no wind. A few fishermen in small boats with outboard engines were heading out the channel into the lake to try their luck with the salmon, and their wakes sent ripples over the still water. I absently waived to them as they chugged by, but my mind was still in the past, when Phil and Weinstock and I were young, working at Laurel's. I thought about how I first met Sharon. I was softly singing one of the songs popular back then---sounding to my ear just like Lionel Richie, the phrasing and all, when my cell phone jarred me back to the present.

"I just heard it on the radio---Weinstock dead---murdered. Why didn't you tell me!" Julia said. "Are you alright?"

"Yeah, we're fine. Somebody shot him in his Jacuzzi."

"I thought they shot him in his head."

"Not funny."

"Sorry," she said. "I couldn't resist. Do they know who did it?"

"No idea---but they're going to compare the bullets to the ones that killed Phil. I think they're the same caliber, and the odds are they'll match."

"But why?"

"I have no idea---but the murders have to be connected some way."

"Well, Phil is the one who first contacted Weinstock to act as our expert."

"And Phil and Weinstock worked with me here in North Beach when we were kids---but what does that prove."

"There has to be a connection between the killings," Julia insisted.

"Look Sherlock, I didn't call you to solve the case. I need you to do a few things for me."

"Shoot---I've got my pad and pencil."

"I may not be back for several days. First, re-schedule my appointments. And make sure you call Bill Masterson, Mijeck's lawyer, and tell him Weinstock won't be able to appear for Deposition Monday. And tell him I will be filing a Motion for Continuance, to give me a chance to get a new expert. Next, see if you can contact Inspector Hollman, the guy in charge of Phil's murder investigation. See if you can get him to call me. Also call my ex and tell her I can't take my daughter to dinner on Wednesday---I'll be tied up."

"Don't you think you should call her yourself?"

"We would just get into a shouting match, like we always do. And I don't want to end up on the internet in a rage, like Alex Baldwin. Just take care of these things for me, and we'll keep in touch." I hung up, or disconnected, or whatever you're supposed to call it when you end a cell phone call.

I was no longer alone. Someone was walking along the pier toward me. I couldn't see who it was because his face was obscured by over-sized sun glasses, a soft tan cotton hat with the brim pulled way down, and the collar of a windbreaker turned up. As he approached I scrambled up from the edge of the pier, and stood facing him. I wasn't going to make it easy for him to push me in the water.

"Nice morning," I said.

"Yeah, but the sun is too bright and it's lousy for my skin," he replied. "Keratosis, don't you know." He walked on past me to the end of the pier.

I breathed a little easier and headed back to the beach.

CHAPTER 42

A Continental Breakfast

When I got back to the Inn, Sheldon Babich was setting out the breakfast table. He had coffee brewing in one of those 25 cup coffee makers that always makes weak tasteless coffee no matter how many grounds you add.

"Try a cup," he urged. "I put egg shells in with the grounds. It gives it a richer flavor." He handed me a paper cup. "And have a bagel. The toaster is over on the other table, and the cream cheese is alongside it." He used his hands to put a sliced water bagel on a paper plate and handed it to me. At least his hands looked clean.

The ineffective toaster was one of those where you put the slices of bagel face up on a belt that glides them slowly under the upper burner, then rotates underneath and spits them out just barely warm and far from toasted. It took three repetitions and several minutes, to give any color at all to the bagels. The coffee, eggshells notwithstanding, was tepid. The cream cheese was good.

I fixed a tray for Sharon and brought it up to the room. She never ate much at night, and usually was hungry for something the first thing in the morning. She wasn't in bed, but was on the floor alongside it, doing her Pilate exercises. Totally nude.

"Nice," I said as I positioned myself for the best view.

She ignored me. " I'll be through in a few minutes." She did a few leg raises and then lifted her butt off the floor, and arched her back, holding the pose for a wonderfully long time.

Then she hopped up and quickly slipped on her robe. "Show's over. What did you bring me to eat?" She took a sip of the coffee and made a face.

"Is this nonfat cream cheese?"

"I didn't see the label, but probably not, because I liked it."

She ignored the cream cheese, took a little nibble of the limp pallid bagel, and then dumped my whole offering in the wastebasket.

"If I'm going to have calories they should at least be tasty. Wasn't there a place in town that used to make terrific blueberry waffles?"

"You mean Halley's. For someone who hardly eats, you sure have a great memory for restaurants. I'll check to see if it's still there. You get dressed, and I'll wait for you downstairs. Unless you feel like a little more exercise," I leered.

"Down boy. I'm hungry. I'll be dressed and downstairs in twenty minutes. See if the other girls want to join us."

I checked on Ros first. I put my ear to her door and could hear the shower running. Geri was already in the parlor, sipping a cup of coffee, chatting with Sheldon. "Did you know he puts egg shells in the coffee? It's delicious."

Sheldon told me that Halley's was still operating in town. "Still the best waffles in the county."

He wasn't at all put out that we weren't satisfied with his Continental Breakfast.

Geri was happy to join us for breakfast in town. Ros came out as we were chatting, her hair still wet. The merry widow. She wanted to come with us too. Of course. There really wasn't anything to do just hanging around the Inn. It took Sharon close to an hour to get ready. Way beyond the twenty minutes she had promised. No big surprise. I have yet to be involved with a prompt woman. But she did look terrific. Even with her clothes on.

CHAPTER 43

Halley's

I doubt that Halley's spent any money redecorating in the past twenty years. Still the same booths with Formica tops and red vinyl seats, some torn in spots, with the tan sponge-like material peeking out. The wooden walls were scarred with the romantic messages that had been etched in over the decades. I searched for the message of eternal love I had engraved to Sharon in our youth, but I couldn't remember where I had carved it.

The menus, encased in plastic and badly stained, still described about twelve varieties of pancakes and a multitude of Belgian Waffles, covered in every kind of fruit imaginable. But it strongly recommended the home-grown blueberries as a topping, "with or without real (not in- the-can) whipping cream." Pitchers holding a variety of fruit syrups were on the tables. There was also one that had a label hung on it: "REAL MAPLE SYRUP---HIGHLY RECOMMENDED." Each booth had its own juke box against the wall, with songs mostly from the 50's and 60's. I put in a quarter and selected the Mills Brothers singing "Taxi Driver," which was a lot older than I was, but sounded pretty good to me.

I ordered blueberry pancakes and homemade sausage patties. Ros selected the waffle. Sharon and Geri opted for poached eggs and dry toast.

Just as our orders were delivered, Wally Smalley entered the restaurant. It had been several years since I had seen him, but even if Sharon hadn't given me his picture I would have recognized him as soon as he walked in. He looked around, and then walked directly to our table. He seemed relaxed and confident, dressed in chinos, a polo golf shirt and sneakers with no sox. About six feet two, and trim. I consciously sucked in my tummy, and silently resolved to eat only half of my breakfast and start exercising more. Wally didn't seem surprised to see us.

"Mind if I join you," he said as he pulled a chair up to the end of our booth.

"Not a good idea," I said. "We really don't want your company." Blunt, not my usual well-mannered self. There would be no flinching by me this time, even if I ended up getting punched out.

"But after Shar came all the way to Michigan searching for me--- yesterday she drove all over town looking for me. I figure she wants my company ---- huh hon?"

Sharon reddened. "That's not true. I never want to see you again--- and don't call me hon."

Wally and Sharon stared at each other. She looked away first.

Wally shifted his attention to me. He looked menacing and started to rise. So did I. We stood there silently, each waiting for the other to make the first move. *High Noon*, Midwestern style.

As the Mills Brothers hit the final chords, Chief Sampson sauntered into the restaurant. He had been keeping tabs on our group to make sure we didn't leave town. Wally turned and left the restaurant without another word. Sampson joined our table, and I gave him half my pancakes.

CHAPTER 44

Smalley, The Bartender

I dropped Sharon, Ros and Geri at the Inn, saying I was just going to drive around for a while. Then I set out to confront Smalley....convince him to stop harassing Sharon, to get out of her life finally and forever. There wasn't much chance he would listen to reason and probably he would ignore my threats of legal action, but I had to give it a shot.

The odds were we would end up in a fight, and most likely he would kick the living shit out of me. I was ready for that. At least a beating would erase the memory of the time on the beach, the time I froze up, ready to run. Part of me was yearning for the rematch.

I figured that Wally worked at a bar somewhere near the lakefront, that's where most of the bars were located, but none of those places opened until cocktail hour, a little before dinner. So I killed the afternoon at the beach.

I wasn't alone. There were several groups of college age girls taking advantage of the unseasonably warm weather. They all wore skimpy bathing suits, the boldest of them in thongs that showed plenty of cheek behind, and patches of waxed skin in front.

The few that were not tapping on cell phones were lying on blankets with their eyes closed, soaking up sun and listening to rap music on their portable I-Pods. Packs of young studs wearing speedos a size too small strutted between the blankets like peacocks, goofing off and vying for attention.

The only person showing any interest in me was a six year old boy whose Frisbee floated onto my beach towel.

The bars opened just before sunset. I hit a few spots and had a couple of drinks before I found someone who could tell me where to find Smalley.

He was bartending at "Six Shillings", a restaurant and tavern converted, the sign said, "from an old North Haven mansion." It was a mansion by North Haven standards, but if you lived on Chicago's North Shore it was no mansion--just a nice old big wooden house with eaves, a big portico front porch, planked oak floors, and six bedrooms upstairs.

The specialties, according to a menu posted at the front door, were whitefish and perch, fresh from Lake Michigan, pan-fried chicken, and, on Saturday night, "a seriously oversized slab of prime rib served on the bone."

I entered a lounge area designed to look nautical. The hostess, dressed as a pirate, sporting a jaunty hat and a patch over one eye, stood behind her station, a large ship's wheel, and greeted guests with a hearty "Ahoy Mates." The knotty pine walls were adorned with mounted sailfish, and fishnets overflowing with sea shells.

There was a polished dark mahogany bar that ran the full length of the room. Several patrons were gathered at the end near the flat screen T.V., their attention riveted on a basketball game. I sat down alone at the other end of the bar, on a stool near a large picture window facing the channel leading out to Lake Michigan. An impressive sized yacht, it's captain on the flying bridge, and a dinner cruise ship were heading out into the lake, and a sailboat at full mast passed in the other direction, returning to the Marina.

I had spotted Wally Smalley as soon as I entered the room. I know he saw me too, but he ignored me as he stayed near the television, chatting with customers, polishing glasses, and watching basketball. He was wearing a tight white tee shirt that proclaimed North Haven to be the Blueberry capital of the world. He looked even bigger and more muscular than he had earlier in the day at the Halley's.

A waitress gave Smalley a drink order, and he smoothly prepared a Rob Roy, shaken, not stirred, and blended a strawberry daiquiri. A very competent bartender.

I sat patiently with my hands folded on the bar, and watched the boats on the river. I never flagged him over, but finally, after about five minutes, he ambled down to take my order.

I ordered an R. J. Hudson Martini, and explained how to make it. Half gin, half vodka. I didn't specify brands. "The vodka smooths out the gin, and the gin gives the vodka character." He nodded, and went off to mix my drink, giving no indication that he recognized me. The guy was either a great poker player or he was a serious mental case.

He carefully measured Beefeater and Absolute, added ice to the shaker, shook it longer and more vigorously than any drink I had ever seen shaken, and expertly poured it into a chilled cocktail glass. As he set it in front of me his hand knocked the drink over and the contents poured into my lap.

"I'm very sorry," he said in a flat tone--no emotion. He didn't seem sorry at all.

A passing waitress gave me a napkin and I dried myself as best I could.

"Accidents happen. It's a good thing I didn't order a hot toddy."

"Why don't you sit out on the deck. The air will help dry your pants. I'll pour you another drink and bring it out to you. I'm going on break now anyway."

I sat at a table at the corner of the deck, awaiting my fresh drink. The sun had set, and it was getting dark. The air was chilly, especially noticeable in the area where my pants were wet. No one else was sitting outside, and the only light was from the small lanterns on the deck railing. There was a full moon, but it was hidden behind a cloud. As always in North Haven, the sky was full of big bright stars. Just like deep in the heart of Texas.

I shooed away some mosquitoes that gathered to sample me, and waited for Wally to appear. Suddenly a hand reached over my shoulder from behind, and I flinched. It was Wally, who snuck up silently from behind to place my fresh drink on the table.

"Kinda jumpy, aren't you." He sat down next to me and sipped a Leinenkugel from the bottle.

"How's Sharon?" he asked.

"She's fine." I tried to keep my voice as calm as his.

"We had a really good thing going. I really love that lady."

"She tells me it ended a long time ago."

"Not for me it didn't. And it wouldn't have ended for her either, if you didn't show up again. You're the only thing that wedged us apart."

"Sharon broke up with you before I ever called her."

"That's bullshit." He banged down the bottle and beer spilled on the table.

"You're a pretty sloppy bartender. That's twice you've spilled a drink."

He ignored my comment. "Sharon and me hooked up for almost a year. We even lived together for the last month. We were going to have a family. Did she tell you that!" He was talking faster now, and louder.

His eyes followed my glass as I raised my drink to my lips. I caught myself before taking a sip. He had spent a long time mixing that drink while I was out on the deck, and there was no telling how he might have doctored it. I returned the glass to the table untouched, and ran my finger along the rim as he continued talking.

"When I first met Sharon in California, it was like a miracle. I was in love with her here when we were kids. But you broke that up then. But now you were out of the picture, and Sharon and me could start over."

I edged back from the table as he became more agitated, realizing this meeting wasn't going the way I had hoped.

"Sometimes, when I was fucking her she would get a faraway look in her eye and I could tell she was thinking of you. But I was making her forget. It was fading. We would have made it if it wasn't for you. We were going to have kids. Then you called. And that ended everything. She ended everything. I can't let it happen!"

"Calm down Wally. Stop obsessing on this thing. You're spinning your wheels. All it's gonna get you is some jail time. Sharon wants you to leave her alone."

"She may say that now, but she doesn't mean it. We just have to get rid of that cancer in her. You're that cancer! And I'm gonna see that it gets cut out, one way or the other."

"You've gotta listen to me and get this through your thick head. Sharon wants nothing more to do with you. You're finished. Kaput. She wants you gone. And so do I. If you don't leave her alone---and I mean alone--- no calls---no letters---no contact of any kind, I'll have you locked away for so long you'll be an old man by the time you get out. And I can do it---and I will. So get the fuck out of her life. Now! Permanently!" I lost my cool and I started to get up.

"Fuck you, you bastard!" He jumped up, knocking his chair over, and swung at me with a roundhouse right that would have knocked my head off, but I ducked down underneath it. He left himself wide opened for a counter punch, but if I connected with his rocklike jaw I probably would have broken my hand. So I kneed him in the groin instead. Hard. He doubled over in pain.

I grabbed his Leinenkugel by the neck, gripping it like a short tennis racket, and as he looked up at me with pure hatred, and started to straighten up, I swung the bottle into the center of his face as if I was driving a tennis ball into the far corner, spending all the anger that had been pent up since he threatened me as a kid. His head snapped back and he went down. His nose was smashed, and blood covered his face and dripped down onto the deck.

He was breathing hard through his mouth, and he rolled over and grabbed the edge of the table, trying to get to his feet, but he couldn't make it. He fell back to the deck, unconscious, and the table fell over on top of him, and the martini he had fixed me spilled onto the deck. Too bad. I was thinking I might take it to a lab for analysis. That's how crazy he seemed.

I drove back to the Bed & Breakfast, and Sharon was waiting for me on the porch.

"Where have you been?"

"Just out to the beach, and then driving around. And then I stopped for a drink."

"It looks like you spilled it on your pants."

"Well, I went to see Walley, and we had a little accident."

"Did he talk to you?"

"We had quite a conversation."

"You and I have to talk," Sharon said. "Let's take a ride."

CHAPTER 45

Sharon Shares A Secret

And so I took Sharon for a ride, both of us quiet and lost in thought. I turned off onto Black Line Road, and pulled off the pavement onto a dirt shoulder at a place where I knew there would be no traffic.

"We used to park here at night when we were kids," Sharon said. "I remember when we were going at it hot and heavy one night when it was raining, and your car got stuck in the mud and we had to call a tow truck to get us out."

"Why were you looking for Smalley? At Hally's this morning Wally said you were driving around looking for him the day Ruben was killed. Why were you looking for him if it was all over between you two?"

"Let's do this another time. You're too worked up now to listen. I don't think we should talk about it now."

"It was your idea to talk, so let's do it. You tell me he was bothering you. You want to get him off of your back. And then we come out here and you drive around looking for him. What's going on?"

She started to cry.

I grabbed her shoulders and turned her toward me. "I want to know the truth. Everything!"

"I'm responsible for their deaths," she said. "Both of them. Phil and Ruben. If it wasn't for me they would both still be alive."

I waited. Gave her time to compose herself. Didn't say a thing. After a few minutes, she continued.

"Remember I told you that while I was in California, after my divorce, I began seeing Wally Smalley. Until just before I began seeing you again." She paused for a long time and I waited for her to continue. "Well I didn't tell you everything."

There was another long pause. Then she took a deep gulp of air, like she was about to jump into the deepest part of Lake Michigan, and blurted it out.

"Wally got me pregnant. Oh, I was as much to blame as him. We got high one night and it just happened. On the last night that we slept together. A few weeks later I kicked him out of my house for good. I didn't see him again until I found out I was pregnant. I didn't want to get back together with him, but I made the mistake of contacting him to ask for some financial assistance with the abortion.

When I told Wally I was pregnant he wanted to get married. Get married----I never wanted to see him again, and I told him that---again and again. He wanted me to keep the baby. He's a Catholic, you know. He wouldn't go along with the abortion, certainly wouldn't help pay for it---killing an innocent fetus and all that. It was still the first trimester. So I had it done without him."

I sat silent, just listening.

"When I missed my period and got a positive on my pregnancy test I wasn't sure where to turn. I was confused. I couldn't believe I was pregnant. I wanted to confirm the pregnancy. I called Ruben Weinstock---someone had mentioned his name, and I remembered him from our North Beach days. He remembered me and gave me an immediate appointment. Ruben confirmed the pregnancy."

"And he did the abortion of Wally's kid," I finished.

"Right."

"Did Wally know it was Weinstock who aborted his baby?" I saw her flinch. "I mean fetus."

"I told Wally that Ruben did the abortion. I told him the fetus was only six weeks old. And I told Wally I never wanted to see him again."

"Did anyone else know about the abortion?"

"I didn't tell anyone. Nobody. Not my girlfriends, not my mother, not you, no one."

"When was the abortion?"

"About a week before I first saw you in California. I couldn't tell you then. I knew I would lose you if I did."

"So the first time I saw you in California, you just had an abortion of another man's kid."

"About a week before. I couldn't tell you."

"You're right. It sure would have put a damper on our relationship."

"I know I was totally stupid," she said. "I never should have gotten involved with Wally---I don't know what I was thinking. And how could I have been dumb enough to get pregnant."

"It was pretty dumb," I said. Feeling numb.

The two of us sat there quietly for a long time. Looking out at the stars.

"What about now," she finally said. "Are you through with me?"

"Is there anything else you want to dump on me---any more surprises?"

"You've heard them all," she said. "Isn't what I told you bad enough?"

I looked at her. She was still as beautiful as when I first saw her. I still wanted her, more than anything. *Nobody else gave me that thrill.* I was probably an idiot.

"It might have mattered then but it doesn't matter much now. You've got me hooked again," I said. But I was shaken.

"You still haven't explained why you went looking for Wally the other night."

"I was afraid he was going to contact you and tell you about the abortion. I thought maybe if I saw him I could talk him out of doing that. It was a stupid idea. Anyway, I couldn't find him."

"And you really believe Wally killed Ruben?"

"Wally was furious about the abortion. I think he killed Ruben because Ruben killed his baby. And I think he felt you were responsible for the abortion. He didn't so much blame me as he did you. He said that I wouldn't have given up the baby if you hadn't come back. He said that you were responsible for killing his baby. And that he would get even with you."

A farmer driving a beat up old pick-up truck at about five miles an hour, it looked like it couldn't go much faster, crept along Black Line Road toward our parked vehicle. He was wearing a straw hat and smoking a corn cob pipe. He stopped alongside us, shined in a flashlight, and asked if we needed any help. Not the kind that he could offer. We thanked him for stopping, and he proceeded along his way.

"And you think that Wally wanted to kill me. And that he came after me, waiting for me in the back of my car, and that he killed Phil by mistake."

"It must have happened that way. I know he was obsessing about the abortion. Or maybe he really did intend to kill Phil."

"That's crazy. Why would he go after Phil?"

"Just try to keep your lawyer mouth closed for a minute and listen." She was feeling pretty confident of my love again when she talked to me like that.

"When Wally started calling and threatening me, and ranting and raving, I called Phil."

"Phil Levine? Our Phil? But why him?"

"He had been my friend. He was an investigator. Chicago isn't too far from North Haven where Wally was living. I thought Phil could help me. Stop Wally from bothering me. He promised to be discreet."

"He certainly was. He didn't even tell me that you called him. But that explains why he had Wally's name and yours on that scrap of paper."

"I wanted Phil to contact Wally. Get him to leave me alone---to leave us alone."

"So Phil contacted Wally?"

"He told me he drove up to Michigan, found Wally, and told him he would be dead meat if he bothered me again, or if he even thought about coming after you."

"Phil liked to play tough guy. I can see him doing that," I said. "So you think that's what got Phil killed. That Wally killed him because of the threat."

"It must have been Wally. And then he killed Weinstock yesterday because Weinstock aborted his baby."

"Did you tell Phil about the abortion?"

"No, I couldn't bring myself to do it. I was afraid Phil might tell you. But Phil found out about the abortion when he talked to Wally. Wally told him about it."

That means that Phil and Weinstock were the only ones who knew about your abortion.

"Right, except for Wally."

"And you didn't want anyone else to know. Especially me. It could ruin your plans for our future."

"What are you driving at?"

"A smart cop might decide that you had a pretty good motive for killing both of them before they could tell me. The only three people who knew about the abortion were Phil Levine, Ruben Weinstock and Wally. You were here when Weinstock was killed, and that same night you were out hunting down Wally. It's a good thing you were in California when Phil was killed, or they could make a pretty good case against you."

"But I wasn't in California when Phil was killed," she said. "Phil found out about the abortion from Wally. Phil called me and said he had thought about it very carefully, and he couldn't keep that kind of secret from you. He said he was going to have to tell you about it."

"But he never told me," I said.

"You were out of town, but he was going to tell you when he picked you up at the airport. I didn't want you to know. I begged him not to, but he was adamant."

"He was a good friend," I said. "I probably would have done the same for him."

Then I realized where she was heading. "Please don't tell me you flew to Chicago and killed him."

"Of course not. I mean I didn't kill him. But I did fly to Chicago and went to his apartment on the day he was killed, in the afternoon, and begged and pleaded with him. I had to stop him."

"And?"

"After a bucket of tears, he finally agreed to keep it in the vault. He promised never to tell. I thanked him, kissed him on the cheek, and then left him and took the Red Eye back to L.A. It was cheaper."

"So you were in Chicago at the time he was killed. And you had even been in his apartment."

"I left his apartment right after he promised. It was in the late afternoon, and I went right to O'Hare and just hung out there, trying to get stand-by on an earlier flight, but no seats were available. So I had to take the Red Eye."

"But I called you in L.A. when I landed in Chicago at about nine. And we spoke."

"You called my house phone, but I had all my calls forwarded to my cell. I was at another terminal at O'Hare when you called."

"And nobody can vouch for the time you got to the airport."

"Nobody."

"You were in Chicago the day Phil was killed. You saw Phil the day he was killed." I was still having trouble assimilating it.

"Don't make it sound so ominous. And stop looking at me like that. I didn't kill him."

"But it sure is gonna look like that. Did anyone see you with Phil that day---or did anyone even see you in Chicago? Did anyone even know you were coming in?"

"Nobody. None---Nada---No. No one at all."

"If the police check flight records or your credit card statement, or your phone bills, they could find out that you were in Chicago."

"But if they don't know about the abortion they would have no reason to suspect me or look at anything," Sharon calmly said. "Is it in the vault?"

"It's in the vault," I promised. "But if they ever find out you lied about not being in Chicago when Phil was killed, you may be screwed."

"It's ridiculous for anyone to think I am a murderer," Sharon said.

"I know it is," I lied.

CHAPTER 46

Dilemma

So what was I supposed to do. Do I turn Sharon over to the police like Bogart did to Mary Astor in the Maltese Falcon. *"Sorry sweetheart, but don't worry, I'll wait for you when you get out in twenty years,"* or words to that effect. My memory of the film was a little hazy, but I know it went something like that.

The police didn't know about the abortion. They didn't know that Sharon saw Phil the day he was murdered, or even that she was in Chicago that day. They didn't know that she was looking for Wally Smalley the night Ruben was murdered, and maybe would never find that out. They had no reason to. If Sharon and I kept quiet the police could be totally stymied in the investigation.

I could live with the idea of her taking up with Wally again in California. She was in the process of divorcing her husband, and from personal experience I knew the emotional turmoil that could cause. I screwed around plenty while my divorce was pending and in the months afterward. Who was I to criticize Sharon for doing the same with Wally, or anyone else who was handy.

The inescapable fact was that although I didn't know for sure I could trust her, I still loved her. Go figure.

But if I couldn't be certain she was innocent, it would make it tough to fall asleep beside her at night, and even harder to swallow the oatmeal she prepared in the morning.

"You've been quiet a long time," Sharon said. "What are you thinking?"

"I'm just trying to figure out what to do. I would work it out better if I had a legal pad where I could jot down notes, organize my thoughts and plot out a strategy, like I do with my cases. I'm just sorting it all out in my head."

"I didn't kill anyone. If you can't believe that, then maybe we should just forget everything. I'll just pack up and go back to California where I belong."

"I don't want you to do that."

"It had to be Wally," she said.

"But if we point the police to Wally, everything is going to unravel, and it's going to rebound right back to you. He would tell them about your abortion. The police would end up checking your cell phone record, your charge account records, and airline records, and would find out that you were in Chicago when Phil was killed. You tell me you didn't fly back to L.A. until late that night. You don't have an alibi for either murder, and you had motive and opportunity for both"

"I didn't think about that. So what do we do?"

I wasn't sure it should still be "WE." But I wasn't ready to let her go. Probably I never would be. I wasn't as strong as Bogart. "We'll figure out something," I hoped.

CHAPTER 47

The Police Brigade

The next afternoon Inspector Hollman pulled up in front of the North Beach Inn, driving a gray Ford sedan, the license plate clearly branding it Chicago Police Department. Detective Charlie Archer, driving a County Sherriff's car was directly behind him, and Chief Sampson, in a North Haven Police vehicle completed the parade.

Sharon, Ros, Geri and I were sitting on the front veranda, sipping white wine from a local Michigan winery. The wine had been provided free by Sheldon Babich as part of the Bed and Breakfast package.

We exchanged pleasantries. I offered each of them a glass of wine which they refused, saying they were on duty. They didn't know how lucky they were. It tasted like piss water.

We talked a little about the weather, about how the clouds were blocking the sun and the wind off the lake was causing a chill in the air. Hollman was wearing a light tan windbreaker, unzipped, a blue Chicago Cubs T-Shirt underneath, "Any team can have a Bad Century," it said. Chinos and tennis shoes completed his attire. Chief Sampson was in uniform, and Detective Archer wore a wrinkled blue suit and a blue and gold rep tie, probably a U. of Michigan grad, and proud of it. The tie was loosened at the collar. For jewelry he wore an American Flag lapel pin, and a Mason's ring on the third finger of his right hand.

Hollman had a smoker's gravelly voice and could never sound anything but gruff. As usual, there was a cigarette dangling from his lips as he talked, and somehow he managed to keep the smoke from getting in his eyes. I was impressed.

"Charlie here called me, and filled me in on Dr. Weinstock's murder," he said, nodding toward Archer. "It looks like the gun was the same caliber as the one that killed Phil Levine. We haven't had a chance to compare the cartridges from the two murders yet, but I'm betting they'll be a match. So we either have one killer, or two different killers using the same method and the same gun. My money is on one killer." Very logical guy, this Hollman.

"We have several lines of questioning we want to pursue," Detective Archer continued. "Because it seems that the killings are somehow related we're pooling our resources for now, and conducting a joint investigation. And we're gonna start by questioning the four of you. Nobody is a suspect yet, but you are persons of interest, and should be able to provide pertinent information."

"I want you all to come down my Station now," Chief Sampson chimed in, attempting to make it sound like an invitation to friends, but having it come out more like an order, especially since he put the emphasis on the "now." The three policemen had obviously discussed the case and formulated their plan of attack before they came to the Inn. "We have plenty of room down there for all of us, where we can discuss this thing in more detail."

Sampson's uniform was freshly pressed, and his black shoes were spit shined to a gloss that would pass West Point inspection. He straightened his spine and ratcheted up his voice to the level of a drill sergeant. Very impressive, if you were impressed by that sort of thing. I never was. I figured he was more bluster than substance. To me, Hollman in his windbreaker, and Archer in his crumpled suit were much more dangerous.

Captain Sampson got up and walked to the door, expecting us to follow, but we remained seated, sipping our wine.

"Asking you to the station wasn't just a request," Sampson blustered. "It is an order."

"Let's just call it a suggestion," Hollman quickly interceded. "A very strong suggestion."

"One we recommend you do not ignore," Detective Archer added.

"Put like that, I don't see how we can refuse," I said. "Ladies, gather your wraps and purses, and let's join these gentlemen."

With no regrets over leaving the unfinished bottle of wine, we accompanied them to the station. Sharon and I rode with Hollman. Geri and Ros rode with Detective Archer, and Chief Sampson drove alone.

CHAPTER 48

Police Interrogations Begin

The Police Station occupied one wing of the new North Haven Municipal Center, conveniently located in the heart of town, on the lot where the old Michigan Movie Theater used to be. They had served fresh tasty high cholesterol genuine buttered popcorn at that old movie house, not the kind of phony butter substitute you get nowadays. But television, Netflix and Blockbuster drove them out of business long ago.

We were ushered into a large conference room. The other officers deferred to Hollman, who explained that we would be questioned individually, and he cautioned us to not discuss the case among ourselves until the interrogations were completed.

They started with Ros, and the three officers, Hollman, Detective Archer, and Chief Sampson accompanied her to an interrogation room. She was dabbing her red eyes with a piece of tissue as she left us. The grieving widow could really turn it on when she wanted to.

The three of us waited in the conference room, monitored by a uniformed officer, one of those boy scouts who had come over to the Inn the night Ruben was murdered. Although it was mid-afternoon, he was half asleep. He looked like he might be hung over. As he sat behind the desk he would doze off, and then he would jerk his head back up, struggling to stay awake. On the whole, the North Haven Police Department wasn't very impressive.

Ros' interview didn't take very long. Her alibi for Ruben's death was she was on the beach with me when he was killed. A pretty solid alibi, unless she shot him before we left for the beach, which was highly unlikely. And she was in California when Phil was killed, and besides, there was no indication she even knew Phil. So if the cops were operating under the assumption that both victims were killed by the same person, she was off the hook, no matter how she may have profited by Ruben's death.

When they finished with her, Ros returned to the conference room and advised us that she was being driven back to the Inn and would wait for the rest of us there.

Geri was the next to be called. I didn't do any criminal work, still don't, but I had seen plenty of cop shows. "You don't have to answer any questions, and you have a right to a lawyer," I hollered, as they led her out.

Geri was kept in the interrogation room being grilled for over an hour. I knew she didn't know much. She probably didn't even arrive in town until after Weinstock was shot. And her only contact with Phil was while she worked with him on the Smith case. If they took that long with Geri, the rest of us could be there well into the evening. There was going to be plenty of overtime pay for those cops, and the guy at the desk was sure to be sound asleep by the time they finished.

CHAPTER 49

Sharon Lawyers Up

An intercom buzzed, and Chief Sampson's voice floated into the room. "Bring in Ms. Heller."

I whispered to Sharon "Tell them I am your attorney, and you demand I be present during your questioning."

"No talking," the uniform snapped, still half asleep. He got up and opened the door, signaling Sharon to follow him. I got up to join them, but he ordered me to remain seated.

While the door was opened, Geri stuck her head in. "They released me," she said. "I'm going to pack my things and drive back to Chicago if that's O.K." I told her that would be fine, and that I would see her back in the City. I hoped that was true.

A few minutes later the uniform came back and told me to follow him to the interrogation room. Sharon must have demanded her right to be accompanied by her attorney.

The interrogation room had a recording device, a video camera, and a two way mirror so that an observer in an adjoining room could watch without being seen. Just like in *Law and Order.*

Inspector Hollman was at the head of the table, and obviously was taking the lead in the interrogation. "Cute," he said. "Very cute. You sit in as the attorney to hear how the questioning of Ms. Heller goes before you give us your statement."

I just shrugged.

"Well, I think we'll just question you first. Take Ms. Heller back to the conference room."

"Let's be reasonable Inspector. I didn't shoot anyone. I was in a plane flying back from a deposition in Texas when Phil was shot. I was with Ros when Weinstock was killed."

Detective Archer nodded his agreement. Obviously Ros had confirmed that we were on the beach together.

"But what about you, Ms. Heller," Hollman turned to Sharon. "Where were you when Dr. Weinstock was killed?"

"I was just driving around town," Sharon said.

"Did anyone see you? Have you got any verification of that?"

"I don't know if anyone saw me."

"A purse full of sanitary napkins and Midol isn't much of an alibi." Obviously Hollman had been talking to Inspector Archer.

"Sharon didn't kill anyone, Inspector." She had no reason to." Sharon looked at me and smiled, relieved that I believed in her. I wasn't sure that I did.

"And if it was the same person who killed both Weinstock and Phil, then that lets Sharon out. Phil was her friend. Why would she want to kill him. It's ridiculous. And besides, Sharon lives in California and I called her on her home phone the night Phil was killed." *Careful wording there.* "Motive and opportunity. Isn't that what you guys look for? With Sharon you have neither."

Hollman looked directly at Sharon. "And are you claiming that you were in California when Phil Levine was killed?"

I didn't like the way he asked that question. My instincts told me that Hollman knew the answer to that question, and that he was trying to trap Sharon into a lie.

"This has gone far enough," I quickly interrupted before Sharon could answer. "I told you I called her there. We came in here to cooperate, and you treat us like a bunch of criminals. I don't like your innuendoes. No one is being charged with anything. I have to get back to my law office in Chicago. Sharon has a plane to catch back to her home in California." And looking at Chief Sampson and Detective Archer "Don't give me that shit about not leaving town without your consent. If you have any more questions for us, phone them in. We're out of here." I nodded to Sharon, and we both started to rise.

If Hollman had anything linking Sharon to Phil's death, or if he could prove that she was in Chicago when Phil was killed, I thought my outburst would goad him into revealing what he knew. But he just looked at me calmly. Either he knew nothing, or he had decided to play it very close to the vest.

Hollman nodded. "We can reach you if we need you. You're free to go." The Michigan contingent, by their silence, acquiesced.

Sharon and I, having our fill of policemen, declined Hollman's offer of a ride back to the Inn, and opted to walk back by ourselves. We needed to be alone, and the Inn was less than a mile from the station.

"Thanks for sticking up for me. I really appreciate it. It shows that you still have faith in me."

"I didn't want you lying to Hollman. He suspects something, I could tell by the way he was looking at you when he asked that question about where you were when Phil was killed."

"I think Hollman was bluffing. I could have looked him right in the eye and told him I was in California, and he would have gone on to something else, and then he would have let us go."

"Don't be naive, Sharon. Hollman wasn't bluffing, and even if he was, he's going to keep digging, and one way or another he'll find evidence you were in Chicago the day Phil was killed. This isn't like batting your pretty eyes at a traffic cop and talking your way out of a speeding ticket. And when he found out you lied to him, you'd have a bull's-eye right in the middle of your pretty chest."

When we got to bed that night, our pillow talk had nothing to do with romance. Sharon was leaning toward telling Hollman about the abortion. But I convinced her it was the wrong thing to do. "Remember when the Feds were investigating the regime of the old Mayor Daley of Chicago?" I said. "Daley was a fisherman and he told his sidekicks 'Learn a lesson from the fish. If you keep your mouths shut you don't get caught.' That's what I want you to do. You'll keep your mouth shut."

"I really think that Wally did it....killed them both," Sharon said. "We've got to tell them about Wally."

"But if we give them Wally for both killings, and they bring him in for questioning, he'll tell them about your affair and the abortion done by Weinstock," I reiterated. "And then they'll look hard and find you were in Chicago when Phil was killed, they already have Phil's note with your name and Wally's on it, and when they dig deeper, and you can be sure they will, they'll find more evidence of your contacts with Phil. The whole thing will unravel. And if Wally has an airtight alibi for either of the killings, that is going to leave them looking only at you."

"But what are we going to do?"

"Like the fish---mouth shut."

She raised her head from the pillow and looked down at me with blazing eyes. "You really think I might be a killer," she said. Then she turned away from me, and with nothing more to say, we both went to sleep.

CHAPTER 50

Live With It

We drove back to Chicago the next morning. The plan was to go directly to O'Hare, where Sharon could catch a flight to L.A., back to her son and her job. She didn't have a reservation, but United had hourly flights, and we knew Sharon would be able to get on standby.

I offered to stop for breakfast on the way, but in a very flat tone, the one Sharon adopted when she was angry or hurt, she declined.

Neither of us was ready to rehash things, so we drove in an uncomfortable silence for almost half an hour, which I knew from past experience, was about as long as Sharon could keep quiet.

I concentrated on my driving and tuned in *Public Radio*, hoping that they would be discussing something like Afghanistan, so that Sharon and I could converse about something we agreed upon, instead of having to deal further with the 800 pound gorilla in the car.

Sharon leaned over and turned down the radio. "You think I killed them, don't you. How could you believe that."

"Of course I don't believe that."

"You think I would kill people just to stop you from finding out that I had an abortion! This is the twenty-first century, not the middle ages. Abortions are legal. Women have rights to their bodies. I'm not ashamed that I had an abortion. I wasn't going to have another kid by some man I didn't even like. You're supposed to support the right of a woman to choose. MISTER LIBERAL. Well, I chose. I'll tell you now, and I should have told you when it happened. LIVE WITH IT."

"You don't have to shout." Sharon, "You're sitting right next to me."

She wouldn't be interrupted. "And my bet is that you would have lived with it. And even if you would have dropped me because of the abortion, don't delude yourself into believing I would have killed to keep you from finding out. I love you but you're not THAT important."

I tried to calm her down, told her again that I loved her, and switched off the radio while I assured her I didn't think she killed anybody.

"But you think it's possible—and that's as bad. That's why you wouldn't let me tell the police about Wally. You think in the back of your mind that I could be a murderer. You lie down beside me at night, we can sleep together, we can make love, but you think I might be a murderer."

"I don't think it is possible that you killed them, but I do think it is possible that overeager cops and prosecutors could stitch together a case against you that could get to a jury, and there is never any certainty as to what a jury will do."

"Even if I'm completely innocent?"

"If a prosecutor gets the case, he wants to win it. He won't be interested in justice. He's only concerned with his conviction record. Believe me. I'm a lawyer. I know."

She mulled that over for a little while, but when I glanced over to her, sitting there with her arms crossed, staring out the windshield with her lower lip slightly protruding like it did when she was being stubborn and digging her heels in, it was obvious that she still wasn't convinced.

"Look Sharon.....I want to tell you about one of the cases I handled. I'm not proud of it, I don't talk about it to anybody, but maybe it will help you understand what I mean." Sharon was always interested in my cases, and I wanted to redirect her thoughts.

"Don't change the subject, talking about your cases. I've heard plenty of your cases....sometimes that's all you talk about, your cases, or the Cubs, or the Bears...." She was still letting off steam, but I figured that was good.

"No. This one will help you understand lawyers, and how they think."

"Lawyers think? They should think more and talk less."

I ignored that. "I never talked to anybody about the Levinson case. I like to feel I'm a pretty ethical guy, but in the Levinson case, I'm not so sure"

That got her attention.

CHAPTER 51

Levinson v. Gomez

"Mrs. Levinson, my client, was involved in a head on collision at about 1400 North on the Outer Drive," I continued." "As you know, the Outer Drive runs north and south."

"I know that," she snapped. "I'm not stupid."

"Mrs. Levinson was driving a white Taurus, and it collided with a white Toyota being operated by Martina Gomez. Gomez was our Defendant. She was also seriously injured, and she filed a counter-suit against Mrs. Levinson. The cases were tried together. One of those cars was being driven southbound and the other was being driven north-bound. The southbound vehicle crossed over into the northbound lanes and caused the collision."

"So one of those ladies would be found at fault for the accident and get nothing, and the other would win and get a big verdict." Sharon was paying attention now. She even dug around in her purse and took out a pad of paper and a pen and made a sketch of the accident.

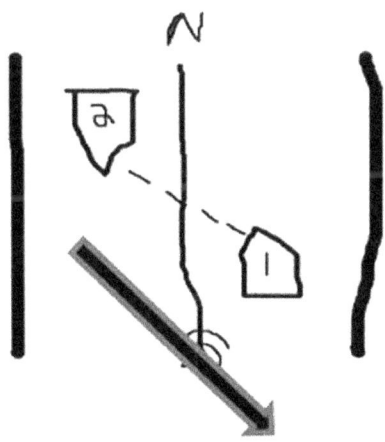

"Sounds like a pretty simple case," Sharon said. The southbound car that crossed over was obviously at fault."

"But the question was, which was the southbound car. There was one eye witness to the accident, and all he could say was that he saw a white car going southbound cross over into the wrong lane. But since both cars were white, and looked similar, the witness couldn't say which one it was."

"Couldn't you tell which car was heading north or south by their location when they came to rest?" Sharon asked.

"As a result of the impact both cars spun around several times, and you couldn't tell by their final positions which way they were headed before the collision. And it was icy so that there were no tire marks. Of course I had a highly qualified accident reconstruction guy who testified that the facts at the scene clearly proved that we, I mean Mrs. Levinson, was going northbound before the collision and that Ms. Gomez was going southbound and had crossed over to the Northbound lanes."

"I suppose Mrs. Gomez had an expert too," Sharon said. She had heard plenty of my lawyer stories.

"Ms. Gomez' lawyer called an expert with a C.V. as long as your arm---he taught at the Northwestern Traffic School and had authored a gazillion articles and served on a host of Federal and State Traffic Commissions---- Her expert reviewed the same evidence as mine, looked at the same photos of the vehicles and roadway, and used the same plat showing the measurements of the area, and he was just as certain that Ms. Gomez was driving the northbound car, and that we, meaning Mrs. Levinson had crossed over into the wrong lane. "

"How could their opinions have been so opposite?"

"A lot of the time it just depends on which side hires them."

Sharon just shook her head.

"Both ladies were seriously injured in the accident, and each was looking for a big verdict. There would be only one winner and one loser. "

Sharon was looking away from me, watching the scenery out the side window. I had left the expressway because of the signs indicating construction ahead, and we were now on a hilly two lane road that meandered through the Indiana Dunes. Lake Michigan was visible through the trees to the right of the road. We could see colorful hang gliders floating above the sand cliffs, and a gas air balloon drifting over the water. I slowed behind other traffic on the two lane road, and brought our car to a stop for a camper turning left in front of me to enter a picnic ground overlooking the beach.

"So what happened with the case?" Sharon asked, as she craned her neck to follow a hang glider that disappeared behind a large mountain of sand.

"Since the witness couldn't help, and the experts were in dispute, the case really boiled down to the testimony of the two ladies. Whoever could convince the jury that she was driving the northbound car would win."

"And…" Sharon prompted.

"Ms. Gomez testified first. She had to testify with the use of an interpreter, because her English was not so good. The accident had happened more than three years before the trial, but her injuries were so severe that she would have to use a cane the rest of her life. She had to struggle to climb the three stairs to get to the witness stand."

"The poor thing," Sharon said.

"Her direct testimony was brief and to the point. She claimed that she left her home on the South Side and was driving northbound on the Outer Drive on her way to work as a cleaning lady for a woman who owned an apartment around Hollywood and Sheridan Road, a place about five miles north of the accident scene."

"'All of a sudden,' she said, through the interpreter, 'this southbound car crossed over into my lane, and crashed into my vehicle.' She said she had no chance to avoid the collision. She claimed she must have been knocked unconscious for a little while, actually she used the word 'asleep,' and she awoke still in her vehicle with a great pain in her leg--- her left leg. Because of the damage to her car she couldn't open the door of her vehicle. The police came and took her to the hospital."

"And did you believe her testimony?" Sharon had grown tired of the hang gliders and now giving me her full attention.

"My job wasn't to believe or not believe. It was to point out any flaws in her story." Sharon flinched.

"She never told the officer at the scene that she was in the northbound car. The police report showed that when questioned at the scene she seemed confused. All she did say, as recorded by the officer, was that she didn't know what happened."

"But she was hurt, she had been unconscious, she didn't speak good English."

"She could argue that, but a Jury might conclude that if somebody crosses into your lane and hits you, you're going to remember that, and tell it to the cop who asks what happened."

"And there were other holes," I continued. "How do we know she was going to work as a cleaning lady for a lady out North. She had no pay stubs or income tax returns to show that she was working as a cleaning lady. As a matter of fact, she didn't even file income tax returns. The defense tried to keep that out, but the judge admitted it into evidence, and the jury, a bunch of taxpaying citizens, wasn't very happy to hear about that."

"But couldn't she bring in the lady she worked for to testify?"

"That lady was conveniently on a cruise ship in the Caribbean. She was afraid she would get in trouble with the federal government if she testified and admitted not having paid withholding or social security on her maid."

"You took advantage of the situation. You beat up on a poor injured cleaning lady who couldn't speak well enough to even defend herself."

"There's more. It gets worse. At the end of my cross we adjourned for lunch. I took Mrs. Levinson back to my office to prepare her for her afternoon testimony. Mrs. Levinson was moved by Gomez's testimony.

"'Mr. Seger, I was listening to Maria,' she began. I couldn't believe my client called Gomez by her first name like they were old friends. 'She sounded so convincing,' Mrs. Levinson said."

"And then Mrs. Levinson reminded me that the case was referred to me by another lawyer several months after the accident, and she told me that when he first met her and signed up the case, in the hospital room, she told him she had a severe concussion, her memory was blurred, and that she really was not sure how the accident happened."

"But you told me that you were in the northbound lanes. And you swore to it in your Deposition, under oath. That's what I said to her."

Sharon sat still, waiting for me to continue.

"She said my referring lawyer had convinced her that she was too careful a driver to cross over into the wrong lanes, and after much persuasion, she finally felt comfortable telling him, and later me, that she was sure she was the innocent party in the northbound vehicle. Now, at trial, after I had broken my ass for her, when she saw Mrs. Gomez in person, how seriously she was injured, and heard her testimony, she had pangs of conscience and wanted to revert to her original statement and get on the stand and say that she wasn't sure how the accident happened. It would have killed our case."

"So what did you do?" Sharon looked down at her sketch and next to the southbound vehicle she wrote "Levinson?"

"You can't direct a client to lie, and you can't put a client on the stand knowing she will lie. That's fundamental ethics. And I explained that fully to Mrs. Levinson. I also told her that I knew she was exhausted and probably confused by the morning's hearings."

"Then I reminded her that if she was driving the southbound car she was going to lose a lot of money. 'Given your injuries, your case is worth at least three hundred thousand dollars if you win,' I said. 'And right now we're way ahead on points. That money is within reach. If you lose you get nothing, and you will still have some substantial medical bills, over seventy thousand dollars, to pay out of your own pocket.' I also threw in that while I had not billed her for my costs of litigation, which totaled about nine thousand dollars, if we lost the case I would have to look to her for those costs, as spelled out in our contract. I also told her she was opening herself to a possible charge that she perjured herself at her Deposition."

"'I can't tell you what your testimony should be,' I continued, 'and ethically I can't and won't tell you to lie on the witness stand, and I'm not doing that. I will believe what you now tell me. But I want you to think carefully about these things before we go further with this discussion about what you remember.'"

"So how long did it take her to cave in?" Sharon said.

"She took a sip of water, thought for several moments, and then clearly remembered that she was sure she was driving the northbound vehicle. She had to admit that at the time of the accident she would ordinarily have been driving southbound to go to her office downtown. The Gomez's lawyer knew that. But as we had discussed earlier, she recalled that just as she arrived downtown, and before getting to her office, she realized she had forgotten a computer disc she needed. So she had to turn around and go back home to retrieve it. That is why she was driving northbound on the Outer Drive at the time of the accident."

"And you had her testify to those lies?"

"Before we left for court she verified to me that she believed it was all true."

"And the jury believed that bullshit?"

"After four and a half hours they returned a verdict for Mrs. Levinson for Four Hundred Fifty Thousand Dollars."

"And Maria got nothing?"

"Maria Lopez limped home with nothing."

"And you're proud of yourself for that?"

"I did a good job for my client. I made a pretty nice fee for myself. But no, I'm not proud. And I felt really lousy the next week when Maria Lopez spent what little money she had saved to place a quarter page ad in the Tribune, saying 'A TERRIBLE INJUSTICE HAS BEEN DONE. IF ANYONE WITNESSED THE AUTOMOBILE ACCIDENT AT ABOUT 1400 NORTH ON THE OUTER DRIVE ON DECEMBER 14th 2009, PLEASE CONTACT MARIA GOMEZ. A REWARD WILL BE PAID."

"Did anyone ever respond to the ad?"

"Not as far as I know. And I'm sure I would have heard."

We sat parked in front of the United Terminal at O'Hare, having not said much to each other since I related the story of the Levinson case.

"You're a real shit. Maybe it was Maria Lopez who tried to kill you. I wouldn't blame her if she did."

"No. She was too nice for that. I really haven't done anything like that since. And I never told anyone else about the Levinson case until today."

"So what do you do now. Say five Hail Mary's and do two acts of contrition."

I took a deep breath. "I only told you because I wanted you to understand that when the adrenaline is flowing a lawyer can get caught up in wanting to win a case and do things he shouldn't be doing. I want you to understand the danger you're in, and why I want you to keep quiet."

"Well, you're still a shit. I never believed it, but maybe you are part of the 99%."

"The 99%? What are you talking about?"

"Like Steven Wright said, '99% of lawyers give the rest a bad name.'"

She left to catch her plane.

CHAPTER 52

A Visit From Hollman

It was cold, and the wind was blowing off of the lake, but I was sitting on my balcony anyway, dressed in my sweats and a parka, sipping coffee. One day 75, the next in the 40's, but that's Chicago weather for you. It was cold enough to see my breath, and I had to wrap my hands around the cup to keep them warm. But I needed the fresh air, and I sat there in kind of a stupor, almost oblivious to the sounds of the traffic, hardly hearing the honking of taxi horns, and even blocking out the occasional whooping of ambulances heading to Northwestern Memorial Hospital, just a few blocks away.

I had already finished a six mile run, and although I had purchased the Tribune from my toothless supplier, it was sitting inside on the dining room table. I didn't feel like reading the news—Local News….South Siders killing each other…West Siders killing each other—International News…Syrians killing each other…Afghans killing us and each other. I just wasn't ready for it. And besides, given the strong wind, if I tried to carry the Tribune out to the terrace, half of it would have been blown back into the park. If that happened the bag lady would probably retrieve it and sell it again.

My cell phone was inside, sitting on top of the Trib. I hadn't yet turned it on. And the ringer was off on my house phone. I just wanted to be left alone.

As I headed inside to warm up, there was a pounding on my front door, too loud and insistent for me to ignore. It was Inspector Hollman, standing in the hall. George, the doorman, was standing at his side.

"I called you last night and I've been calling you all morning," Hollman said. It wasn't even eight o'clock yet and this guy says "all morning." When the hell did he start his day? "Don't you answer your phone, or are you just trying to duck me."

"I'm sorry Mr. Seger," George said. "I tried to call up to you, but you didn't answer. And this Police gentleman insisted on coming up anyway."

"That's all right George. I'll take care of it." I didn't expect that Hollman was there to arrest me as an accomplice to stealing Tribunes. "Come on in, Inspector. Join me for a cup of coffee. I can't offer you a 'latte', but it is fresh ground. And I would appreciate it if you would drown your cigarette in the toilet. This is a non-smoking establishment."

He looked at my outfit. "You going somewhere?" he growled. He did a lot of that growling.

"No, I was just taking a breath of fresh air."

I had left the balcony door opened when I answered his knock. Now he walked out there and looked down the block to Phil's place.

"Your friend Levine was a weird guy, a real pervert." He turned back to look at me.

"What do you mean?"

"A creep. A real sicko. You hung out with him. Don't bullshit me that you didn't know."

I took a sip of coffee. A long sip. Then another. "I don't know what you're talking about."

"You were his good friend. You lived down the block from him. You worked with him. You drank with him. You partied with him." He took the coffee cup out of my hand and put it down on the table, and looked me in the eye. "And you must have spent plenty of time in that creepy apartment of his, like in his bathroom."

"Let's go inside, Inspector, it's too chilly out here." And we went in and sat at my dining room table.

The crime scene was the garage, Hollman explained, so that is where they had originally concentrated their attention. Later they went into Phil's apartment and conducted a cursory exam, nothing thorough. "But we did take his computer back to the station, and after some effort one of our geeks cracked his password and we were able to examine his files. A lot of the stuff dealt with investigations he worked on, most of them for you. But that isn't what grabbed our attention."

"One of the folders was marked 'John'," Hollman continued. "That had its own password or code or whatever the geeks call it, and they had a hell of a lot of trouble getting in. Some new whiz- kid the department just hired finally cracked it yesterday. It was a bunch of photographs. AND YOU KNOW WHAT KIND." His leer said it all.

"I know he liked porno, but there's no law against that."

"It was smut alright, but not exactly porno. Sicker than that."

"Don't tell me child pornography. I knew Phil well enough to know he couldn't be into that. He loved women."

"You really didn't know about his little hobby, did you," Hollman said. "But you knew something. I can tell it in your eyes. I hope I can trust you, because I'm going to tell you what we found. We need your help."

"You can trust me. I want to find Phil's killer more than you do."

And then he told me. That folder, "John" was a folder of photos of women using the toilet in Phil's apartment. I had seen a lens, but I didn't realize it was a camera, and that he was snapping pictures that were transferred to his computer.

"And you think that taking these pictures might have gotten Phil killed?"

"We consider it a strong possibility, either one of the women, or her husband or maybe a boyfriend, if they found out about the pictures. Thanks to you we were looking at this guy Smalley, in Michigan, as a possible suspect. On the theory that he was after you, and killed Levine by mistake. You were the one that steered me toward him, remember."

"He sure looked like a reasonable suspect," I said. "Now I'm not so sure."

"I didn't personally verify his alibi. I had the North Haven Police check him out. It looks like he had a pretty good alibi, but it isn't airtight."

"Anyway," he continued, " if these sick pictures were the motive, then Levine was the real target, and we have to look in a whole new direction. Are you sure you didn't know about these pictures?" He absentmindedly reached to his shirt pocket for a cigarette.

"I swear it. These pictures sound plausible. Someone finds out about it, a girl or her boyfriend, or maybe even a father, they get angry enough to kill Phil. I think you might really be on to something. And please don't light up!"

"But then your friend Weinstock gets killed by the same weapon, and that clouds things up. Now I don't know what to think. But there might be some lead in these pictures. I figure that you might be able to identify some of these women, you being Levine's friend and all. We want to interview all of them. You'll have a hard time recognizing some of them. The faces are a little blurry and out of focus because the lens is directed at another part of the anatomy, if you know what I mean."

Hollman handed me a disc which contained the complete "John" file. "It's just a copy, but as good as the original. They're in jpeg format and in high definition. My experts tell me Levine used Photoshop to brighten and highlight the areas he was interested in. Have fun, and call me with any names you come up with."

"And by the way," Hollman said in true *Columbo* fashion as he reached the door, "one of those pictures looks an awful lot like your girlfriend, Sharon. It was taken the same day Levine was killed. Funny she didn't mention being there. You might ask her what she was doing in his apartment, and when you come up with an answer, let me know."

CHAPTER 53

Pictures Galore

I went into my home office, the room my accountant wouldn't let me claim as a deduction because it would waive a red flag to IRS, and booted up my computer. Then I downloaded Phil's disc into a folder on my hard drive that I labeled "Cats."

While the computer was copying the pictures into the folder, I poured a tall cup of coffee, black, and then settled into my chair and studied the screen. Phil had been a busy boy. By the time the download was complete, there were twenty three pictures in my "Cats" folder, each of a different woman. The pictures were not in any chronological order, but it didn't take me long to figure out that they were arranged by true hair color, with totally shaved saved for last.

I ran the photos as a slide show, setting each of them to pause for ten seconds as they filled my 17 inch computer screen. Phil had purchased a black and white Picasso etching of a bullfighter shortly after moving into his apartment, and it hung above his toilet. The bullfighter stood facing the subdued bull in front of him, with his sword raised in position to perform the *estocada*. In each of Phil's photographs a woman was seated on the toilet, beneath the etching. It looked as if the bullfighter was about to drive his sword into her neck. Picasso might have approved of the composition. Dali certainly would have.

From the angle, it was obvious that the pictures were taken by a camera embedded in the door just above the level of the toilet seat. Anyone sitting on that toilet would necessarily be facing the door, and would be captured in all her glory. Phil had graduated from peeping over a crack in the top of the door to high tech photography.

I saw what Hollman meant about Phil using Photoshop tools to doctor up the pictures. Phil had used brightness, contrast, and in some instances color correction to highlight the part of the female anatomy he was most interested in.

I studied the pictures one at a time. Each one in glorious color, filling the screen. I was looking for faces I could recognize, but it was hard to ignore the highlighted anatomy. It was like flipping through pages of Hustler magazine.

In several pictures the faces of the ladies were out of focus but most were still distinguishable. Some of the women had their skirts hiked up and panties around their ankles. Some had been wearing slacks. A few faces were obscured in whole or part by books or magazines they were reading.

Sharon was grouped among the blonds. The newspaper she was reading blocked the lower portion of her face, but the image was sharply in focus and she was easily identifiable. I must confess that if her face was obscured, I probably couldn't have picked Sharon out from the other blonds. Magnification of the newspaper revealed it was dated the day Phil was murdered.

I couldn't identify any of the other ladies by name, but recognized a few of them as maybe being with Phil at parties we attended together.

The identity of one if Phil's guests was totally obscured, because "she," and I use the term lightly, was standing facing the toilet, the back to the camera. The skirt was hiked up, and piss was streaming from a dangling prick. That one must have given Phil quite a jolt.

It reminded me of when I was just starting out, and had volunteered to do some defense work at night in the District Police courts. One of my clients was a cross-dresser who was picked up for soliciting. When we interviewed him at the lock-up he was still laughing about standing on the corner of Lawrence and Kenmore in his high heels and miniskirt, getting picked up by a *john*, and for five dollars giving him a blow job in the front seat. The *john* then slid his hand under the skirt and felt a pair of hairy balls. I wondered if Phil got a blow job from his subject before seeing that picture.

When I finished my review of the complete file, I called Inspector Hollman, and told him I couldn't identify any of the women by name.

"Except your girlfriend."

"Yes," I admitted, "except Sharon. "

Hollman asked me to meet him later because he had some other things he wanted to talk to me about. I told him I had some work to do at my office and couldn't see him right away. Actually, I wanted to have a chance to talk to Sharon before meeting the police again. I called her several times that afternoon but was unable to reach her.

Hollman and I had agreed to meet at the end of the day for drinks in the Restaurant in my building, "Casa de Oro." I knew we could get a private booth where we wouldn't be disturbed, because the place was so overpriced that it was never crowded.

CHAPTER 54

Casa de Oro

When I entered the *Casa de Oro* Henri, the Head Waiter, or Maître de, as he preferred to be called, greeted me warmly, and no wonder. He must have been lonesome. Only two tables were occupied.

Seated at one of the tables were a real estate developer and two potential investors. There was a drawing of some project spread out on the table, and the developer was pitching it for all he was worth. He was forced to stop his spiel while the bored investors studied a wine list and consulted with the sommelier. The drawback to mixing business with dinner.

At the other table I spotted a malpractice defense lawyer I had butted up against several times, sitting with his client, easily recognizable as a doctor, even though he wasn't dangling a stethoscope around his neck The third party at their table was an insurance adjustor. They were drinking Champagne in celebration of a not guilty verdict that had just come in. I stopped briefly at their table and congratulated the beaming barrister on his victory, which had probably come at the expense of some poor crippled victim who wouldn't have a pot to piss in for the rest of his life.

Henri stood to the side as I made small talk, and then led me to a booth at the back of the restaurant. Once seated, I was approached by a captain, smartly attired in a well pressed tuxedo. He summoned the waiter who unfolded the stiff linen napkin from the table and draped it over my lap, and then took my order for an R.J. Hudson martini, straight up and chilled.

My drink arrived at about the same time as Inspector Hollman, who, when asked for a drink order said, without first inquiring, "Give me the same thing the counselor is having."

"What the hell kind of martini is this anyway?" Although he made a face when I explained it was part gin, part vodka, after the second sip he had to admit that it tasted very smooth.

We chit-chatted about the Cubs and the Bulls, and the news of the day, and then got down to business.

"I know you didn't kill them. Hell, you have an alibi for both murders." He paused and took out a cigarette. "And they were both your friends, so I am assuming you want to help me." He lit the cigarette. We both knew there was an ordinance against smoking in restaurants, but I had a lot of clout in this place, so as an act of good faith I signaled a waiter and had him bring us an ashtray, and the captain rushed over and drew the curtain that closed off our booth.

"Thanks," as he blew out a long stream of smoke. Fortunately the booth was well ventilated by a fan in the ceiling. It didn't completely clean the air, but then, it's not a perfect world.

"I hate to keep calling you Inspector. Don't you have a first name?"

"If you don't want to call me Inspector you can just call me Hollman."

And this, after I thought I had softened him up with the martini and the ashtray.

He took out his pad of paper, the one with the spiral at the top. "Let's take it from the beginning--have you got time for that?" I assured him that I had all night.

"So let's go back to when after your friend Phil was killed. Remember how you were helpful earlier, Stan, when you gave me several possible suspects."

I stopped myself from telling him to just call me Seger.

Hollman consulted his list. "You mentioned an ambulance chaser named Cochese, and I checked him out and he has a good alibi for Levine's death. He was signing up an accident victim at County Hospital, and he has a dated retainer agreement, and the victim, and two nurses verify it." Hollman made a check mark next to Cochise's name. He flipped to the next sheet.

"You and I discussed the possibility that the perp got Levine by mistake, and that you were really the intended victim. You told me about some people that might have it in for you, like those greaseballs whose mother was getting screwed out of a wrongful death settlement by her daughter-in law, but again they would have no reason to kill Dr. Weinstock.

He continued flipping the pages of his note pad. "I thought this guy Wally Smalley might be a solid suspect, especially after I found that he had a record. Your girlfriend, Sharon, had a restraining order on him in California, and he twice pled *nolo contendre* to charges of aggravated assault in bar fights. One was in California, and one in Michigan. Both resulted in suspended sentences."

"You told me Smalley had made a threat against you, and figured him for a solid suspect, thinking that in the dark he could have mistaken Levine for you. It was a theory that made some sense. And it was even possible that Wally actually made Levine the target. We did find a notation in Levine's papers linking Sharon's name with Walley Smalley. I figured you had told Levine that Smalley threatened you or Sharon, and maybe Levine tried to protect you and Sharon, and in doing it ticked Smalley off."

Actually, it was Sharon, not me, who told Phil about Smalley, but I didn't see any reason to tell that to Hollman, so I just nodded. "It's the kind of thing Phil could do, try to protect us, and he has been known to rub people the wrong way," I agreed.

"I had the North Haven police check if Smalley had an alibi for the night of Levine's murder, and they reported he did, but it wasn't airtight, and I don't know if I could trust that rinky dink department anyway. As a matter of fact, I was on my way to Michigan to interview him myself regarding the Levine killing when I got sidetracked by the call about Weinstock's murder."

"So that's how you got to North Haven so fast after we called you about Weinstock's murder. I thought it made sense to call you when it looked like both were killed the same way. I figured you would want to be alerted right away."

"I'm glad that you gave me the heads up, even though it complicates what was already a very confusing case. But now that we know for a fact that Levine and Dr. Weinstock were both killed by the same gun, I figure we can cross Smalley off the suspect list---unless you know of some reason he had something against Weinstock."

Was he testing me? I didn't think so. "I can't imagine what."

He placed his pen alongside Smalley's name, but looked up at me and conspicuously didn't put any check mark next to Smalley. Instead he put a couple of question marks.

He flipped by some pages too fast for me to read what was on them. Then he stopped.

"At the time we talked, we didn't know about that porno you looked at today, but now that we do I suppose any of those women, including your girlfriend, could be angry enough to kill Levine, if they learned about those pictures. By the way, did your girlfriend, what's her name, Sharon Heller, know about those pictures?"

"If she did, Sharon wouldn't have shot Phil--- she would have cut off his balls."

"Did you ever find out why she was in Levine's apartment the day he was killed?"

"You know I was out of town until that night, she must have come to Chicago for some reason, maybe she came in to surprise me, she sometimes did that, and she could have got lonesome and called Phil. She and Phil had been friends for years. The picture makes it obvious why Phil, the lecher, had her come up there. I can't believe the sicko would do that to Sharon."

"But when we were at the police station in North Haven, you lied to me. You said she was in L.A. when Levine was killed."

"I didn't lie to you. I told you I called her in L.A., and that was the truth. I didn't know that she had forwarded her calls to her cell phone and that she was really in Chicago when I spoke to her."

"And she never mentioned that she was in Chicago that day?"

"The subject never came up."

"She was sitting right there in the police station when we were talking. Why didn't she say anything about being in Chicago?"

"That was my fault. I instructed her not to answer any questions."

He just looked at me. "You're about as credible as Lance Armstrong."

"At least you didn't compare me to O.J. Look inspector, Sharon didn't kill anyone. I know she's innocent"

"What was she doing flying into Chicago when you weren't even in town. Explain that to me."

"It's possible I forgot to tell her I was going to Lake Geneva, and she flew in to surprise me. You'll have to ask her that."

"Easy for you to say, now that she's safely back in California."

He changed tack. "Well anyway, if we just had the Levine murder, we would have to track down each of those women and embarrass them, but I think we can put that on the back burner for now---I don't see how any of those women, including Sharon, could have a motive for murdering Weinstock. Unless maybe he was publishing a new gynecology text book and Levine sold him those photos for some type of illustrations, but that's a ridiculous idea, isn't it?"

"Are you sure this is your first martini? You've got a wild imagination, Hollman. You should write mystery novels. There are a lot of great writers around who don't need a first name, Tolstoy, Shakespeare, Hemmingway." He ignored my comment. We both drained our glasses, and ordered another round. Hollman flipped a page in his notebook.

"Say, are you hungry? I've been at the station all day, and didn't have any lunch. How's the food here?"

"Great," I lied. It was obvious the meal would be on me, and the drinks too.

The captain brought over two menus, handing Hollman the guest menu, the one with no prices, and suggested tonight's special, a linguini dish with roasted salmon on top, but Hollman opted for the sixty dollar porterhouse, rare. I wasn't very hungry, but selected the grilled scallops. We both passed on wine, but ordered another round of martinis. It was turning into a drinking contest. This would make my third, my absolute limit. I would have to watch what I said.

The new drinks arrived, we clinked cheers, and each of us took a sip before he continued. "That leaves Dr. Mijeck," he said. I jumped on it, trying not to sound too eager. *Anything to steer Hollman away from bundling Sharon with Smalley and Weinstock.* Obviously, he didn't know about the abortion.

"Mijeck knew we were doing a thorough background check. I took his deposition, and showed a lot of interest in his background. It touched a nerve. Phil was digging deeper at the time he was killed. Masterson, Mijeck's lawyer, knew Phil was my investigator, and that he would be the one looking for dirt. Or Mijeck could have been tipped off by one of the doctors Phil talked to. "

"It's not a very strong motive for murder," Hollman said.

"But there's more. Now we have Weinstock getting killed. The same murderer, you said. Mijeck had a motive for that one too. He had seen a copy of the very critical report that Weinstock wrote about the surgery in the *Smith* case. A woman died in that surgery. Mijeck was the surgeon. Weinstock placed the blame squarely on Mijeck, and he said in his report that the negligence was so gross that it almost amounted to negligent homicide."

I gave Hollman a copy of Weinstock's report. He read it as he chewed on huge bites of steak. He swallowed and said, "I talked with Mijeck after your friend Phil was killed. You gave me his name and contact information, remember. On the night of Levine's killing Mijeck claims to have been home alone, watching television. His wife was out of town and his kids were away at college. He said he didn't talk to anyone and went to bed about eleven."

"In other words," I said slowly, twirling my half-empty martini, "Nobody backs up his alibi."

"I'll have to give it a harder look. A lot harder look. And I'll check into his whereabouts when Dr. Weinstock was killed. Didn't you say he know that Weinstock was going to be in North Haven?"

"He knew, all right. I told his lawyer that Weinstock would be with me in North Haven for the weekend to prepare for the deposition on Monday. I'm sure his lawyer would have told him."

"North Haven isn't far from Michigan City, where Mijeck lives, " Hollman said, trading his fork and knife for his pad and pen. There wasn't a scrap left on his plate, not even the fat.

"It can't be more than sixty miles, certainly less than a one hour drive."

Hollman was writing now. "I'll follow up on this tomorrow." As he rose from the table he thanked me for dinner and said, "And my first name is Louie, but don't start with that 'Louie, I think this is the beginning of a beautiful friendship.'"

"Actually, I was thinking more along the lines of Huey, Dewey and..." He laughed as he got up from the table.

I scribbled my name at the bottom of the check, leaving generous tips for the captain and the waiter. The meeting was almost worth the price of the meal.

CHAPTER 55

Phone Tag

When I got back to my apartment the light on my answering machine was flashing. The message was from Sharon, saying she had just gotten back from the pizza she had treated her son's soccer team to after the game they won 3 to 1, her son having scored a goal, his first of the season, and she forgot to take her cell phone along. She was out the door for Viet Nam, Sharon's term for the manicurist shop down the block, and I shouldn't call her there because reaching for her cell phone could ruin her nails.

I clicked the remote to turn on the stereo, always tuned to The College of DuPage's jazz station, settled back to Coleman Hawkins, and mulled over whether I was ready to call Sharon back that night. It was important to alert her to the fact that Hollman knew she was at Phil's apartment, but I dreaded telling her about the pictures.

Sharon and I spent the next day playing phone tag. She called once when I was on a conference call, and once when I was in the john. I tried to call her back, but once she was in class and had turned off her cell, and later she said she couldn't talk because she was in parent-teacher conferences.

When I called her home in the evening her son said she and a girl-friend had gone to the theater to see, "Freud Meets Oedipus Rex," a play I had refused to go see the last time I was in L.A. Instead I had taken her to see the latest James Bond movie. I complimented her son on scoring his first soccer goal, told him to write a note to his mom saying that I had called, and had him read it back to me, as I knew that if he didn't write it down he would forget I even called.

"Do you want me to say that mom should call when she gets home?"

"No. With the time difference it'll probably be too late. Tell her I'll talk to her tomorrow." Coward that I am, I was relieved to postpone our conversation for one more day.

CHAPTER 56

Grounds For Another Continuance

The next morning there was a 9:00 o'clock status call on the Smith case, so after my early morning run I took a quick shower, passed on coffee, dressed in my trial lawyer outfit, blue suit, white shirt, and muted tie, all very expensive but not looking that way, and rushed to court, where I was brought to a halt by the long line to get through security.

The full blown security system at the courthouse, with metal detectors and the search of all bags and briefcases, was not in response to a possible terrorist attack, but had been instituted well before 911, immediately after an irate husband, obviously displeased by the alimony payments just ordered, pulled a gun in divorce court and shot and killed his wife's lawyer, the judge, and a bailiff, and seriously wounded his own attorney.

Usually lawyers could bypass the security line and the long delay by showing a photo I.D. I don't know why lawyers were considered less likely than others to shoot somebody, but who was I to complain about the convenience.

But about once a month, a day would be designated as a heightened security day, and then even the lawyers and judges were required to pass through the metal detectors, and have their briefcases and other belongings searched.

On one of those days a lawyer friend of mine was very embarrassed and ended up pleading guilty to a misdemeanor charge after a search of his briefcase revealed two marijuana cigarettes that he had forgotten were in there. Both of the Chicago newspapers headlined the incident in big bold print on their front pages, with pictures and two column stories. Rather than tarnish his reputation, the publicity brought him an avalanche of new wrongful possession cases and several new drug dealer clients.

This was one of those high security alert days, and I put my I.D. back in my pocket, stepped to the rear of the line of ordinary peasants and impatient grumbling lawyers, slowly worked my way to the front, and finally got to my courtroom fifteen minutes after the scheduled time for my hearing. It didn't matter that I was late, because my judge, Judge Neilson, was trapped behind me in the security line, and didn't make it to the bench until well after I was seated in the courtroom.

Geri Sapperstein wanted to attend all Court hearings in the Smith case just for the experience, so she was sitting in the back of the courtroom, and when the Smith case was called I signaled her to move alongside me as I stepped to the bench.

William Masterson, to my surprise, and contrary to his usual practice, appeared in person at this rather routine court call, rather than sending one of his junior lackeys who he could bill out at two hundred fifty dollars an hour for a court appearance. Masterson himself normally billed at a minimum of five hundred an hour, but his insurance carrier was too sharp to accept that kind of rate for a status call.

I had forgotten that Judge Neilson required the Plaintiff's lawyer to bring along and furnish him with a copy of the most recent Status Order entered in the case, and I didn't have a copy with me. I braced myself for the lecture I was about to receive, but when the judge requested that I give him a copy of the Order, Geri rescued me by handing me her copy, which I handed up to the Judge. He quickly scanned it.

"This Order is the third time I had set a deadline for you to produce your gynecological expert witness for discovery deposition." The judge was not happy with me. He consulted his computer, and continued. "I had previously granted you extensions because you were engaged in trial, and then later because your expert, Dr. Weinstock, had scheduling conflicts. This latest order, the one I have before me today, stated, and was underlined by me before I signed it, 'no further continuances.' I assume the order has been complied with and that the deposition of Weinstock has been taken?"

"I'm afraid not, your Honor. We need another continuance, because of extenuating circumstances."

"What kind of extenuating circumstances?" a visibly agitated judge asked.

"My expert was shot and killed last week."

A pause. The judge looked over the top of his reading glasses. "That's pretty extenuating." Several in the courtroom laughed. Lawyers have a macabre sense of humor.

I told the judge I would need at least three months to locate a new expert, have all of the material reviewed, and have the expert ready to give a deposition. Masterson, standing alongside me, didn't object to the continuance and I again wondered why he bothered to appear himself instead of sending a lackey.

The judge didn't even pause before ruling on my request. "One month should be plenty of time for you to get your new expert and present him for deposition. I want to move this case along on my docket. One month to give the Deposition---and the trial will start two weeks after that." He banged his gavel for emphasis. It was futile to argue with him.

While Masterson and I waited in the corridor for Geri to bring us stamped copies of the new Order, Masterson suggested we go out for coffee, saying there was something important he wanted to discuss. Having missed my morning caffeine fix, I was quick to agree.

"Do you mind if Geri comes along?" Masterson hesitated, seeming reluctant, but with Geri standing there he was too much of a gentleman to refuse. Finally he said "Why not. Maybe she'll learn something."

We settled in a booth at the Greek place across from the courthouse, laid aside the five page menus, and ordered black coffees. "Are you really looking to be a defendant in a libel and slander case?" he asked me.

"What are you talking about?" I was really puzzled.

"You told an Inspector Hollman that Dr. Mijeck killed your investigator, and your expert. Are you crazy?"

"I never said he killed them. I only said he might have had a motive...."

"You're full of shit." And this from a guy who almost never swore. "Mijeck called me last night, at around midnight. He was all agitated. Hollman was snooping around and talking to Mijeck's neighbors, his maid, and his hospital, inquiring about Mijeck's whereabouts when Levine and Dr. Weinstock were killed. Hollman even left a message for Mrs. Mijeck to get back to him."

I took a sip of the coffee that had cooled down enough by now. "Interesting. Did Mijeck have an alibi for either of the killings?"

"Cut it out. You can't go around accusing doctors of murder without any proof. It was bad enough the way you badgered the poor guy at his deposition. Your conduct was outrageous, and I should have asked the court to enter sanctions then."

"But you didn't. Your guy is a quack, he probably should never have been licensed, and he had no business operating on Mrs. Smith. You and I both know that he botched that horribly, and through his incompetence he killed her."

"I'm not sitting here to argue the case. I'm here to tell you to lay off those accusations. Call Hollman and set him straight. Tell him it's a bunch of crap. Or I will have to file that libel and slander case. My client is insisting." He got up and walked out, without even paying for his coffee.

"What was that all about," Geri asked. "He was really steamed."

"Well, it's kind of complicated." She waited for me to say more, and I tried to just leave it hanging there.

"But what was that about Dr. Mijeck and Inspector Hollman? What *did* you tell Hollman?"

"We had a little talk over R.J. Hudsons. I may have shaded things a little, but everything I told him was true. Hollman was just following through. He's a very thorough cop. It sounds like he really shook things up."

"But what did you and the Inspector talk about? Does Hollman think Dr. Mijeck might be the murderer? Does he have any other suspects?"

"Leave the investigation to Hollman. You have enough to worry about with the Smith case. Let's finish this coffee and get back to work."

CHAPTER 57

Sharon & Stan Connect

Sharon and I finally connected that evening after I got home. She started by telling me how wonderful the play was, Freud meets Oedipus Rex.

"As good as James Bond?"

"Almost," she said. "Only Freud didn't say, *My name is Freud---Sigmund Freud.*"

"But did the other guy say *My name is Rex---Oedepus Rex.*"

She didn't laugh.

"And speaking of pictures," I said, taking a deep breath, "there are some other pictures I want to tell you about." And I told her about Phil's photography hobby, and the disc the police had found. She erupted even before I casually slipped in that she was one of the women on the disc.

I waited patiently as she ranted for several minutes about Phil's perversions, and then broadened her attack to include all males. As she revved herself up she even threw in some of the Freud-Oedipus theory she had seen in the play the night before, but by that time I wasn't listening very closely.

"I know you're upset. I don't blame you. It's despicable. Phil was a sicko. I swear to you I knew nothing about it. I'm as shocked as you are."

"Yeah, sure. I bet you and the cops really loved looking at all those vaginas."

"We had to look. The police think those pictures could have been a motive for Phil's murder. They want to check out the women, and their husbands or boyfriends. They say the pictures could give them a lot of new leads."

"They'll never stop digging," Sharon said. "And now they know I was at Phil's the day he was killed. I should have told them before. And I should have told them about the abortion. It gives Smalley a motive for killing Weinstock."

"But that won't explain his killing Phil," I said.

"Phil was trying to protect me. That could be reason enough for Smalley to want to kill him. Or maybe Smalley was trying to kill you, and shot Phil by mistake. It's for sure that Smalley wants you dead."

"We went over this before. They'll just zero in on you. They'll think you killed Weinstock to keep it secret, and that Phil knew about the abortion and you killed him for the same reason."

"But why would I kill two men just to keep my abortion secret. Our Supreme Court hasn't made abortions illegal, at least not yet." We were rehashing old grounds.

"The cops will think you wanted to keep it secret because it could screw up our relationship."

"You're the one screwing up this relationship." She slammed the phone down. I was talking to a dial tone.

"Give me a break here. I love you. I'm only trying to protect you. And I don't have time to argue. I only have a month to find an expert to replace Weinstock, have him review all the records and deposition transcripts, and present him for a discovery deposition." I had to call Sharon back three times before she picked up the phone and listened to my plea.

"I love you too. But I think your advice stinks. Go find your new expert. I have to find a new gynecologist too, for myself. But I'll never give *you* his name. It's too dangerous."

We blew kisses through the phone, and hung up.

CHAPTER 58

Our New Expert

The following month was filled with *Smith* business, the usual last minute preparation for trial, multiplied tenfold by the urgency of finding a new gynecological expert. The first experts I contacted, those I would have preferred, were unavailable on such short notice to review the records, give a deposition, and testify at trial. Dr. Foster, the gynecologist I was forced to settle for, was a very competent doctor, but he was young, and a novice as a witness. I spent two whole days painstakingly preparing Foster for the tough questioning he would face at his discovery deposition, but when that time came, Masterson took advantage of Foster's relative inexperience.

Masterson: "Now Dr. Foster, you say it is important that the carbon dioxide be injected into the abdomen and not into a blood vessel, because if it goes into the blood vessel it can kill the patient. Is that right?

Foster: "That is correct."

Masterson: "And the doctor performing the procedure must take reasonable care to see that the needle, in this case a Verres needle, is correctly placed so that it is in the abdominal cavity, not a blood vessel?

Foster: "That's right."

Masterson: "So in order to avoid malpractice a doctor must do what a reasonably careful doctor would do to correctly place the needle, is that right?

Foster: "I guess that's right."

Masterson: "And you testified that before *you* would insert the carbon dioxide, *you* would do the syringe test--that is put a syringe onto the Verres needle and draw it out, to make sure that you were not drawing out blood---blood would indicate that you had mistakenly place the needle into a blood vessel, rather that the abdomen."

Foster: "That's the way I would have done the procedure."

Masterson: "But you've only done this procedure a handful of times, isn't that correct?"

Foster: "I would say at least twenty times. That's more than a handful."

Masterson: "Of course. Sorry. But in those twenty or so times, when you placed the needle initially, and then attached the syringe and pulled up on the plunger, how many times did you find that you had by mistake put the needle into a blood vessel instead of into the abdominal cavity?"

Foster: "Never. I never put it in the blood vessel. It was always correctly placed it in the cavity."

Masterson: "Alright. So here we have you, who has been in practice only five years, and you never hit a blood vessel. Dr. Mijeck, who is the defendant in this case, has been in practice over thirty years. He says he could tell by feel, by the resistance when he put in the Verres needle, that he was in the open space of the abdomen, and not in a blood vessel. He says if the needle had even touched a blood vessel he could have felt the resistance, and that he would have not gone further. He is sure he did not contact a blood vessel. Isn't it reasonable for someone of his experience to rely on his touch, the feel, without having to subject the patient under anesthesia to the extra time and trauma of a syringe test? "

Foster: "I suppose it might be."

Masterson "So the fact that someone of Dr. Mijeck's experience didn't do a syringe test, that in and of itself is not malpractice, wouldn't you agree?"

Foster: "I guess one might say that."

I tried to resurrect Dr. Foster on redirect, and got him to correct himself and say that the syringe test should always be used to insure the proper positioning, regardless of the experience of the doctor, and that was the standard the textbooks had set. But his earlier answer seriously weakened our position, and I knew Masterson would take full advantage of it at trial.

CHAPTER 59

The Trial Begins

Two weeks later we were in the chambers of Judge Nielsen, ready to start the trial. As was customary, the Judge asked us about the possibility of settling the case. "It would save us all a lot of time." he said. "A settlement is always the best way to work these things out."

The judge banished me to the outer office while he first discussed the possibility of settlement with Masterson. It was a very brief discussion. I was only out there for a few minutes when he called me back inside, always a bad sign for settlement.

"It looks like we have a trial," he said. "They won't make any offer." Masterson was looking very smug. Their interest in settling faded as soon as Weinstock was out of the picture. I tried to match his look of confidence.

We headed back to the courtroom. I was seated at one table with my client, Tom Smith, at my side. Just the two of us. I liked it that way. Two little guys against the big establishment. Tom was neatly dressed, but no shirt or tie. A hard working man who lost his wife, and struggled alone to care for his twin babies, and their other child. I assured him that everything was going to be fine.

Masterson was at the other counsel table with his entourage, Dr. Mijeck, two lackeys, and one of those jury selection experts, a psychologist who claimed she could divine whether or not jurors would be favorable to their side by means of their responses to set questions, body language, and for all I knew, the way they parted their hair. Probably Masterson had already presented the case to test juries in the mock courtroom in his offices, to help guide him with jury selection and trial tactics.

Our potential jurors filled several rows of seats at the back of the courtroom. We all rose when Judge Nielsen entered.

The Judge made his welcoming remarks to the jurors, and told them the general nature of the case.

He said the attorneys would give them more details about the case in their opening statements, but cautioned them that our opening statements were not evidence, just an outline of what we hoped to prove. The evidence they were to consider, he said, would come from the witness stand and the exhibits. While this was technically true, most lawyers recognize that you can win or lose your case in the opening statement.

While the judge was talking, both sides were studying the potential jurors, looking for any expression, movement, tic or any tell that would give a hint as to their feelings. We were supposed to be seeking a fair and impartial jury, but every trial lawyer really wanted jurors who would give him an edge.

Finally, the first twelve potential jurors were called into the jury box, and the lawyers could begin questioning them directly. We both assured the jurors that we were only asking questions to insure that we could get a fair and impartial jury, while in fact we sought to ingratiate ourselves to them, to curry their favor, to find juries favorable to our side, to subtly indoctrinate them, and to weed out those who might be favorable to our opponent. Some of my questions were very general, just to establish rapport with the jurors. Some were more pointed, such as:

"The law states that all witnesses are entitled to start off with the same credibility. Would you believe a doctor or nurse more than an average person as a witness just because he or she is a physician or nurse?"

"Do you believe that negligence lawsuits have caused an increase in the costs of medical care?"

"Has anyone in your immediate family or any close friends had training or employment in a health care field, or in any field of law?"

"Have you or any relative or your kids ever planned on becoming a doctor or nurse?"

"Do you understand that doctors and nurses must meet certain standards and requirements when treating patients?"

"If you find Dr. Mijeck did not meet required standards, and that this caused the death of Mrs. Smith, will you enter an award that fully and fairly and completely compensates her husband and children for their terrible loss?"

The jury selection went on for almost two full days, and it wasn't until Thursday afternoon that the twelve jurors and two alternates were finally impaneled. The Court adjourned for the day. Friday morning was reserved for preliminary motions, and we would give opening statements in the afternoon. I would have the weekend to finish my preparations, and put more backbone into my wishy-washy expert.

And we had only three more days to locate that missing nurse, the one that Phil Levine was still searching for at the time he was murdered. The way Dr. Foster had screwed up, finding her could be more important than ever. I would be too busy to devote much time to search for her myself, Phil was dead, and that left nobody to rely on but Geri.

After Court ended on Thursday I took her aside. "Geri, you have only one very important assignment. I know you've been busy with other things, but that can't get in your way of finding that nurse who was in the operating room! Starting right now drop everything else. You've got to find her. There's a good chance her quitting right after Mrs. Smith died had something to do with our case. Phil was hot on her trail. Retrace what he did. Hire anyone you need. Julia can give you some names of skip tracers if you need help. Spend whatever you have to. You've got to find her and talk to her."

"It probably won't do any good," Geri said. "None of the other nurses have been any help. They all stonewalled us. She'll probably do the same."

"She's the only one in the operating room we haven't been able to contact. We've got to get more ammunition against Mijeck. Do whatever you have to, but get her story, and if it helps us, get her here for the trial. I'll pay whatever it takes."

CHAPTER 60

Preliminary Matters

Friday morning I passed up my regular jog, slowly sipped one cup of coffee instead of gulping down my usual three or four, so that I wouldn't have to take too many bathroom breaks during the morning court session, and headed for battle, dressed in my uniform of conservative blue suit and power red tie.

We killed the morning in the Judge's Chambers, going over routine matters such as an order excluding witnesses from the courtroom until they were called to testify (which of course did not include the parties themselves, who could always be present). We discussed the starting and quitting time each day (we agreed to start at 10:00 A.M. sharp, and adjourn at 4:00, with a two hour lunch break insisted upon by the Judge). This made for a short trial day, but it would give the jury a chance to get to and from the court house each day without fighting the heart of the rush hour, and it would give me plenty of time to prepare my witnesses before they took the stand.

I moved that all parties be limited to no more than one expert in each field of medicine. Without that limitation, the defense could swamp me with an overwhelming number of experts more than eager to help a fellow doctor. I had one pathologist, Dr. Eugene Kramer, who I knew would be helpful, and one gynecologist, Dr. Harry Foster, whose testimony, if I was lucky, would be barely adequate to get me beyond a directed verdict.

"I object to the limitation," Masterson boomed. "As counsel for the Plaintiff knows, we have three prominent Gynecologists lined up and ready to testify for the defense. We have submitted them all for discovery deposition, so counsel is aware of their opinions. There is no surprise."

"I do know their opinions Judge. The testimony of each is merely a cookie cutter repetition of the other. It is unfair to the Plaintiff to be swamped by repetitive testimony just because the defense has a bottomless pocketbook."

Masterson and I each cited authority in support of our position, me handing the Judge a two page memo on the issue, one I had used successfully in earlier cases, and Masterson digging out a bound tome of at least twenty pages, with copious footnotes, carefully drafted by his staff.

Any Judge experienced in handling Medical Malpractice cases had been presented with this same issue numerous times. The Defense always tried to swamp us with numbers. Judge Nielsen scanned the memos of both sides, found nothing he hadn't seen before, and correctly ruled that the Defense was limited to one expert in each area of medicine.

"We spent an awful lot of money on those experts, retaining them and presenting them for deposition," Masterson complained.

"Maybe you should have saved some of that money to pay the verdict," I said, sounding a lot more confident than I felt.

We discussed the evidence I had of Dr. Mijeck's earlier mishaps, the death of three patients during surgeries, and his resignation from a hospital under a black cloud. But the court ruled, probably properly, that the evidence was inadmissible because none of those earlier episodes involved a tubal ligation, and I could not prove Mijeck had been forced to resign from the hospital. The judge barred me from mentioning any of it, it was too prejudicial, but at least I made the judge aware of Dr. Mijeck's spotty record.

"I have one more Motion, your Honor, before we get started." Masterson handed his neatly typed Motion to the Judge, and a copy to me. He was asking the Court for an Order preventing any party from calling any witnesses that had not been deposed.

"Do you have any objection to this Motion, Mr. Seger?" the Court asked.

"I do you Honor. Each party has submitted a list of witnesses. As Mr. Masterson knows, one of the witnesses on our list is Ann Swanson, the Circulating Nurse who was in the operating room at the time of the tubal ligation. She disappeared shortly after the operation, and we have been searching for her, and I believe we will have her available to testify at this trial. She is not a witness under our control, and we had no obligation to produce her for discovery deposition."

"You were also required to give her address to us," Masterson said, curtly. "If you would have done so, I would have been able to subpoena her for deposition before the trial began."

"The last address I had for her was from your hospital employment records," I replied hotly. "That was as available to you as to me. As we both know, she left your hospital, with no forwarding address, or at least that's what you claim."

"Gentlemen, gentlemen, let's cut the bickering. Mr. Seger, you may never even find that witness. If you do, and present her in Court, we'll deal with the question of whether or not to bar her testimony at that time. Now we've taken the whole morning here in Chambers. I'm going to tell the Jury to take lunch, and we will resume at 2:00 for opening statements." The Judge liked a long lunch at the table reserved for him across the street at Petterino's.

"Oh, by the way, Mr. Masterson," the Judge asked, "any change in your company's position on settlement?"

I was packing my briefcase and pretended indifference as Masterson replied "still no offer."

CHAPTER 61

Opening Statements

"Ladies and gentlemen," I addressed the jury of six men and six women, "this case is about the unnecessary death of a young healthy mother just four weeks after she gave birth to twin boys, a death brought about solely because of the negligence of an incompetent doctor, the defendant here, Dr. Walter Mijeck." I pointed to the doctor, who was seated at the defense table with his hands clasped, looking straight ahead.

"The evidence will show that Dr. Mijeck, during the performance of a tubal ligation, inserted a lethal dose of carbon dioxide into a blood vessel of Celia Smith, instead of inserting it into the open abdominal cavity. This tragic death could have been avoided had Dr. Mijeck used the simple test available to him and employed by all careful doctors. That test is called the syringe test." The jury looked interested, but puzzled by the term.

"I know you may be familiar with the process, but let me review it for you." I pointed to a fertilization diagram and explained that during a tubal ligation, the fallopian tubes, which carry the egg down from the ovaries to the uterus, are closed off so that the eggs can't get down to the uterus, and therefore they can't be fertilized by the sperm, and pregnancy can't occur.

"Now here's how the surgery to prevent pregnancy is performed. The surgeon will make one or two small cuts in the belly area, usually around the belly button. A laparoscope, a narrow tube with a camera on the end, is inserted into the abdomen. Instruments to close the tubes are sent through the laparoscope. The tubes are either burned shut ---that's called catheterization, or closed off with a small clip."

I paused to make sure the jury was following me.

"To make it easier for the surgeon to identify the fallopian tubes in the abdomen and close them off, the surgeon first puts carbon dioxide gas into the abdomen and blows up the abdomen like a balloon. This makes the fallopian tubes in the abdomen easier to see."

The jurors all were carefully following my explanation, and many took notes.

"The way that you get the carbon dioxide into the abdomen is by taking a container of carbon dioxide that has a long thin rubber tube attached to it. There is a valve that you turn that allows the carbon dioxide to flow from the container into the rubber tube. The valve works like a faucet in your sink that turns the water on and off."

I indicated a picture of the carbon dioxide canister, tube and valve that I had set up on an easel. "I know I am getting into a lot of detail here," I apologized. "Is everyone following me so far?" They all nodded.

"The carbon dioxide is harmless if it is put into the empty space of the abdominal cavity, and it just blows up the abdomen like a balloon, as I told you." The jurors all nodded. They remembered that.

"And the way you get the carbon dioxide into the abdomen, is by taking a hollow needle, in this case a needle called a Verres needle, and sticking it into the abdomen, and then you attach the rubber tube from the carbon dioxide canister to the hollow needle. Then you turn the valve and start the carbon dioxide gas flowing into the abdomen."

"BUT, AND THIS IS A BIG BIG BUT," I emphasized, "you can't attach the carbon dioxide hose onto the hollow needle and start it flowing until you are certain that you have that hollow needle in the right place, the open space of the abdomen. BECAUSE IF BY MISTAKE YOU HAVE PUT THE HOLLOW NEEDLE INTO A BLOOD VESSEL INSTEAD OF THE OPEN ABDOMEN----IF THE CARBON DIOXIDE GOES INTO A BLOOD VESSEL, IT WILL TRAVEL DIRECTLY TO THE HEART AND YOU WILL KILL YOUR PATIENT!! PUTTING CARBON DIOXIDE INTO A BLOOD VESSEL IS HOW THEY EXECUTE MURDERERS!" Now I really had the jury's attention. They all were at the edge of their seats.

"So how do we make sure , by we I mean a reasonably careful doctor, how does a reasonably careful doctor make absolutely certain that the needle isn't in a blood vessel before he starts the carbon dioxide flowing--how does he avoid the terrible tragic execution of his patient?" I paused a few moments.

"The answer is simple. After he puts that hollow needle, the Verres needle, through the skin and into what he hopes and expects is the opened space of the abdomen, and BEFORE-- underline BEFORE-- he attaches the carbon dioxide line, the reasonably careful doctor takes a syringe and attaches it to the hollow needle. The reasonably careful doctor then draws up on the plunger of the syringe. If the syringe is clear it indicates that the hollow needle is in a clear and opened space, the abdomen, and then, and only then, the reasonably careful doctor can remove the syringe from the hollow needle that is in the abdomen, and attach the carbon dioxide tube to the hollow needle and start the carbon dioxide gas flowing into the abdomen." I paused again. "Got it?" The jurors nodded.

"But if, when he pulls up the plunger on the syringe, the doctor sees blood, it means he has by mistake put the hollow needle into a blood vessel, and that he better not start the carbon dioxide flowing because it will kill the patient. So instead he will reposition the hollow needle, run the syringe test again, and not start the carbon dioxide until the syringe test shows the needle is properly placed." I took a sip of water, and gave the jury time to absorb what I had told them.

The evidence will show that in this case the defendant, Dr. Mijeck, never gave his patient the benefit of that syringe test. Instead he carelessly and negligently put the hollow needle in, mistakenly placed it so that it was into a blood vessel, started the carbon dioxide flowing directly into a blood vessel, and killed his patient. She died moments after the carbon dioxide began flowing. A simple syringe test would have saved her life." I took another drink of water.

"Her husband, Tom Smith, her older child, and her baby twin sons, are seeking damages for her death. Thank you."

"The Court will take a 15 Minute Recess before you hear the opening statement from the Defense," Judge Nielsen said as he tapped his gavel once and rose. Everyone in the Courtroom stood as he left the bench.

Ted Mizell, my referring lawyer who had a substantial financial interest in the case, had been sitting in the back of the courtroom and rushed up to me during the recess, complimenting me on a "great opening."

"Sound like you've got them by the balls," was his legal analysis of the situation.

"Now all I have to do is prove what I said," I whispered to him. "And that ain't gonna be easy. Have you heard from Geri today?"

"I thought she was with you," Ted said.

"I have her out chasing down a nurse who was in the operating room, but I haven't heard from her today. I would have thought she would have called with an up-date. "

"Well I hope she gets it done today," Ted said. "Next week I'm taking her to a client conference in Vegas, and she'll be with me for about a week. What happens in Vegas stays in Vegas," he winked.

I really needed Geri to help me, but she wasn't my employee, she worked for Ted, and if he couldn't keep his pants zipped, that was something I'd have to live with. I hoped that before Geri left for Vegas she would tell me she located the nurse, but it wasn't to be.

Bill Masterson's Opening Statement was pretty much as I expected. He started out telling the Jury how much he and his client sympathized with Tom Smith and his family for their loss. He condescendingly understood how they felt someone was to blame for their tragic loss, and complemented them on finding such a clever lawyer (with a nod toward me) to try and hit a money jackpot.

But, he cautioned the Jury, sometimes, even with the best care, people die. And that was the case here. "Despite what Mr. Seger said in his opening statement, that was just the story woven by a shrewd lawyer." *(before I was clever, now I was shrewd--I better watch out before he called me a shyster)*, and it was not, he said, backed up by the evidence.

"Listen carefully to the evidence from the witness stand," Masterson lectured, "even the evidence of the doctor hired by Mr. Seger as his own expert, that's Doctor Harry Foster, F-O-S-T-E-R, if you want to write it down, even Dr. Foster, Mr. Seger's hired expert, agreed under oath that Dr. Mijeck was acting fully within acceptable medical standards when Mrs. Smith was operated upon. AND JUDGE NIELSEN WILL INSTRUCT YOU AT THE END OF THE CASE that the Plaintiff cannot prevail, I repeat, CANNOT PREVAIL, THAT MEANS HE CANNOT WIN ANY MONEY DAMAGES, if he fails to prove that Dr. Mijeck was acting outside of acceptable medical standards and that he caused the death. That is the burden of proof the Plaintiff must meet, and in this case he is unable to prove negligence or causation."

I noticed that several of the jurors and even Judge Nielsen wrote into their notes the name of Dr. Harry Foster.

Masterson went on for a while longer, probably too long, as the Jury was getting restless. He claimed that the evidence would show Mijeck, a good and competent doctor, was acting properly, and that his conduct had nothing to do with the death of Mrs. Smith. He didn't go into detail as to just what he claimed caused the death, but implied it could have been due to a myriad of things, from congenital defects, or blood clots breaking loose and causing blockage of a blood vessel, or maybe one of those unexplained acts of God.

When he concluded, the Court was adjourned until Monday.

I would have felt a hell of a lot more comfortable if Ruben Weinstock was still alive to testify.

And by the end of the weekend Geri still hadn't located Ann Swanson, the missing nurse.

CHAPTER 62

The Case Proceeds

The case for the Plaintiff opened pretty much according to plan. Tom Smith made a beautiful witness, and I kept him on the stand for a full day as he described his life with Celia, how they came up from the South, built a home and a family, their joy at having twins, and then the horrible loss---her sudden death during the tubal ligation.

Tom described his loneliness since Celia's death, and the difficulty raising his kids without their mother. The jurors paid rapt attention, and several were in tears by the conclusion of my direct.

Actually, Tom had met a new woman and against my recommendation had married her about six months after Celia died. But the court ruled that under Illinois law the Defense could not tell the jury of the remarriage. Illinois courts have held this to be fair, because if not for the death there would have been no remarriage, and if the jury was told of the remarriage it could be highly prejudicial to the plaintiff's case.

Masterson's hands were tied by reason of the Court's admonition that he refrain from asking any questions that might reveal the remarriage. His cross exam was very brief. He again expressed sympathy to Tom for the loss, and his questioning emphasized how helpful and supportive the hospital staff were after the death.

"Did Dr. Mijeck ever apologize for killing your wife?" I asked on redirect. The court sustained an objection to the question before Tom could reply.

"How's the trial going," Sharon asked when I called her that evening. We hadn't talked for a few days, me busy with the trial and she with teaching activities. Her tone was cool, and had been that way ever since I told her about the photographs in Phil's computer.

"So far, so good. It gets tougher next week. What's happening with you?"

Neither of us wanted to talk about what was really on our minds, the murders. But after some mundane chit-chat, and lame attempts at humor, we ran out of topics.

Just before saying goodbye she asked, struggling to sound casual, "Anything new with the investigation?"

"I'm supposed to meet with Inspector Hollman later this week. I'll let you know what he says."

"Thanks." She hung up. No goodbye. No I love you. Nothing. I went back to work, preparing for next day's exam of Dr. Mijeck.

"I call Dr. Mijeck as an adverse witness," I announced to the Court and Jury. This meant that I was not vouching for his credibility, and it allowed me to ask leading questions, and treat him as if he were under cross-examination.

Juries are always impressed by doctors, and why not. We are brought up since childhood to respect them and trust them. Young Dr. Kildare, Ben Casey, Dr., House, E.R. and a myriad of other television series have helped to enhance their stature. I began by trying to demonstrate that Dr. Mijeck didn't quite live up to that lofty image.

"Would you explain to the jury what is meant by the term 'Board Certification'?"

"I don't follow your question. What is it you are asking me to say?"

"Well Dr. isn't it true that there is a process by which a doctor in any area of medicine, in your case obstetrics and gynecology, can prove his qualifications to his peers by submitting a summary of his training and experience and then passing a series of written and oral examinations. And if he does this his peers can certify him to be qualified to practice in his specialty. And isn't that called 'Board Certification'?"

"You don't have to be Board Certified to perform tubal ligations," Dr. Mijeck said, shifting a little uncomfortably in his chair. "You merely have to be licensed as a physician, and I was licensed in Indiana and Illinois."

"But you limited your practice to obstetrics and gynecology."

"That is true."

"But you never even took the examinations to be certified as an expert in that area or in any other area of medicine."

"True"

"And you don't belong to any of the local, State or national medical associations, where publications and seminars are available to hone your skills."

"I'm not much of a joiner." There were murmurs in the courtroom at this answer, and the judge ordered quiet.

"And you never held any teaching positions, and you never published a paper in any medical journal, isn't that true?"

"I was too busy helping patients to involve myself in those activities."

"Like you helped Celia Smith?"

"Objection!" yelled Masterson, jumping to his feet.

"Sustained," said Judge Nielsen, admonishing me to avoid such comments.

I was unable to prove that Mijeck ever had his license revoked or suspended, or that he failed to get the degrees he claimed. And thanks to the medical conspiracy of silence I had no concrete evidence that he committed acts that would have gotten him kicked off the staff of any good hospital. But I did show to our provincial American jury that all of his education was in foreign countries. And I traced the movement of his practice from state to state, hoping to leave the innuendo that there was something suspicious about the reason for the moves.

Then I asked the Court that we adjourn for lunch. Let the jury ponder what a sub-qualified doctor Mijeck really was.

CHAPTER 63

The Afternoon Session

During the lunch break I gulped down a sandwich at my desk and called Geri Sapperstein in Vegas, to see if she had any leads on the operating room nurse. I was angry that she hadn't kept in touch with me, but stayed cordial. They paged her at the hotel, and I reached her at poolside.

"Tough life you lead," I said. "How is the conference?"

"We have a lot of free time, mainly it's entertaining some corporate clients, food, drinks and some boring meetings. I really don't think Ted even needed me to be here with him."

"I'm sure he had planned some task for you."

"When we arrived, he tried to get me to share his suite, but I straightened that our pretty quick."

I had enough banter, and abruptly switched to Ann Swanson and told her I was disappointed that she hadn't updated me. Geri said that she had no luck locating the nurse, but she had other leads to follow up on and could do so from Vegas. She was 'cautiously optimistic' that with a little more time she would find her. Unfortunately, we didn't have a little more time. Geri didn't think she would be back in town for another week, unless Ted got tired of her saying "NO." She wasn't doing anything for Ted, but she wasn't doing anything for me either. It was a toss-up as to whether Ted or I was more frustrated by her.

I rushed back to Court for the afternoon session. Dr. Mijeck was back on the stand. I resumed my examination.

"O.K. Doctor, let's go to the day of the Celia Smith surgery. I want to take you through the entire procedure, step by step."

And then we tediously went through the entire operation, minute by minute, with the use of large drawings I had ordered prepared by medical illustrators. The drawings cost me $6,000.00. It was worth the expense so that the jury could follow just what was happening at each step.

There was a delicate balance between giving the jury a full explanation, and overloading them so that their minds would just shut off. People who were used to short sound bites weren't up to long windy explanations, and I watched the jury carefully for signs of fidgeting and boredom.

We took a 15 minute recess before going to the crux of the case.

"Now doctor, we come to the part where you have inserted the Verres needle into the abdomen. What did you do to insure that the needle was correctly placed into the hollow abdomen, and not into a blood vessel, before you started the carbon dioxide flowing?"

"I very carefully noted the amount of resistance as I inserted the needle into the abdomen. I could tell by the feel that it penetrated the abdomen and was in the hollow space. I even wiggled it a little, and could tell it was moving freely. If it was in a blood vessel the feeling would have been different. I would have noted more resistance, and it would not have wiggled freely."

"Are you familiar with the syringe test--- that is attaching a syringe to the needle and drawing it out?"

"Of course I am aware of that type of test. But that is just one way of making sure the needle is correctly placed--not the only..."

"I didn't ask you that, doctor. The syringe test would tell if the needle is incorrectly placed into a blood vessel, isn't that true?"

He admitted that if the syringe were attached and if the plunger when pulled up would draw blood into the syringe, then this would clearly indicate that the needle was improperly inserted into a blood vessel.

"And if the carbon dioxide was sent through the needle while it was in a blood vessel, this would kill the patient, wouldn't it."

"Yes, but this wasn't ....."

"We'll argue that later, doctor," I interrupted. "Just answer my questions, please."

"Many medical texts recommend the use of the syringe test before starting carbon dioxide flowing, isn't that correct?" I asked, as I moved toward a stack of medical books I had piled on my table.

"They do make the recommendation, but it is not compulsory, especially for highly experienced doctors who have performed the procedure many times."

I ignored the last part of his answer, and just shook my head dismissively. The jurors were closely following the testimony.

"And so, without performing the syringe test mentioned in all of these text books," indicating the two high stacks on my table, "you attached the carbon dioxide tube to the needle, and started the carbon dioxide flowing."

He nodded.

"And within two minutes of starting the carbon dioxide, the bells and whistles went off, and her heart had stopped!"

"There were no bells and whistles"

"Whatever," I shrugged. And in a voice tinged with sadness, "Within two minutes her heart stopped, she was never revived, and she died." I sat down.

I headed back to my office and called Ted Mizell in Vegas and reminded him that his firm had a big stake in the case. I told him to put his prick back in his pants and send Geri back to Chicago so she could take up the search for our missing nurse. It could be the key to winning the case. Ted said he would put Geri on the next plane, probably because he wasn't getting any. "Is the trial going well so far?" he asked.

"So far. But it's gonna get rocky when I put on our gyne expert. I really need that missing nurse. Let's hope Geri can find her."

CHAPTER 64

Dr. Kramer Comes To Town

I couldn't take the time to look for the nurse myself. Dr. Eugene Kramer, my expert pathologist, was scheduled to testify the next day. He was flying in from California, and I had to meet him at the airport, and get him settled into the very expensive hotel suite I had reserved for him in a new boutique hotel that had opened on Ontario Street. Those were tasks that Phil Levine would have performed if he was still alive, and I had no one to take Phil's place.

I wanted to immediately start prepping Kramer for his testimony, but he was 'famished'. The food in first class "was not at all to his liking." Kramer suggested we dine at Gibson's Steak House, a place he had read about in the airline magazine.

It cost me forty dollars to get us a table without the usual hour and a half wait, and the place was too noisy for any meaningful discussion while eating. So we devoured our huge sirloins. And we knocked off a bottle of wine.

When we finished dining, Kramer suggested we go around the corner and listen to some jazz, but I told him he had to be ready to testify in the morning, and persuaded him to return with me to his suite where I could review the case with him. And that is what we did, working together until just before midnight.

When I returned home my phone was ringing, and I rushed to answer, hoping it was Geri, telling me she was back in Chicago and had found our nurse. But it was Sharon.

"I haven't talked to you in a few days. I know you're busy with the trial, but I just wanted to say hello. I've missed you." Thankfully, she was over her funk.

"I missed you too, honey, but you're right, I have been busy. As a matter of fact I just waddled in the door. I was prepping Dr. Kramer for his testimony tomorrow, but first we had to gorge ourselves. He flew in tonight from L.A. I wish it would have been you on the plane instead. I miss you."

"I miss you too. I know you're busy with the trial, but our school gets out Friday for holiday, and I'll be free all next week. My son is going on a fishing trip with his father. But I don't want to get in your way…"

I assured her that I wanted to see her too. "My case-in chief is probably going to wrap up by Monday at the latest. Why don't you fly in this Friday, and stay with me all next week. Once I finish my side of the case I'll have to be in Court during the day while the defense puts on their case, but I should be pretty free in the evenings. And the whole case should be wrapped up by next Wednesday or Thursday at the latest."

"If I come, can I watch you in Court?"

"Absolutely—I'll even let you carry my briefcase."

She laughed that wonderful laugh I loved, and said she would see me Friday. I told her Julia would make arrangements for the ticket.

CHAPTER 65

Kramer On The Stand

Kramer's testimony was right in line with our preparation. We started out with a detailed review of his background and accomplishments.

We emphasized that he rarely got involved in court cases, in other words, that he was not a hired gun, and that he was a practicing pathologist with only less than one percent of his income being derived from reviewing medical malpractice cases.

It was only after we laid this foundation, and prepared the jury to accept Kramer as a well-qualified, credible, and believable witness, that we got down to the crux of his testimony--- Kramer's opinion as to the cause of death.

"It is my firm opinion, based upon my review of the hospital records and the sequence of events," Kramer said in a steady voice, looking directly at the jurors, as I had coached him to do, "that Celia Smith died as a result of carbon dioxide being injected directly into a blood vessel, causing a carbon dioxide embolism that traveled to her heart, and killed her."

Bill Masterson did as much as he could with Kramer on cross-examination. After some verbal dueling he got Kramer to concede that based upon the autopsy report findings it was impossible to exclude the possibility that the death could have been due to an aneurism, or some other natural cause. But this was only because the pathologist at the hospital had performed an incomplete autopsy, Kramer argued. He was convinced that if a complete autopsy had been performed, it would have ruled out any cause other than carbon dioxide into a blood vessel.

"But you admit that the autopsy findings didn't rule out those other causes, did they," Masterson said. "And therefore you can't say with absolute certainty what the cause of death was."

"Only because your pathologist was trying to hide the truth." Kramer shot back.

Kramer readily conceded that he was not a gynecologist-obstetrician, and that he could offer no opinion as to the standard of care when administering carbon dioxide during a tubal ligation.

The Court took a short recess, and I escorted Kramer from the stand to the hallway and thanked him for his assistance. He took off for Michigan Avenue to spend some of the money he had just earned. I returned to Court.

My next witness was Dr. Harry Chappen, the anesthesiologist in the case. I knew Chappen was not going to testify against Dr. Mijeck. That would have been too much to expect. After all, they were colleagues and both were still on the staff of the same hospital. If there was anything to prove Mijeck screwed up, that was not going to be heard from the lips of Dr. Chappen. But Chappen wasn't going to hang himself either, and he testified that nothing about the anesthesia caused or contributed to cause the death of Celia Smith. He had to admit that Celia went into cardiac arrest very shortly after the carbon dioxide was started, but quickly volunteered that "the death could have been due to an aneurism of some type of blood clot or other natural cause that could not have been avoi—"

I cut him off before he could finish. "I move the last portion of the answer be stricken as not responsive!" The bastard had been primed by Masterson to slip in those opinions.

"Sustained. The last portion of the answer is stricken and the jury is instructed to disregard everything after 'It was not anesthesia.'" As if the Judge's instruction would do much good.

Masterson had no further questions of the witness. We adjourned for lunch.

When I got back to the office, Geri Sapperstein was there, back home safely from Vegas. She still had been unable to contact the missing nurse. I suspected that someone must be hiding her.

CHAPTER 66

A Motion For Directed Verdict

We diddled around the rest of the week, with me presenting various witnesses who added a little color but no real substance to the case. I was buying time to get to the week-end, where I would have one last opportunity to locate the missing nurse.

I presented a family physician who had seen Celia for annual physicals and testified to her general good health in the years prior to her tubal ligation.

I called to the stand a couple of nervous looking nurses still employed by the hospital who were in the operating room at the time of the surgery. I was sure they were lying when they claimed no meaningful memory of what happened, but could not shake their testimony, and didn't press too hard because the jurors were becoming annoyed with me for harassing those nice young ladies in their white nurse's uniforms.

An economist I called testified as to the market value of a wife's and mother's services. She was a cook, housekeeper, chauffeur, baby sitter, part-time teacher, and companion. He estimated that the cost of paying someone to perform all of those acts, available 24 hours a day, for the expected lifetime of a young woman, adjusting for inflation, to be over 14 million dollars.

Finally, on Friday afternoon, I got around to calling my shaky expert, Dr. Harry Foster. He looked splendid as he walked to the stand. Tall, handsome, lean, youthful,--but not immature. Just the way you would want a bright young doctor to look. Dressed in a grey three-button Brooks Brothers suit, with a quiet paisley tie. Shoes shined and hair neatly trimmed. The women on the jury were already in love.

And his direct examination went fine. He spoke with a strong firm voice as he described his experience and training, and he looked directly at the jury as he condemned Dr. Mijeck for not using the syringe test before inserting the carbon dioxide into the body.

But he crumbled under cross examination. He had to admit that in his deposition, taken just a few weeks ago, he said under oath that it might have been permissible for Dr. Mijeck to rely on 'feel' and maybe the syringe test was not necessary. He wilted before my eyes, and conceded that there was no objective evidence that the carbon dioxide was put into a blood vessel. He admitted that there were known cases where congenital problems or unavoidable blood clots caused the death of a patient in surgery, and that a surgeon was not to blame for those types of problems.

On redirect I tried to rehabilitate him, and he did reaffirm that in this case, it was his opinion that Mijeck was negligent in not doing the syringe test, especially since the tubal ligation was being performed so shortly after the birth of the twins, at a time when all the blood vessels in the area were still swollen and more susceptible to being punctured. If he said anything different in his deposition, he explained, it was only because he had misunderstood the question being asked at the time.

When Dr. Foster concluded his testimony, I studied the jury, and was not sure that we sold them. And the judge didn't seem very impressed. It was, by now, late Friday afternoon. The jury was excused and instructed to return on Monday morning. The Judge asked the lawyers to meet in chambers.

Judge Nielsen had removed his robes and was sitting behind his desk, puffing on a cigar. "Have there been any further discussions about settlement?"

Masterson said there was no settlement offer, and would be no offer.

"As a matter of fact, your Honor, I have here a Motion for a Directed Verdict at the end of the Plaintiff's case," Masterson said, handing across a sheaf of papers to Judge Nielsen, and a copy to me.

"I don't believe the Plaintiff has rested his case yet, have you?" the Judge asked me.

"No we haven't your honor. I believe that by Monday we will have located and will be calling the circulating nurse who has been missing during this trial."

"I object!" Masterson thundered. "All witnesses were required to be listed by name and address long before the trial started. That circulating nurse left the employ of the hospital long ago, and we have been unable to locate her. Mr. Seger, despite our repeated discovery requests, never gave us a location so we could question her. It is too late to spring her on us now."

"I'm inclined to agree with Mr. Masterson," the Judge said. "Under the discovery rules you were required to give the names and addresses of all witnesses, and if you failed to provide the address of this circulating nurse, she will be barred from testifying."

"But we didn't have an address, Judge," I explained. "I don't even have her address now. But I hope to locate her this weekend and bring her in on Monday."

"The question as to whether the circulating nurse would be allowed to testify is moot, because you don't have the nurse."

"I'll have the weekend to locate her, so please give me that time before you close me out."

"Even if you bring her in I may very well bar her testimony. And if it appears that you or your people knew how to locate her earlier, I will hold you in contempt."

"I believe we are entitled to a ruling on my Motions right now," Masterson argued.

"I will reserve ruling on the question of this witness, and on the Motion for Directed Verdict until Monday morning."

There was a real danger that if I didn't come up with more evidence, on Monday the Judge would rule that I hadn't presented a strong enough case to beat Masterson's Motion for Directed Verdict. That would mean we lost without ever even getting the jury to make the decision.

And the way things stood, even if the case proceeded to a jury verdict, I wasn't at all sure the jury would find in our favor.

It felt shaky now, and Masterson hadn't even presented his side of the case. The jury had yet to hear the opinions of Masterson's Gynecology and Pathology experts. They were in full support of Mijeck, and in total disagreement with my guys, Drs. Foster and Kramer.

My instincts screamed that I had to come up with further testimony. Sharon might be upset when she flew in tonight and found me unable to see her, but I was going to be very busy trying to track down the missing nurse. And finding her would only help if her testimony strengthened our case. And even that would do no good unless the Judge allowed her to testify. A lot of ifs.

CHAPTER 67

Hollman Reports

Inspector Hollman was in the waiting room when I returned to my office. He ignored my protestations that I was too busy to see him, and followed me and plopped down into a chair in front of my desk. I told Julia to hold my calls.

"Look Inspector, I'm in the middle of a trial and have a million things to do. And I have to leave in a half hour to pick up Sharon at O'Hare. So please make it quick."

"I'll make it quick all right," Hollman said, flipping through the pages of that little note pad he always carried with him. "I've been pretty busy too."

"First, I went to Indiana, and checked up on your Dr. Mijeck. It seems he did have an alibi for the Ruben Weinstock murder in Michigan, although he wasn't about to broadcast it around, especially to his wife."

"Meaning?" I asked.

"He was at a motel with a nurse-anesthetist on the staff of his hospital, and she shared a bed with him, but I don't think it was to put him to sleep."

He flipped a page. "And then I drove on up to Michigan to see your old friend, Wally Smalley."

"You really have been a busy guy."

"You bet," he said. "And Smalley told me some very interesting things that you and Sharon forgot to mention."

"Such as?"

"You overlooked telling me that Smalley knocked Sharon up in California, and that Dr. Weinstock performed the abortion. How could you forget a little detail like that?"

"I didn't think that it was relevant, Inspector. It doesn't really prove anything, does it?" My response sounded weak, even to me. Hollman ignored it.

"It was obvious that Smalley was really hung up on Sharon since they were kids. At first I figured that Smalley blamed you for screwing up that relationship, and that he tried to kill you, but when Phil Levine got into your car in the dark garage, he killed Levine by mistake."

"It certainly sounds possible," I said.

"And I figured that he killed Weinstock because Weinstock had aborted his baby. Turns out that Smalley had cried to friends in North Haven about losing the only child he would ever have because of the abortion, and on top of that he is a devout Catholic, and considered the abortion an unforgivable sin."

"Sounds like you have your man, Inspector," I enthused. "Congratulations."

"Only one problem," Hollman said. "Smalley seems to have a pretty good alibi for the Phil Levine murder. On the day of the killing he spent the afternoon at Saint Mary's Church in North Haven for a Christening, and it's verified by the priest and several parishioners. Afterwards he went back to the parent's home for a party. It seems that he stayed until the evening. No one is sure of the exact hour he left, but they all say it was late, and it would leave very little time for him to drive to Chicago and kill Levine."

"But it is possible."

"But I consider it highly unlikely. Highly unlikely."

"So where does that leave you?" I asked.

"It leaves me with your girlfriend, Sharon. We know from the picture I showed you that she was in Levine's bathroom the day he was killed. And she was in North Haven without an alibi when Weinstock was murdered."

"But what was her motive? She had no motive," I protested.

"I figure you were her motive, Stan. Good old adorable, rich, eligible you. She was out to marry you, and it all would have blown up if you heard about the abortion. I figure Levine learned of it and she killed him before he could meet you at the airport that night and tell you about it. And when she saw Weinstock in North Haven, she knew she had to kill him before he told you about the abortion."

"That motive sounds pretty weak, Inspector."

"A jury won't think so. Especially with some devout Irish, Italian, and Polish Catholics on the jury. They won't like Sharon having an abortion."

"I tried for a subpoena *duceus tecum* to be served in California to get Weinstock's medical records to nail down the abortion," Hollman continued, "but the Court shot down my request. The judge held that any of Weinstock's medical records were protected by doctor-patient privilege, and wouldn't let me get any of them."

"You're spinning your wheels, Inspector. You have that picture of Sharon in the bathroom with the newspaper, but even though you have the date, you don't know what time it was taken. She might have been at Phil's at any time on the day he was killed. It could have been in the morning or afternoon."

Hollman handed me a sheet of paper. "This is a phone log of calls made from Phil Levine's telephone the day he was killed. I made a copy for you. You'll note that at 6:05 P.M. there is a call to 310-327-3337. That happens to be the number of Sharon's ex-husband."

Hollman then flipped a page on his pad, and continued, "It turns out her son was staying with his dad, and Sharon was calling to say she was in Chicago, would try to catch a late flight, but she might not be able to get back until the next day."

I examined the phone log Hollman gave me. "There's one other call after the one made by Sharon, I said. "At 7:02 there was a call to area code 715. Did you follow up on that?"

"It was a call made to an area code for Cable Wisconsin. I tried calling the number but nobody answered. I don't see how it could have anything to do with the murder."

"But if Phil made that call, it shows that Phil was alive an hour after the call made by Sharon. She had already left his apartment, on her way to O'Hare."

"She may have left the apartment, but it would still have given her plenty of time to sneak around to the garage and set up the kill. Then go to the airport."

"I can't argue with you anymore. I have to get to O'Hare to pick up Sharon. She'll be waiting for me."

"I'll come along with you to O'Hare, and when Sharon gets off the plane I'm placing her under arrest for murder."

CHAPTER 68

A Houseguest

As usual, the traffic on the Kennedy Expressway was lousy, but that was O.K., because it gave me plenty of time to calm down Hollman and convince him that he didn't have enough evidence to arrest Sharon and hold her. He had no weapon, no proof that Sharon had ever been in the garage, no eyewitness. If she was going to kill Phil, she could have done it in the apartment, I argued. There was no reason for her to wait until he went to the garage.

I stressed that Sharon had no motive for the murders because even if I had learned of the abortion it wouldn't have mattered to me. The fetus had been conceived before Sharon and I had gotten back together, so she wasn't cheating on me, and I didn't care what Sharon had been doing in L.A. before we reunited. I wasn't an angel before that either, I said.

Hollman had plenty of time to mull it over, because although the flight landed on time, deplaning was delayed until a gate became available, and that wasn't until a half hour after touchdown.

Hollman said he wanted to make sure Sharon wouldn't flee the jurisdiction, and that the only way to do that was to take her in custody.

"Don't throw her in the slammer, for God's sake. You'll never get her to cooperate that way. You want to keep an eye on Sharon--- why don't you just stay at my place with Sharon and me. She'll answer all your questions, won't hold anything back, and I guarantee she won't fly back to California until you O.K. it."

It was an offer too good for him to refuse. We would be a happy threesome, Hollman, Sharon and me. Sharon was going to love this.

Sharon was relieved that the abortion was in the open, and reminded me, in front of Hollman, that it was solely my idea to keep it secret. She was still convinced Wally was the killer, and that there must be a hole somewhere in his alibi.

I told her she would have the weekend to persuade Hollman, because he was staying with us. "The alternative was to let him lock you up in a cell with a bunch of hookers."

On the way from the airport we stopped off at Hollman's brick bungalow on the Northwest Side so that he could pack an overnight bag. His wife, a red-headed woman who was trim and would have looked attractive but for the curlers in her hair, walked out to my car with him, and introduced herself. On closer inspection, she was very pretty, even with the curlers.

It was obvious she was checking us out to be sure everything about his sleep-over was kosher, but she really didn't seem worried, and had a twinkle in her eye as she watched Hollman squirm when she asked us to take good care of him, "He doesn't snore if you give him a cup of hot tea before you tuck him in." She kissed him on the cheek, and we drove away.

"I can call her later to confirm that her little Louie is safe and sound in his bed," I offered.

"Louie—your name is Louie?" Sharon looked back at Hollman and laughed.

"Louie," Sharon and I said in unison, "I think this is the start of a beautiful friendship."

Hollman couldn't suppress a smile.

On the way back to the apartment we stopped at Uno's for a large deep dish pizza, covered with sausage in accordance with Hollman's request. At Sharon's suggestion I had them add their large tomato and onion salad

The food would go well with the vintage bottles of Chianti that had been sent to me by Dorothy Parelli, in appreciation of the very large settlement we had just entered into for the death of her husband. We had worked out a deal with the ex-in-laws to give them twenty percent of the net, well over three million dollars. I convinced the widow to agree. It may not have been the law, but it did seem fair, and it left her more than enough money for two lifetimes. And, I reminded her, it insured that she would live to enjoy the money.

When we got back to my apartment I showed Hollman his room, put the half-cooked pizza in the oven, and uncorked the Chianti. Sharon set the table, even lighting candles, and I brought out some oregano and hot peppers from the pantry.

By the time the dinner was over, the candle had burned down half way, and we had finished the salad, devoured the entire pizza, and polished off two bottles of Chianti. Hollman, who turned out to be a pretty nice guy, did the bulk of the damage.

We were all too sleepy to do much talking, so Hollman retired to the guest room, and Sharon joined me in mine. I was almost too tired for any hanky-panky, but decided on a quickie, with both of us agreeing to keep the volume low. When we finished, I kissed Sharon good night.

"My God," she whispered, "he was almost ready to arrest me."

"Don't worry, honey," I mumbled, "keep charming the pants off of Hollman, and we'll figure something out tomorrow."

CHAPTER 69

Ann Swanson

I was the first one up in the morning, as usual, and ground the beans, prepared the coffee, and left a note that I was going out for a run and would be back by 9:00. By the time I returned Sharon and Hollman were at the table, still in their pajamas and robes, sipping coffee and chatting like old friends. I figured that Hollman was fishing for information, and hoped that Sharon was smart enough to avoid any traps.

I spread around sections of the Tribune that I had purchased from my toothless purveyor. Sharon took Tempo, Hollman started with Sports, and I scanned News and Business.

"What's your sign?" Sharon asked Hollman.

"A Virgo.

"You're an 8. If you trust in others you will be rewarded."

"Must be a misprint." Hollman said.

"And you're a Taurus," Sharon informed me. "A nine! You will receive help from a long lost friend."

"And mine is a four," Sharon continued. "I will be going on a long trip, and it will be difficult to return."

Sharon and I waited for Hollman to comment, but he pretended he was no longer listening.

Hollman cleaned up the dishes, and Sharon went off to dress. I took out Phil Levine's telephone log, the one Hollman had given me the day before, and dialed the last number listed, the one with area code 715, Cable Wisconsin.

"My name is Stan Seger, an attorney in Chicago. Is this Cable Wisconsin?"

"Yes it is," the lady answering the phone cautiously said.

"May I ask to whom I am speaking."

"Who are you again?

"Stan Seger, a Chicago lawyer. I assure you this is not a sales call. It is part of a police investigation, and this number, according to phone records, was called by a man named Phil Levine."

"I spoke to Mr. Levine, but that was some time ago. I don't know how he ever found me. My number is unlisted."

"And your name is…?"

"Ann Swanson."

Bingo! The operating room nurse. Phil had come through for me right before he was killed.

"I need you to come to Chicago to testify at our trial." I said it without even learning what her testimony would be. Anything she would say could only help us.

"But I thought the case was settled."

"What made you think that?"

"That's what the lady said when she called me earlier this month. I thought she was calling to set up a time for my testimony. But when she called she told me the case had been settled. And I was really relieved, because my sister was scheduled to give birth, and I was going down to Hayward to help her, and I didn't know when I would be able to get away. She told me I didn't have to worry any more about testifying, that I could spend as long as I needed with my sister, and she thanked me and wished us luck with the baby."

"Did the lady give you her name, or tell you whose office she was with?"

"She said she was from a lawyer's office."

"Which lawyers office? Did she mention a name?"

"I was so relieved that I didn't have to testify that I never asked many questions. I don't know what lawyers office. To tell the truth, I was a little nervous about testifying anyway, because I've seen all those programs where you lawyers cut up witnesses on the stand."

"That's just on T.V." I told her that testifying would be "a piece of cake." She said she liked cake.

"How are your sister and the baby getting along?" I asked, trying to sound interested.

"She gave birth the day after I got the call from that woman. They're both doing fine. He's a boy, seven pounds six ounces. I just got back home from Hayward last night. If you called any earlier you would have missed me."

We covered the gist of what happened in the operating room, the same things she had told Phil on the night he was murdered. Halleluiah! We were going to nail Mijeck to the wall.

"How fast can you get to Chicago---can you get on a plane today? I'll cover all your expenses, and pay you well for your time."

"I'll need help with the expenses, but you don't have to pay me for my testimony. It was terrible what happened to that poor lady. I can catch a flight from Duluth or Minneapolis, and be in Chicago by this evening."

"We'll make all the arrangements for your flight and the room, and someone will meet you at the airport."

"My sister, the one who had the baby, has never been to Chicago. She needs a break. Her husband can take care of the boy for a few days, and our mom will help out. Can I bring my sister along? And I'll have to bring my teenage son too, if I can't find someone to watch him."

"Ann. You can bring your whole family. Plan to stay a few days, and we'll show you the city."

CHAPTER 70

A Slide Show

"I want to see those pictures." Sharon had come out of the bedroom wearing Polo Jeans, ridiculous red crocs, and a Cubs Sweatshirt that matched the sky blue of her eyes.

I tried to talk her out of it, but she would have none of that. "Right Now!" she insisted. "Give me the disc and show me how to start up your computer."

Reluctantly I handed Sharon the disc, sat down at my desk, typed in my password, and surrendered my chair. Hollman, the coward, said he was going for a walk and would be back a little later.

Sharon inserted the disc and Phil's slideshow began, one crotch shot after another appearing for ten seconds and then slowly sliding across my 17" high definition screen to give way to the next glorious Technicolor photo.

Sharon hit the pause button when her picture appeared, studied it silently and then looked at me with an expression that reminded me of my mother's face when she discovered Playboy Magazine under my pillow. When she got to the last photo, the one of the subject who was standing over the toilet with the back to the camera, with the skirt hiked up, and showing a prick dangling between a pair of very pretty legs, she looked at me quizzically. I could only shrug.

Then she went through the full slide show a second time, like she couldn't believe what she had seen. "It needs a musical background," she said.

Hollman returned from his walk with an Ashkenazi Deli bag filled with bagels, nova, cream cheese and even a tomato and an onion. "I figured we could use a good breakfast," he said as he put two egg bagels in my toaster. He was really settling in.

After taking a gulp of coffee to wash down a huge bite of a nova sandwich, Hollman confessed that he wasn't serious when he threatened to arrest Sharon. He admitted that he didn't have enough evidence for an arrest, but he warned that she was still a prime suspect.

I realized that I had underestimated Hollman. He was shrewder than I thought. He had manipulated me by using the threat of arrest as a means of finagling an invite to stay at my place so that he could observe Sharon in a relaxed atmosphere and question her when her guard was down.

Hollman was still the investigator, even as he struck the pose of a guest relaxing in my home. While I cleared the table, put the dishes in the dishwasher, and went to shower and changed from my running clothes, Hollman and Sharon chatted, and from the snatches of conversation I could overhear, she was recounting in detail her long history with me, the story of her years in California, her marriage and divorce, and her involvement with Wally Smalley.

"She sounds very serious about moving back here, even with our lousy weather," he said, as I came out of my bedroom, wiping my hair, still wet from the shower. "Giving up California sunshine for snow and ice…man, it must be love. Real all-consuming love."

But what he really meant was *maybe she loved me enough to kill twice to keep me.*

"I'm still in the process of trying to convince her to move," I said. "She's a tough sell."

I told them I had to go to the office to clear up some business and prepare for Court on Monday. Sharon said she was going around the corner to the Vietnamese, (meaning the Manicure Parlor), to have her fingers and toes done, and then she was going over to visit the lions, (her reference to the statues at the entrance to the Art Institute), to check out the Impressionists.

"How the hell do you ever know what she's talking about," Hollman asked.

"I just guess, and I'm right about half the time."

Hollman said he was checking out of our B & B, and heading to the station house. Sharon and I both solemnly promised she wouldn't leave the jurisdiction without notifying him first.

CHAPTER 71

Ann Swanson Hits Town

Julia was at her desk when I arrived at my office. She worked weekends when I had a trial going. Julia, God bless her, had gotten Ann Swanson and her sister the last two seats on a United flight from Duluth, arriving at 5:30 P.M. The son had a soccer match, and wasn't coming along.

The sisters were going to have to hustle to catch the plane, but they were willing to do it. Julia was going to pick them up at the airport.

I was having trouble concentrating on the trial---- couldn't stop speculating about the murders. There had to be a connection between Phil and Weinstock. Something that would give the killer a motive to kill both of them.

*Suspect: **Dr. Mijeck**. Both Phil and Weinstock posed a serious threat to Mijeck's career. Phil was digging into his background and posed a threat to expose falsifications in his license applications, and a record of buried medical errors. Weinstock would testify to gross negligence in the Smith case, conduct so far outside acceptable practice that it could cost him his accreditation to practice surgery.*

*Suspect: **Wally Smalley**. Weinstock had performed the abortion. That was enough motive for Smalley to murder Weinstock. And Smalley could have killed Phil because he was obsessed with possessing Sharon. He either killed Phil because he mistook Phil for me, or because Phil was demanding him to leave Sharon alone.*

*Suspect: **Sharon**. Hollman thought she killed them both to keep me from finding out about the abortion. She was in the vicinity at the time of both murders. It didn't help matters that she neglected to mention that Weinstock had performed her abortion. It made it even worse that he found a picture of her in Phil's apartment the day he was killed, and* *this after she had led him to believe, thanks to my advice, that she was in California at the time Phil was shot.*

But maybe there was something else, some other way Phil and Weinstock were connected. I had trouble imagining other possibilities. Was it possible Weinstock had a patient who in the past had somehow been involved with Phil? Somebody who had a grudge against both of them. Very far-fetched. I was grasping at straws. But I couldn't think of anything else. Like my grandmother used to say. "What have you got to lose?" I wanted to examine Weinstock's medical files to look for someone who connected him to Phil.

Hollman told me he couldn't get the Court to order the release of Weinstock's office records, but I thought I knew how to get hold of them. I interrupted Julia as she was calling around to make a hotel reservation for Ann Swanson. There was an electronics convention in town, and she was having trouble finding a vacancy.

"Put that on hold for a minute, and get Weinstock's widow on the line." Their home number was in our computer.

A maid answered the phone, and said Mrs. Weinstock was spending the week at her beach house in Malibu. "Pretty fancy living," Julia said to me as she dialed the beach house number.

Ros Weinstock answered the phone, and we chit-chatted a few minutes. There were sounds of a party in the background. She assured me she was coping with her husband's death just fine---no surprise to me--and then invited me out for a vacation. "I can promise you a good time," she said in her most seductive voice.

I thanked her, and said I was a little busy with a trial. "But there is something you can do for me."

"What's that?" Now she sounded guarded.

"I need a copy of all of your husband's office records for the past three years."

"You know I can't do that. Doctor-Patient confidentiality and all that . They even have a federal law, HIPPO or something ."

"But these are relevant to the investigation of your husband's murder," I said.

"It doesn't make any difference. I can't do it. Why don't you get a Court Order."

"That will take too long. We need the information now."

"Well, you'll have to try another way. You won't get them from me!" she started to hang up.

"Just a minute Ros. You're the beneficiary of Ruben's Life Insurance Policy, and that policy has a double indemnity clause." I remembered she had mentioned that.

"These insurance companies look for any excuse to deny payment, or at least hold onto their money as long as they can. They won't pay out a penny if they hear you're a suspect in the investigation of his murder. And, come to think of it, the Probate Court in California will tie up all of his bank accounts and other assets until the murder investigation is resolved."

"You know I didn't kill Ruben. How dare you. I'm not even a suspect."

"That's not what Inspector Hollman is going to tell the California people if you don't cooperate with us." Hollman would kill me if he heard this conversation.

"But I need money now. I have bills to pay---assessments, mortgages, credit cards, car rentals. You can't do this to me."

"We can and we will if you don't cooperate."

"I can't get the office records right away," Ros said. "Those are all computerized at the Westwood office, and I would have to locate the key somewhere. But I can get the billing records right away. I helped Ruben with the billing, and those are on my laptop. Will those help?"

"If the billing records have names and addresses of the patients, and the billing codes for the services performed, they could be helpful. But I also want the office records as soon as you can get them."

I told Julia to keep an eye out for Weinstock's billing records. Ros had promised to e-mail them later in the day. Julia would print them out and notify me as soon as they were ready.

"And you'll defend me when I'm charged with conspiracy to violate federal confidentiality laws?" Julia asked.

I told her not to be such a worrywart.

"What is a worrywart, anyway," she asked.

"I have no idea, but it's what my mother used to call my aunt Celia."

Julia was able to reserve a suite for Ann and her sister at the Burnham, a beautiful hotel in the renovated Reliance Building, originally built in the 1890's. She called the Burnham as a last resort, because more modest accommodations were all booked by conventions. The hotel was just two blocks from the courthouse, and we had used it before to house fancy expert witnesses.

"And I made a reservation for the three of us, me, Ann, and her sister, for dinner at 9:00 P.M. at Petterino's," my gem of a secretary added, "and you can join us if you want to. You get to pick up the tab whether you're there or not."

Sharon and I met them at Petterino's at nine. It's a popular pre and post theatre destination, a little like the old Sardis's in New York, and the walls are covered with framed caricatures of local celebrities, mainly politicos and broadcasters. One artist had done all of the drawings, and he did a pretty good job of capturing the distinctive characteristics of his subjects. He wasn't Al Hirschfeld, but they weren't bad.

The restaurant was a good choice. It was just a few blocks from the Burnham. At this hour it was quiet and pretty empty. Almost all of the clientele were at the various theatres in the area, and wouldn't be returning for another hour or so.

Both sisters were surprisingly fresh after their long day of travel. They were excited about being in Chicago, loved the beautiful old hotel, and admired the "elegant restaurant." They looked forward to shopping on State Street, that great street, even if Marshall Field's had become Macy's.

Ann Swanson was a solid chunky blond with grayish blue eyes and a pug nose that probably looked pert when she was twenty years younger. I put her age at about forty five, but she looked older, because of a deeply lined face and a complexion leaning toward leathery. She looked like her life had not been a bed of roses, but the twinkle in her eye said she handled the bumps well. I would never have wanted to date her, but I would have been very comfortable with her being my nurse.

Her sister, Mildred something or other, was a little younger, and looked very much like a larger version of her older sister, *sans* the weathering. It was probably unfair to judge her, because she was still coming down from her pregnancy, but she had a lot of deflating left. She wasn't going to make much progress that night, because she ordered a shrimp cocktail, fried onion rings, the biggest steak in the house, and, because she was "watching her weight", a baked potato with sour cream instead of french fries.

Ann matched her sister bite for bite, and not to be outdone I did the same, except no shrimp cocktail. Sharon had a lobster cocktail and a salad, and Julie the wild Alaskan Salmon, a special of the day. We had three bottles of red wine, at about $45.00 a crack. I was doing the ordering, and the only way I know to evaluate wines is by the price. Those bottles were in the mid-range. If I had left the ordering to Sharon, the discussion with the waitress or sommelier would have lasted fifteen minutes and probably ended up costing at least twenty dollars more per bottle, money that would have been wasted on our guests.

During the meal it was all light conversation, as we got to know a little about each other. We spent a good portion of the time oohing and aahing over pictures of Mildred's baby. Mildred explained that she had pumped out enough milk to last several days, information I could have done without.

By the end of the meal the wine had its effect, and everyone was growing groggy, especially the ladies who had flown in. Although I was eager to discuss Ann's testimony, that would have to wait for the morning. I signed the $460.00 tab, and charged the meal to the Smith file.

We left the restaurant just as the after-theater crowd began drifting in, and Sharon, Julia, and I accompanied the ladies back to the Burnham, cutting across Daley Plaza and stopping to admire the Picasso. Ann said it reminded her of her ex mother-in-law. I arranged to meet her at the hotel early the next morning to get her ready to testify. She had already told me what had occurred in the operating room, but I wanted to nail it down cold.

I spent almost all day Sunday with Ann, prepping her. We went over her demeanor, the questions I would ask, how she would answer, the cross-examination we could expect, and how she would handle it all. We went over everything twice. Now all I had to do was persuade the Judge to let me call her as a witness.

I thought I covered it all. But in the end I was in for a big surprise. I totally missed something crucial.

CHAPTER 72

Ann Swanson Meets the Judge

I got to the Courthouse early on Monday, bypassed the security line by using my attorney's I.D., and waited for Ann Swanson until she cleared the metal detector. We went up to the twenty-fourth floor, and I stored Ann on a visitor's bench at the back of a vacant courtroom next to the one we were using for the Smith trial. Then I waited at the entrance to our courtroom, and intercepted William Masterson when he arrived, and led him to a bench in the hall.

"I found Ann Swanson," I said. "I'm calling her to the stand to testify, and I strongly suggest that you make no objection."

"Are you crazy?" he said. "You never gave us a chance to depose her—you never gave us an address and you've been keeping her under wraps. You violated the discovery orders. I'm going to insist that she be barred from testifying, and the Judge will grant my Motion. I have authority here," he said starting to open his briefcase.

I reached over and slammed his briefcase shut, almost catching his fingers. I leaned into his face. "I'm going to give you this one opportunity to save your ass. If you raise an objection to her testimony, I'll be forced to put your witness tampering on the record---how your office called Mrs. Swanson and told her she shouldn't come to Chicago because the case was settled and she wouldn't have to testify. You could lose your license for that cutey."

"What are you talking about?" he asked, looking puzzled, but I disregarded that look because most trial lawyers are pretty good actors.

"I have the testimony of Mrs. Swanson," I said. "She has no reason to lie. I'm going inside, and you have a few minutes to reconsider before the Judge gets on the bench." I picked up my briefcase, and entered the courtroom.

The jury was in the box. Masterson was deep in conversation with Dr. Mijeck, who was seated next to him at the counsel table, but their talk was interrupted when the entire courtroom stood as Judge Nielsen took the bench. "Mr. Seger, do you have any further evidence to present?"

"I do, Your Honor." I paused five beats for dramatic effect. "The Plaintiff calls Ann Swanson, a nurse in the operating room at the time Celia Smith was killed---I mean at the time she was operated on and died."

"I object!" Masterson shouted. "I object to his comments, and I object to him pretending before this jury that he has any other witnesses he can call, and I would like to be heard on these matters in chambers."

The jury was sent back to the jury room and Masterson and I, along with the Court Reporter, followed a very angry Judge Nielsen back to his chambers, where he proceeded to rip into me even before he sat down.

"Look Mr. Seger, you knew I was reserving my ruling on the eligibility of this witness, and you had no business calling her to the stand until I ruled on the matter. It was highly improper to call her and make Mr. Masterson object in front of the jury. If I bar her, they will think that Masterson is trying to hide her from the jury, and no Instruction I can give will erase that impression."

"You asked me in open court, in front of the jury, if I had any other evidence to present," I replied, "and I was just answering your question and calling my next witness. I told Mr. Masterson in the hallway that I was going to be calling Ms. Swanson, he knew what I was going to do, and he could have asked for a hearing in chambers before I called her, but he never did so."

"Mr. Seger. You had the sense of the Court on this matter," the Judge said, still seething. "We will have an in camera hearing here in chambers now, before a Court Reporter, but the hearing will be limited to whether you, or anyone in your employ, had any contact with the witness before this trial began. If so, and since you failed to disclose her last known whereabouts, and the subject matter of her testimony, she will be barred from testifying, and I will hold you in contempt."

I started to speak, but he wasn't through yet. "And if I decide to bar this witness, I am prepared to rule immediately on the Defense Motion for a Judgment in their favor, and, Mr. Seger, considering the meager evidence presented by the Plaintiff on the issue of liability, I don't think you will be pleased by my decision."

A very nervous Ann Swanson was brought back into the chambers, and took the seat in front of the Judge. She looked questioningly at me, having no idea what was going on, but I had no chance to talk to her.

"Miss Swanson," the Judge said, in a manner a hell of a lot kindlier than the one he used with me, "certain questions have arisen regarding your testimony, and we have called you back here to straighten them out."

"It's all right, Ann," I began, but the Judge spoke over me as if I hadn't said anything, and continued. "I am going to place you under oath, and then I will ask some simple questions that are troubling me. Questions that should be easy for you to answer. Please answer them fully, but don't elaborate beyond the questions I ask. Do you understand that?" She nodded as she raised her hand and took the oath. The Court Reporter was poised to record her testimony.

"When did you first speak to Mr. Seger about anything having to do with this case?"

"This past Saturday morning," she said. "He called me in Wisconsin and we talked about my testimony. He asked me to come to Chicago to testify."

"And you have never spoken to him before yesterday?"

"No, your honor."

"Did you ever speak to anyone calling on his behalf before yesterday," the Judge continued, and Ann, realizing where this was going squirmed in her chair, as I looked passively at my note pad, jotting down doodles. Masterson was sitting at the edge of his seat.

"His investigator called me a while ago. At my home in Wisconsin."

"That was at the same number Mr. Seger reached you at this weekend," Judge Nielsen said, looking at me, more of a statement than a question. She agreed that it was.

"And I don't want you to tell me the substance of your conversation with that investigator," the Judge continued, "that is not the purpose of this hearing. But just answer Yes or no, did you discuss with that investigator the same things you were going to testify to today?"

"Yes."

He asked Ann to step out while the lawyers conferred.

"I think I've heard enough," the Judge said.

"Wait a minute Judge---you haven't heard enough---I want to make a record here."

"The record is very clear," Masterson objected, sniffing an easy victory.

"You can make your record," Judge Nielsen said," but it had better be good."

I explained to the Judge that Phil Levine, my investigator who had spoken to Ann, was murdered later the same night, and had never had a chance to tell me he had located Ann, much less that he had talked to her. I produced Phil's phone record to verify the date of Phil's phone call to Cable Wisconsin.

"And the date of the phone call is the same as the date Levine was murdered?"

"The very same day," I replied, "and based on the time, it was not too long before Phil was murdered. Phil would have had no time to notify me that he found the witness."

And I told the Judge that I didn't learn that Phil had located Ann until the other day, when I stumbled across the record of a call to Cable while reviewing Phil's telephone bill for the night of his murder. I offered to take an oath to those facts, but the Judge, sounding a little warmer, said I was an officer of the Court, and an Oath would not be necessary.

The Judge was weighing the issue, and it was time for the *coup de grace*. He allowed me to bring Ann back into the room.

"Ann, you are still under oath," I said

"What the hell is this," Masterson yelped. "He hasn't been given permission to question this witness."

I assured the Judge that my questions were pertinent to the inquiry, and he gave me permission to proceed, but cautioned me to keep the questions brief and to the point.

"Did you receive a phone call at your home a few weeks before you heard from me, telling you that that the case was being settled and that you would not have to testify and that you were free to travel to a different town to take care of your sister and her new baby?" The question was leading, but I wanted to get it all in while the Judge was paying careful attention. Sometimes these judges have the attention span of a flea.

"Yes, I got that call, but it wasn't quite two weeks ago."

"Whatever, and who was it that called you?"

"It was from a lawyer's office."

"Do you remember what lawyers office they were from?"

"I don't think they mentioned a name of any office."

"Thank you Ann." She was excused again from the room.

"Well it certainly wasn't someone from my office," I said. I need this lady's testimony. It isn't me who would win a directed verdict if she doesn't testify."

"That's ridiculous!!" Masterson exploded, his face turning bright red. "I didn't call her, and neither did anyone form my office or anyone connected with Dr. Mijeck. This is outrageous."

"It must have been someone for Dr. Mijeck," I said. "When you hear her testimony, you'll realize why they wanted to muzzle her."

"I'm going to overrule your objection," Mr. Masterson. The witness will be permitted to testify." Masterson angrily snapped his briefcase shut and rose to leave the chambers.

"And," the Judge called out to him, "at the end of the case I will hold a full hearing on the question of witness tampering, and if warranted, my report of your conduct will be turned over to the ARDC with my recommendation that you be strongly censured, and maybe even disbarred."

CHAPTER 73

Ann Swanson Testifies

Ann took the witness stand, and by the time she finished testifying, the case, for all intents and purposes, was over, and the only thing still in doubt was the size of our verdict. We got the jury's attention immediately when she first declared that "after what happened the day of Mrs. Smith's surgery I was so sickened that I quit nursing, and moved back to the North Woods."

Ann told the jury that Mijeck never used the syringe test. He inserted the Verres needle and immediately attached the tube and started the CO_2 flowing. After he finished administering the CO_2 he closed the valve and disconnected the CO_2 hose from the Verres needle. And as soon as Dr. Mijeck removed the hose a stream of blood shot up through the center of the hollow needle, through the hole in the needle.

"Blood shot up like a fountain," she said, "and it hit me in the shoulder." She had saved the surgical gown, unwashed since that day, and held it up to show the large blood stain to the jury. A regular Monica Lewinsky, my Ann.

She explained to the jurors, although they probably didn't need any explanation, that the blood gushing out through the needle meant that the Verres Needle was in a blood vessel, not in the hollow abdomen where it was supposed to be. "I've assisted in almost a hundred procedures where the abdomen was insufflated with CO_2, and if the needle is properly paced into the abdomen no blood flows through the needle. There is no blood floating around in the abdomen. It had to mean that the needle was in a blood vessel."

"And when the blood shot out," she continued, "Dr. Mijeck panicked, grabbed the CO_2 tube, and put it onto the Needle to cap the spurting blood."

"And did that work?"

"Yes, the blood, of course, stopped spurting out because there was nowhere for it to go. And then he, Dr. Mijeck, turned the valve and started the flow of carbon dioxide through the Needle again." Her voice broke, and I waited a few moments, the courtroom silent, while she collected herself.

"And then what happened?" I asked softly.

"Within a few minutes her blood pressure dropped, all of her vital signs fell, and we called a Code blue. We did everything we could, but we were unable to revive her."

"Dr. Mijeck may have performed numerous tubal ligations before," she told the jury, "but this was the first time he insuflated the abdomen with a Verres Needle." I purposely did not ask how she knew of his inexperience.

"You never worked with Dr. Mijeck before, and you didn't even know him before, so how could you possibly know that he never used a Verres Needle before?" Masterson asked in cross-examination, falling into the trap I had set, as I suspected he would. I had seen him make the same mistake before. Never ask a question on cross-examination unless you knew what the answer would be.

"I knew it because Dr. Mijeck said so," Ann explained. "He asked for the package insert describing how to use the Verres Needle and spent a few minutes studying it before he inserted it into the abdomen. You could see that he didn't really know what he was doing."

CHAPTER 74

Closing Argument

Normally, after bombshell testimony like that, I would have expected some settlement overtures from the Defense. But Masterson wasn't talking to me at all, still fuming over being accused of witness tampering, and trying to figure how to save his license.

After Ann's testimony I rested our case, and the Defense renewed their Motion for a Directed Verdict. The Motion was quickly denied.

Masterson called Dr. Mijeck to the stand to refute Ann's testimony, but nobody, not even Masterson, I suspect, believed him.

A world renowned pathologist was the last Defense witness, and Masterson took the entire morning reviewing his impressive credentials. In the afternoon the expert testified that in his opinion Celia Smith had died of a congenital brain aneurism, and that the insertion of carbon dioxide had nothing to do with her death. The jurors barely listened to his testimony. They had already decided that Mijeck was as guilty as sin. So I didn't dignify his opinions by re-examining them. I just asked his fee for testifying, and then shook my head, and said dismissively, "He charges for his testimony by the hour, and I see no reason to spend any time questioning him and increasing that already bloated fee. I have no other questions." Several of the jurors snickered.

I spent the night finalizing my Jury Instructions.

Ann Swanson and her sister had originally planned to return to Wisconsin after she testified, but changed their plans and decided to hang around to hear closing arguments, and the verdict.

Word was out that a big malpractice case was going to the jury and the courtroom was packed. A couple of members of the press who I had alerted were sitting in the front row. Favorable publicity never hurt.

Ted Mizell, my referring lawyer, was seated right behind our counsel table, along with Geri Sapperstein, looking well-coiffed and very attractive. Ted had released Geri from her regular chores for the day. Both gave me a thumbs up.

Sharon, who was also in the front row, leaned over to wish me good luck as I prepared to give closing argument.

My ex-wife, Phyllis, clothes designed by Ralph Lauren, was seated a few rows back, along with my daughter, who was looking very pert with a blond ponytail and dressed in a cashmere sweater. I didn't know they were still in fashion. She wasn't really interested in the law, but she skipped school for the day just to watch her dad at work. Phyllis and my daughter both waived.

Inspector Hollman was standing at the back of the courtroom. I nodded at him but he didn't see me. He seemed more intent on keeping an eye on Sharon, making sure she wouldn't cut and run as soon as the case was over.

Judge Nielsen entered the courtroom, carrying a set of the Instructions we had settled on earlier that morning in his chambers. During the conference he reminded Masterson that after the verdict came in there would be a hearing on the witness tampering charge.

Each side was given an hour for closing argument. I didn't spend much of my argument on the negligence issue. That wasn't necessary. The damning evidence of Ann Swanson was still fresh in the juror's minds. I spent most of my time stressing the damages to which we were entitled. Masterson spent most of his allotted time trying to hold down the amount of the award.

By 5:00 P.M. the jury had been deliberating for four hours without reaching a verdict, and Judge Nielsen excused them for the night, instructing them to return and continue their deliberations the next morning.

CHAPTER 75

Ann Swanson's Surprise

Ted Mizell was concerned the jury was taking so long, and I told him to relax, they were probably just haggling about how much, not liability. We were having a pre-verdict celebration dinner at the Greek Island, Ted, Sharon, and me, along with Ann Swanson and her sister.

As usual, the restaurant was crowded and noisy. We were sitting at my favorite table, on the balcony overlooking the restaurant. Our table was covered with platters piled high with Greek delicacies, and bottles of wine.

Ann guzzled Roditis like it was Leinenkugel, and was feeling no pain. "I really don't understand why it took you so long to find me," she slurred. "I gave them my address and phone number the first time I spoke to your people, and I've always been at the same place."

I explained that Phil had been murdered right after he spoke to her, and he never had the chance to pass on the information to me.

"But Mr. Levine wasn't the only one I talked to that night," Ann said. "He had a lady working with him on the case, and actually he put her on the phone to take down my name and address. Her name was Jerry something, funny name for a lady."

"You never mentioned the lady before," I sputtered, struggling to swallow the wine I had been sipping.

"Nobody asked me," she replied nonchalantly. "The one who called and told me the case was settled might have been the same lady. I'm not for sure, but it could have been."

It was much later that night. Sharon and I were in bed. I had drunk too much, and was just drifting off when Sharon hit me with the question that I had been trying to put out of my mind so I could get some sleep. I had been mulling over the implications of Ann's revelation since we left Greek Island.

"Are you going to set the record straight with the Judge in the morning?" Sharon asked, "about Geri having Ann's address for a long time now, and her maybe being the one who told Ann the case was settled."

"But she never gave me the address, or told me she spoke with Ann," I mumbled. "I don't understand it. If it comes out, the Judge will think I purposely misled him. He could declare a mistrial and we would have to start all over again, and this time Ann could be barred from testifying."

"But you have to tell the Judge. You have to clear Mr. Masterson. He could lose his license otherwise."

"I know that, but if I tell the Judge everything, I could be the one losing his license."

"I heard you phone Julia a little while ago and tell her to make arrangements to fly Ann and her sister back to Wisconsin on the earliest flight in the morning. You're going to squelch the whole thing, aren't you?"

"You bet your cute ass I am, at least until the verdict comes in." Now I was fully awake.

"I am shipping Ann and her sister back to Wisconsin on the first flight in the morning, and if there would have been a red-eye the two of them would be on it right now. I'm not fucking up the trial at this stage. But as soon as the verdict comes in I'm going to find out what that bitch Geri was up to. I wouldn't put it past those bastards on the other side to have somehow planted her or turned her as a spy to screw up my case."

"A conspiracy," Sharon said. "You think there was a conspiracy."

"It's hard to believe Geri was acting on her own. That would make no sense. But I'm not going to say anything about it until after the verdict comes in tomorrow. Now, can we please get some sleep."

CHAPTER 76

The Verdict

Sharon, Tom Smith, and I were at my office the next morning, just a few minutes walk from the Courthouse, awaiting a call that the Jury had reached a verdict.

Julia was on her way back from O'Hare, after picking up Ann and her sister at their hotel very early in the morning, treating them to omelets at Tempo, and depositing them at the airport. The sisters, Julia assured me, were winging their way home, with our promise that we would notify them as soon as a verdict came in. She didn't tell me what excuse she had devised for hustling them out of town so abruptly.

Just before noon I got a call that the jury had reached a verdict, and we rushed to the Court.

Tom Smith and I stood at one table, and Masterson and Dr. Mijeck at the other, and when the foreman of the Jury rose to announce the verdict we all leaned forward as if that would get us the word a little faster.

"We the Jury find in favor of the Plaintiff, Tom Smith, and against the Defendants, Dr. Walter Mijeck and his employer, the South Side Community Hospital. We award damages in the amount of thirty seven million dollars."

Tom grabbed me and hugged me. Masterson slumped to his chair. Dr. Mijeck just looked ahead impassively. He was fully covered by the hospital's malpractice policies, and the verdict wouldn't cost him a cent out of pocket.

"Judgment will be entered on the verdict tomorrow," Judge Nielsen said, banging his gavel once. "And Mr. Masterson, please be back here tomorrow morning at eleven for a hearing on that other matter concerning witness tampering. I would like you in attendance also at that hearing, Mr. Seger."

"I swear to you my office never called Mrs. Swanson," Masterson said as we left the courthouse. "We didn't know how to reach her, and believe me we didn't even try. I had a pretty good idea what she would say if she was found. I heard she was very upset when she quit the hospital, and I was relieved when you couldn't locate her. I was crossing my fingers hoping you never would. I wanted her to stay lost, but I never would have tampered with a witness or pulled a stunt like that to keep her away. You know me better than that," he implored.

I just shrugged, saying nothing. I wasn't ready to accuse him of subverting Geri Sapperstein, not yet. I wasn't going to spring that on him until the right moment.

It was a great victory. My share of the fee would be about five million dollars. Even after taxes I could probably retire comfortably, if that was what I wanted to do. But probably I didn't. I would miss the action. And that was going to cause more problems with Sharon.

Sharon had only considered moving to Chicago after I promised that we would move back to California together once I could afford to stop practicing. I had made that rash promise once as we lolled on Venice Beach, and she made me renew it a couple of times right after we made love.

We were in my car, heading to my apartment. "I guess I won't have to move to Chicago after all," Sharon said. "We can afford to buy that place on the Ocean that we saw, and move in there." She sounded very excited.

"I still have a lot of cases pending here. I could probably take a month or so off, but I don't think I'm ready to close up the practice."

"You promised."

"I know I did. But closing it down just doesn't feel right. Maybe we can find a nice little place in L.A. and visit often, but our base will have to be here."

"It's the murders, isn't it. You still think I might be a murderer, don't you."

"Of course not."

Sharon exploded. "You promised that when you hit the big one you would be able to move to California. Now you say you expect me to tear up my roots, leave everything I worked for there, abandon all my friends and family, and live with you in this shitty Chicago weather instead. You were lying to me all along. "

"Don't get so angry," I pleaded."

"Angry----I haven't even started doing angry!"

The argument quickly escalated, and ended with Sharon saying she was going to my apartment to pack up and head home to California.

We were interrupted by my cell phone ringing. It was Inspector Hollman. "Now that the trial is over I want you and Sharon to get over to the Station House immediately," he said. "And I mean right now."

"Fuck him!" Sharon said, as she got out of my car at a stoplight and hailed a cab.

"You can't go back yet," I hollered after her. "You're still a murder suspect and we promised Inspector Hollman you wouldn't leave town."

"Well I'm packing and leaving!" she shouted as a taxi pulled to the curb.

"I gave my word you wouldn't, and you gave your word too," I yelled back. "Don't be foolish. Hollman will get out an arrest warrant for you, and stop you at the airport."

She walked back to my car, and for a moment I thought she might get back in. "You really would tell him where to find me, wouldn't you, you wimp. You're just like Hollman. He's stupid enough to think I might be a murderer, and you're ready to go right along with him."

"He does have reason to suspect you," I said, and immediately wished I could take back those words.

"You think I killed Phil too," she said sadly, the anger now gone. "I'm going to grab some lunch, and then head back to your place. I'll pack my things and find a hotel. I won't leave Chicago without Hollman's permission, but I'll be damned if I want to stay with you."

She hailed a cab.

I didn't know whether to follow her or go talk to Hollman. My phone rang again and it was Julia. "We got in Dr. Weinstock's billing records from Ros."

I sped over to my office, hoping to find, I don't know what, something that would connect the Weinstock murder to Phil's. Anything that would point to someone other than Sharon. Hollman would have to wait.

CHAPTER 77

Weinstock's Records

Julia had printed out Weinstock's billing records, and spread them on my desk. Alongside the records were some of our books listing the various Doctor's Billing Codes. I would need those to understand the procedures Weinstock was charging for.

On the floor alongside my desk were several large boxes of office records that Ros had sent along. She must have hustled over to Weinstock's office right after my call. I had really scared her into full cooperation.

Realizing that the office records would take forever to review, I started with the billing records.

The billing was in a data base with several columns and I first scanned down the column listing the residence of each patient, figuring that if there was a woman both Weinstock and Phil knew, that woman would most likely be from the Chicago area. But Weinstock had no patients residing in Illinois. I then shifted my attention to the first column, the one listing the names of each patient.

I first jumped down to Sharon Heller, and to the right of her name, the dates of each treatment, and their codes. The coding indicated that there was a bill for the abortion. The date confirmed that it was performed shortly before Sharon and I started seeing each other again. All of her other charges were for standard gynecological exams. At least there were no bills for STDs.

Then I went back to the top of the list, starting with "A", and examined each name carefully, looking for any that might ring a bell. I saw that Weinstock had treated a number of movie stars. I bet he enjoyed those examinations. But I didn't see any names that could connect to our case until I got back down to "S." And there it was, jumping out at me.

"Sapperstein, Geri." She had a Los Angeles address and there were a number of treatments in the year before she had moved to Chicago and began working for Ted Mizell's firm. Funny she never mentioned being a patient of Weinstock. I wasn't familiar with the coding for her visits, and had to consult several of my texts before I found the description of her treatments.

I grabbed the phone and called Hollman. "This is confidential---can you keep it to yourself---never repeat what I'm going to tell you?"

"What's this about. You were supposed to be at the Station by now. With Sharon. What are you tryin to pull?"

"Just relax a moment and listen to me. This is really important. But it has to be between you and me. If it gets out I could lose my license."

"You could lose it anyway for harboring a fugitive."

"Just cut me a little slack here. But you have to promise the confidentiality. This conversation cannot be repeated---no recording--no note taking--just listen. O.K.?"

Hollman paused for a few moments, thinking it over. Finally he said, "O.K. It's in the vault." Even Hollman watched Seinfeld reruns.

"I got a copy of all of Dr. Weinstock's records, and found something very interesting," I said. I think it's the key to solving both murders.

Hollman told me to stay put, and he rushed over to my office.

"How did you get these records? I'm no lawyer, but I know that no court would allow you to examine all the records of a doctor, a gynecologist, especially. You'd be bombarded with objections of *Doctor-Patient Privilege.* When I Petitioned the Court to see them, my application was turned down cold. Any judge letting you examine those records would be thrown off the bench. And if you got them without Court approval, you could lose your license, and probably end up doing time in a federal prison"

"I know. I know. But I needed those records. "I contacted Ros Weinstock, Dr. Weinstock's widow," I said. "She didn't seem very upset by his death, by the way. It sounded like she was having a party at her house, and it wasn't a *Shiva.* There was a band in the background playing *salsa* music."

"You mean they don't play *salsa* at a *Shiva?*"

"Don't be cute. I persuaded her to get all of her husband's records over to me. The billing records were on his computer, and his notes and dictation were in his office, and she had the key."

"And how did you talk her into sending all this stuff to you?"

"She isn't very bright."

He nodded in agreement.

"And she is a very greedy lady."

He nodded again.

"I told her that you would tell California that she was still a suspect in her husband's death, and that if you told them that, then all of his assets would be frozen and no insurance policies would be paid until the case was resolved."

He visibly blanched at that, but said nothing. I could see he was thinking it over.

"You know that we could never use those records in court, or even the fruit of the records."

"Nobody will ever know. Those records are the key to the whole case."

"You mean Sharon's abortion---I already know Weinstock performed Sharon's abortion. And that would give her a good motive to kill him, if she wanted to keep it a secret. And she would have the same motive to kill Phil Levine, if he knew about the abortion. I'm still working on that part."

"Not Sharon's abortion. Look here. These records show Geri Sapperstein was a patient of Dr. Weinstock."

"Interesting, but what's the point?"

Geri was receiving female hormone injections administered in preparation for a sex change surgery. She was a man, waiting for the final step---the surgery. Weinstock still had to perform the final procedures, where he would whack off Geri's prick and create a vagina. It was Weinstock's sub-specialty."

Hollman still didn't get it.

"Think about it." And then I laid it out carefully for him, just as I figured it out while I waited for him to reach my office.

"Geri starts her sex change procedure in L.A., but it is long process — psychological testing, hormone injections, breast enhancement, and ultimately removing the penis and the surgical forming of a vagina. And Geri wants to keep the metamorphosis a secret. The people in L.A. know her as a man, so when she has made enough of a change to pass for a woman, even though the final surgeries had not yet been performed, she moves away to Chicago to begin her life as a woman."

"O.K.," Hollman said, taking notes, "she moves here as a woman figuring she will go back to L.A. for the final surgery. But why didn't she just stay in L.A. until that last surgery was done, and then move out of town?"

"Because she had graduated Law School, the time was right for finding a first job, and she could work here in Chicago and save up to pay for the final surgery."

"And then she comes to Chicago, keeping the secret that she doesn't want anyone to discover." Hollman is following now.

"And she goes to work at Ted Mizell's firm as a young lady lawyer. No wonder Ted Mizell couldn't get in her pants."

"I get it," Hollman says. "Nobody knows until one day she ends up in the bathroom of Phil Levine's apartment, and gets photographed standing at the toilet taking a piss."

"Exactly," I say. "And do you know when that was? It was the night Phil was killed."

"And how do you know that," Hollman asked.

"Phil's phone records, the ones that you got for me, showed that Phil had called our witness, Ann Swanson, from his apartment on the night he was killed. And Ann Swanson told me that during the call she also talked to a woman who was working with Phil. That had to have been Geri. She was the only one working with Phil. And it had to have been that same night, when Geri used the bathroom, that Phil took that photo of her, with her prick hanging out. Geri told me that she had only been in Phil's apartment one time."

"And you think Phil would have told Geri what he just saw?"

"He must have. Knowing Phil, he probably got a good laugh out of it. He might even have suggested that she give Ted Mizell a blow job."

"And she killed him that night to keep her secret."

"She knew the arrangements for him to pick me up later that night. She was afraid he would tell me as soon as he saw me. So she went downstairs, waited for him in the back of my car, and killed him."

"And later she did everything she could to stop me from locating our witness, Ann Swanson, because she knew Ann might reveal that she had spoken to Geri at Phil's apartment the night he was killed."

Hollman was still writing feverishly, and motioned for me to slow down a little.

I let him catch up, and then spelled it out in more detail. "When I assigned Geri the job of locating Ann, she claimed she couldn't find her. She knew that if I talked to Ann I would find that Geri was with Phil the night he was killed. She even went so far as to call Ann, and say that the case was settled and Ann's testimony wasn't needed. This was just to stop Ann from contacting us to see what was going on, and maybe let slip that Geri was in Phil's apartment the night he was killed."

"Wait a minute," Hollman said. "You told the judge that it was Masterson's office that called Ann Swanson. That's the only reason they let her testify in the trial--that Masterson was tampering with evidence. Now you say that it was Geri who made that call. Are you going to tell the judge that. Have him reconsider the motion to bar the testimony? Maybe take away your verdict?"

"I'm not sure I want to go that far. When I made the argument, I thought it had to be Masterson's office that made the call to Ann. I wasn't lying to the Court. I don't see any reason to revisit that question now."

"So Geri killed Phil because he found out *her*---I mean *his* secret."

"Exactly. And when Weinstock came to Michigan, Geri knew that he eventually would learn she was involved in the case, would probably even come face to face with her, and she was fearful that he would reveal her secret. And so she snuck into his room while he was in the Jacuzzi and shot him too. She was desperate to hide the sex change, and killed twice to do it."

By the time we finished talking, Hollman was persuaded that Geri Sapperstein was a double murderer. He put out an all points on Geri-- she had killed twice--was most likely armed, and must be considered extremely dangerous.

I called my apartment to give Sharon the news that she was off the hook, but nobody answered the phone, and she wasn't answering her cell.

CHAPTER 78

Stan's Apartment

Sharon responded to James' friendly greeting with a forced smile, and went directly to Stan's apartment to pack her things.

But before she packed there was something else she wanted to take care of. She went to his computer, entered the password he had given her, booted up, and located the folder of pictures taken by Phil Levine in his bathroom.

She opened the folder and was just starting to delete the pictures one by one, when the intercom rang. James announced that Geri Sapperstein was on her way up to celebrate the win. Sharon thought it interesting that James knew Geri well enough to send her up without checking first. Maybe Geri had spent more time with Stan than Sharon had realized.

I'll show Geri what a sicko Phil was, Sharon thought, and by association what a prick Stan Seger must be too. She answered the door, and after exchanging pleasantries led Geri to the computer.

Geri visibly paled when Sharon told her how Phil had photographed the women using his bathroom, but seemed a little relieved when Sharon explained that almost none of the faces showed in the pictures. "Except mine," Sharon complained. "I was looking down at a newspaper when the shutter, or whatever you call those things on a digital camera, went off, so I am easily identifiable."

Geri wanted to see each of the picture before Sharon erased them, and Sharon complied, warning "They're really obnoxious, but if you really want to see them, O.K. I'll be in the bedroom finishing packing. I don't care to see them again. Call me when you finish.

The pictures were set up to be viewed as a slideshow, with each picture filling the screen and lasting about 10 second before yielding to the next photo in line. The show stopped with the last picture displayed on the screen, the one with the subject's back to the camera, the skirt hiked up, and urinating through a clearly visible penis.

Sharon walked back into the room as Geri sat in silence, studying that last picture, frozen on the screen. Sharon studied it more closely than she had before, this time examining every detail of the picture, and for the first time noticed the handbag hanging down alongside the hiked up skirt. A silver metal and red leather Wendy Stevens. Very unique and ultra-expensive. Sharon liked it when she had seen it at Neiman Marcus a few weeks earlier, but she didn't buy it because she didn't have matching shoes.

But apparently Geri Sapperstein did have the shoes to match, red leather granny shoes. Geri was now sitting at Stan's computer with the identical red handbag on the floor beside her, and the matching shoes on her feet. On closer inspection, Sharon noticed that one of those shoes was visible in the photograph as well.

Sharon tried to hide the fact that she made the connection, but she wasn't that good an actress.

"Wendy Stevens calls the purse the 'Perforated Seed Pod,'" Geri said. " It costs about $500.00. Not bad, don't you think?" Geri slipped a small gun from her purse and pointed it at Sharon.

"I didn't know Phil was taking pictures. I thought he was just peeping into the bathroom. I was working with him on the Smith case. We had just located the witness in Wisconsin, the nurse, Ann Swanson."

"Stan sent Ann Swanson and her sister back to Wisconsin," Sharon said. She wanted to keep Geri talking, hoping Stan would come home.

"We were all excited, Phil and me. He poured us a couple of drinks to celebrate. He was trying to get me drunk. We both had more to drink than we should, especially Phil, even though he was scheduled to pick up Stan at the airport later that night. And then the pig grabbed at me, but of course, I pulled away. He was insulted, but obviously I couldn't let him get too close. So I excused myself and went to the bathroom."

"And that's when he got the picture of you, the one on the computer."

"I didn't know he took a picture, but I did know he saw me. Because when I came out of the bathroom he was laughing, and thanked me for pushing him away. He said I could probably have given him a great blowjob, and he never would have known the difference. I could have killed him right then, but I waited."

"And you killed him that night in the garage?"

"He was going out to the airport a little later. I knew he would tell Stan, and Ted Mizell, even though he swore to me he would keep my secret. The story was just too juicy. I could picture everyone laughing about it. I had to stop him, so I went around to the garage, I had to break in, and then I climbed into the back seat of Stan's car, and waited for Phil to show up."

"But Phil promised not to tell---he couldn't have said anything without people finding out what a creep he was," Sharon said.

"I couldn't take the chance. I had prepared for the change for a long time. I went through law school as a man, and used the name Geri, my given name was Gerald, even though a lot of people questioned my spelling. And I started the serious transformation right after law school, just as I was studying for the Bar."

Geri seemed pleased to be able to reveal her secret to someone, especially since the person listening would soon be dead. She was absorbed in telling her story, related in detail how she had felt trapped in the body of a man, and as she spoke she lowered her gun to her lap. But when she noticed Sharon edging closer she immediately raised the gun. Sharon froze.

"The hormone treatment worked beautifully. My skin was smooth. I was forming breasts. My voice was higher, a husky sexy voice. I had gone through all the psychological conferencing they required. After I passed the Bar in California, I moved to Illinois. I couldn't stay in California because too many people knew me there. I wasn't going to go through life with everybody thinking I was a freak.."

"But why Illinois?" Sharon asked. She kept stalling for time, and watched for an opportunity to grab the gun.

"I checked the national bar journals and saw an ad that Ted Mizell's firm was looking for lawyers. They weren't a multi-state firm, not one likely to have any contacts at the dinky school I had attended. But the pay looked pretty good, so I sent them a résumé. They got my law school transcript, very high grades by the way, which showed my name, Geri Sapperstein. The records do not show the gender of the student."

"So they hired you," Sharon prompted.

"Only after they flew me in for an interview with Ted Mizell. Of course, he propositioned me. I pretended I might be interested, but not just then, and he hired me. I've been putting him off ever since. One of these days, after I have my vagina built, I may give in."

Geri rose, signaled for both of them to move to the living room, and when they got there she took a pillow from the couch and put it over the gun to muffle the sound of a shot. She reconsidered, and ordered Sharon to move toward the balcony.

Sharon hung back, fighting for more time. "And you killed Ruben Weinstock too?"

"He was my doctor in California, the one who was going to build my new vagina. I couldn't believe it when Stan hired him as an expert in the Smith case. Of all the rotten luck. He was bound to see me, or at least hear my name somewhere in the course of the trial, and I couldn't risk him telling anyone."

Geri moved closer to the sliding door leading to the balcony.

"When everyone got together at that B&B in North Haven, I knew it was my only chance to shut him up. I couldn't take the chance he would tell on me. It would have ruined everything."

"You can't get away with this," Sharon said. "They'll get you for sure now. Killing me won't help. It'll just add another murder." God, she was sounding like a victim in one of those old black and white movies Stan always made her watch.

Geri laughed. "They suspect you of both killings. They'll think you walked out on the terrace so you could look at the place Phil lived, the place you murdered him, and you became remorseful. You couldn't live with yourself any longer. A double murderer. And the guy you loved wasn't even standing by you. So you committed suicide. Either you shot yourself with this gun, or you went over the banister. If you're nice I'll give you the choice. Now get out on the terrace. I hate to mess up this nice carpet."

"It's not a terrace, it's a balcony," Sharon corrected, stalling for time while Geri searched for the pulls to open the drapes covering the sliding door "A terrace is surrounded by walls. A balcony juts out from the building into an open space. The one out there is a balcony."

"I don't give a crap about an architectural lesson," Geri said, as she finally managed to open the drapes. "Whatever the hell you call it, you're going over the side, with or without a bullet in you." Geri struggled to slide back the heavy door leading to the balcony.

CHAPTER 79

The Balcony

I called the doorman's station in the lobby of my building. The phone rang more than ten times before James answered. "Sorry Mr. Seger. I was helping Mrs. Sanchez with some packages."

"Forget that. Have you seen Sharon?"

"She went up to your place a while ago. Hasn't come down yet. Probably she and Ms. Sapperstein are talking. You know women."

"Geri Sapperstein is in my apartment?"

"Yes sir. She came here a little after Ms. Heller. I figured it was O.K. to let her up as long as Ms. Heller said it was O.K."

I told James to hustle up there and go into my apartment and stay with the women until I arrived. I gave no explanation other than it was a matter of life and death. I said I was heading right over.

Hollman and I ran out the door and jumped in his car that was illegally parked in front of my office building. One of the perks of being a cop.

We didn't travel two blocks before we got stuck in a traffic jam, and even with Hollman's flashing light and siren it took what seemed forever to get to my place. I kept calling Sharon's cell and my home phone.

The phones kept ringing, but nobody answered. After several rings every call switched to voice-mail. "Sharon, answer---PLEASE." There was no response. *GOD don't let anything happen to her. PLEASE GOD!*

When we finally got to my building we ran through the lobby. James was not at his post. He was probably upstairs in my apartment.

We caught an elevator just as the doors were closing. Three more people were already inside, and they had pressed their buttons, so we had to stop three times before we reached my floor. My blood pressure rose higher with each stop, and by the time we were finally able to escape from the elevator, my heart was pounding and my head was ready to explode. If anything happened to Sharon....

James was in the hall by my apartment, shaking my door, calling for someone to open up.

"I used my key to unlock the door, but the chain is on. I can't get in. Nobody is answering," he said, "but I thought I should stay here until you arrived. And a little while ago, I'm not for sure, but I thought I heard shots, four shots, muffled like."

I pushed him aside and tried to force the door opened. But the security chain was on, just as James had said, and the door only opened a crack. Hollman shoved me aside, lowered his shoulder, and burst through the door, drawing his gun at the same time. He rushed into the room, and crouched down behind a couch and I crabbed into the room beside him. We peeked up cautiously. Nobody was in the living room. The door to the balcony was closed, and the drapes were drawn. It was quiet.

The door to my bedroom was closed, but I could see a light coming from beneath the crack. And we heard someone moving in that room. Hollman hurried to the door quietly. I was right behind him.

"What's the layout of the room?" he whispered.

"When you open the door you'll be facing one side of the bed. It's a king size. The headboard to your left, the foot to the right. Small side tables on each side. Two large dressers along the wall opposite the foot of the bed. Large windows beyond the far side of the bed."

"We're going in. Fast. We'll duck for cover when we reach the bed. Follow me on my count. Hit the floor quick and keep your head down."

He paused a beat, turned the handle, threw the door opened, and dived for cover behind the bed. I followed. We waited a few beats. Nothing. Then we peaked up over the bed. My view was obstructed by a partially opened suitcase on the bed.

Sharon was on other side of the bed, calmly packing the suitcase. I detected a slight smirk.

"Are you O.K.? Where's Geri?"

"I'm fine," she said. "And Geri is locked out on the balcony."

Sharon explained that Geri had covered her with the gun in one hand, and struggled to open my heavy sliding door with the other. "'This fuckin goddamn door,' she cursed as she pulled and tugged. She swears like a drunken sailor."

"It glided opened a lot easier when she accidentally lifted it slightly. And that's when she lost her balance for a moment, as the door slid more freely, and I saw my chance and lunged forward and hit her with my shoulder and knocked her out onto the balcony and pulled the door shut and locked it real quick before she could recover."

"She's still trapped out there," Sharon said. "She tried to smash the glass with her little gun and couldn't do it. And when she tried shooting at the glass it didn't even crack. The bullets just bounced off."

I owed one to the salesman who talked me into that cumbersome door. I should probably call and offer him an endorsement.

"But watch out," Sharon warned. "She still has the gun."

Sure enough, when we drew back the drapes we saw Geri, standing out there shivering, trapped on the balcony. She was enraged, stomping her feet, with the small gun still in her hand.

Her situation was hopeless. It didn't take long for Hollman to talk Geri into setting the gun down so he could let her back inside. Before Geri came in she kicked the gun off the balcony, perhaps hoping it would not be found.

When Hollman later took Geri downstairs in handcuffs, James opened the door for him, and handed him the gun that one of the tenants had spotted in the driveway.

CHAPTER 80

Setting the Record Straight

I was upstairs with Sharon, trying to convince her to unpack. She was still fuming. "It doesn't matter that I am innocent," she said. "What matters is that you thought I could be guilty of murder. And on top of that you lied. You never had any intention of moving to California. And you're not even an honest lawyer. You sent that nurse, Ann whatsher-name, back to Wisconsin and you're going to let Bill Masterson take the rap for calling her off when you know for a fact that it was Geri who made the call---all to save your precious verdict. You are despicable."

"Don't leave like this," I pleaded. "We may not have a third chance." It took hours and all my persuasive powers, but I convinced her to stay around another day, and to accompany me to Court for the entry of judgment on the verdict, and the Masterson hearing.

I called Hollman at the Station House, and at my request he agreed to keep Geri's arrest quiet and out of the press for twenty four hours. It really was turning out to be the beginning of a beautiful friendship.

Sharon and I arrived at the Courthouse early the next morning. She had calmed down somewhat, but was still cool to me.

I intercepted Bill Masterson in the hall. He looked drawn and nervous. Who wouldn't be. His license was on the line.

"Bill, how would you like me to get you off the hook?"

"You know I didn't call that lady," Bill said. "I didn't even have her number."

"I'm giving you a chance," I said. "And it's gonna make you a hero to your company at the same time."

"What do you want," he asked suspiciously.

"Call your company. Tell them you can save them almost a third. If they agree right now, and I mean right now, I'll settle the thirty seven

301

million dollar verdict for an even twenty five million. That's a saving to them of twelve million dollars. And I'll make sure you get off the hook on that phone call to Ann Swanson."

"How are you going to do that?"

"Never mind how---you have my guarantee."

Masterson made phone calls to his insurance carriers, and after a long and animated discussion got them to agree to pay the twenty five million. While Masterson was on the phone I called Tom Smith. I told him that if we didn't settle, the Judge might grant the Defense a new trial because of the Ann Swanson business, the fact that it was my assistant who told Ann to stay away from the trial. And I said that even if the Judge didn't order a new trial, the Defendants would file an appeal that would delay our collecting the money for a couple of more years. Tom was more than happy to give me permission to settle, and take twenty five million right now. It was more than he could make in a hundred lifetimes. Masterson and I shook hands on the deal.

The Bailiff accompanied us, Bill Masterson and me, into Judge Nielson's chambers. There was a Court Reporter there. Masterson and I put on Record the twenty five million dollar settlement. The Judge entered a final judgment in that amount. It was formal now---a done deal. Neither side could back out.

"I'm pleased the matter is finally concluded," Judge Nielsen said, "But there is still the very serious charge of witness tampering, and I'm not about to overlook it."

"It wasn't Mr. Masterson's office that called Ann Swanson, your Honor. I learned only yesterday that it was a lawyer working with me, Geri Sapperstein."

And I told them the whole story, how Geri had murdered Phil and tried to keep Ann Swanson from coming to Court because it might come out that Geri was in Phil's apartment the night he was killed.

"That means that your investigator and a lawyer working with you had Ann Swanson's phone number long before she testified---and you didn't furnish it to me. The nurse should have been barred from testifying," Masterson exploded. "Judge, I insist that the case be reopened and that you strike the testimony of Ann Swanson and direct a verdict for the Defense."

"I can't reopen the case," Judge Nielsen said. It is over. It has been settled---totally resolved. It's on the record."

"And I won't tell your company you got them to waive a right to appeal and pay me twenty five million just so you could save your ass, unless you want me to," I added.

Masterson shut up, and walked out still fuming.

Sharon was waiting in the Courtroom.

"I told them about Geri," I said. And I got Masterson off the hook."

"Well at least you did one thing right."

"And I called that broker in Venice Beach, the one who had the listing on that ocean front duplex that you liked. I'm ready to buy it. We'll both be on the title."

"That means we'll be living in California!" She threw her arms around me.

"Not exactly. But when you finally move to Chicago, we'll have a really comfortable place to stay when we go out to California for visits."

"You're still a bastard," she said.

CHAPTER 81

At O'Hare

Louie stayed at the Courthouse with us, and while I tried to persuade Sharon to be reasonable, he made a series of phone calls.

"This was my last homicide," he said. "Geri just confessed to everything. Twenty years on the force, and I hung around until I closed it. You're looking at a private citizen."

"With Phil dead, I need a new investigator. How would you like to come to work for me. You'll still have your pension, and I pay real good."

"I had a feeling you might ask. You need a guy like me to keep you on the straight and narrow. But before I start I need a little vacation time. Promised my wife a long trip."

"A long trip sounds like a good idea for us too," I said to Sharon. How about it. Let's go to the Caribbean, take some beach time, and patch things up."

She didn't respond, and instead said "It's late. We have to get to O'Hare fast, or I'll miss my flight to L.A."

Hollman volunteered to get us to the airport fast. "My last official act." We piled into his car, Sharon and me in back. He slapped his red light on the hood, and turned on the siren.

We were sitting at a window in a far corner of the airport lounge, Hollman, Sharon and me. People were rushing by to catch flights, but we were in no hurry. Her flight was delayed an hour. The lounge was almost empty, because nobody was permitted through security without a boarding pass, but Hollman flashed his badge and they let us pass.

I was drinking an RJ Hudson, Sharon was sipping Dewers, neat, and Hollman was carefully pouring a Blue Moon, getting just the right amount of head.

"At least Phil wasn't killed because of you," Hollman said. "Geri didn't kill him thinking it was you."

"I suppose that's true. But how do we tell his parents he was killed because he spied on women peeing in his bathroom?"

"He was a goddamn pervert." Sharon had no mercy

"At least Weinstock died for a worthy cause," Hollman said. "He was in the business of cutting off penises and creating vaginas. Our world can use fewer pricks and more vaginas."

Sharon just shook her head. "You men are all incorrigible."

I took one final shot. "We can't break up again. If we do, it could be the last time. We may not get another chance. When I knew you were trapped in my apartment with Geri, and you didn't answer my calls, I thought I lost you forever. I was afraid you were dead. I realized I couldn't live without you. I want us to spend our lives together."

"I'm glad you finally appreciate me. I thought it would shake you up if I didn't answer the phone."

"You mean you could have answered, but didn't?"

"Sure, and I didn't let James in either. Geri was locked out on the balcony before your first call."

"You scared the hell out of me."

"Maybe you needed that."

"You're always gonna keep me on edge, aren't you. With you it's never gonna be easy."

She kissed me, at first a light peck on the lips, then a deep lingering kiss. Then she smiled and looked deep into my eyes. "Don't worry, it'll be worth it."

When Sharon's flight was finally called, the three of us got up and walked toward the gate. Sharon walked on one side, me on the other. Louie squeezed in between, wrapped his arms around our waists, and sang out, "This is gonna be fun."

The end

ABOUT THE AUTHOR

Sidney Robin is a highly experienced trial and appellate attorney, specializing in the representation of seriously injured persons in Medical Malpractice, Product Liability, Aviation and General Negligence cases. He has written numerous articles for Legal Publications, and has been a frequent lecturer in various areas of negligence law.

A Wrongful Death is his second novel, and is a prequel to his first book, *An Attractive Nuisance.*

He is a lifelong residence of Chicago, and currently resides with his wife on the Near North Side.